"Tell me, how'd Gregory manage to propose in a hot-air balloon when he's scared of heights?"

Sputtering, Brynn almost choked.

"I—I guess…he'd been working hard at conquering his fear…."

The silence wasn't thick; it was impenetrable. Finally Matt said, "Sounds like Gregory did a lot of things he never had before."

"Like I said, love…" She glanced up, meeting Matt's gaze. There was something there—that same something she'd seen before. Whatever it was, she couldn't complete the thought, couldn't put the words between them again.

"Changes people," he finished for her.

Brynn had the sudden urge to tell him the truth, to explain why she'd carried out the charade, how it had seemed like the right thing to do—

"I guess it's a good thing love can change people," Matt continued, not meeting her gaze now, "otherwise you and Gregory would have married. And right n̶̶̶̶̶̶ going."

Brynn's c̶̶̶̶̶̶ at if she told all an̶̶̶̶̶̶ orse? She never ̶̶̶̶̶̶ arade, but ending ̶̶̶̶̶̶

ABOUT THE AUTHOR

A hopeless romantic, Bonnie K. Winn naturally turned to romance writing. This seasoned author of historical and contemporary romance has won numerous awards, including having been voted one of the Top Ten Romance Authors in America, according to *Affaire de Coeur*.

Living in the foothills of the Rockies gives Bonnie plenty of inspiration and a touch of whimsy, as well. She shares her life with her husband, son and spunky Westie terrier.

Bonnie welcomes mail from her readers. You can write to her c/o Harlequin Books, 300 E. 42nd St., New York, NY 10017.

Books by Bonnie K. Winn

HARLEQUIN AMERICAN ROMANCE
624—THE NEWLYWED GAME
646—WHEN A MAN LOVES A WOMAN
680—THE DADDY FACTOR
720—HIS-AND-HERS FAMILY

Don't miss any of our special offers. Write to us at the following address for information on our newest releases.

Harlequin Reader Service
U.S.: 3010 Walden Ave., P.O. Box 1325, Buffalo, NY 14269
Canadian: P.O. Box 609, Fort Erie, Ont. L2A 5X3

The Accidental Mrs. MacKenzie

BONNIE K. WINN

HARLEQUIN®

TORONTO • NEW YORK • LONDON
AMSTERDAM • PARIS • SYDNEY • HAMBURG
STOCKHOLM • ATHENS • TOKYO • MILAN • MADRID
PRAGUE • WARSAW • BUDAPEST • AUCKLAND

To Huntley Fitzpatrick for the inspiration,
the faith and the friendship.

To my partners in crime, Jean Case and Karen Rigley,
for your invaluable assistance.
Thanks for always being there, guys.

ISBN 0-373-16775-X

THE ACCIDENTAL MRS. MACKENZIE

Copyright © 1999 by Bonnie K. Winn.

Look us up on-line at: http://www.romance.net

Printed in U.S.A.

Prologue

Brynn Magee edged closer to the podium and the culmination of her plans—she was finally going to meet Gregory Mac-Kenzie. Having jogged the same paths as he had for months, Brynn knew he was the *one*. Mr. Right.

She didn't care if the label sounded dopey, because he was dreamy, handsome, successful, outgoing—everything she'd always wanted in a man. Brynn hadn't yet gathered enough courage to introduce herself, but that was all going to change.

Now she was a valued charity-auction volunteer; one who'd stuffed envelopes, answered phones, lugged cartons, schlepped coffee, vacuumed sawdust, and dusted chandeliers. And Gregory would notice—because he was chairing this high-profile charity event. He would appreciate all her hard work, commiserate over the fingernails she'd sacrificed, laugh with her over her needless struggle for a simple introduction. Because, of course, he would tell her that it wouldn't have taken more than a simple hello to catch his attention, a smile to keep it, and just a touch of encouragement to—

"Excuse me," the impatient voice intruded. "You in outer space, lady?"

"No... Uh, of course not," she mumbled, pushing at the heavy-rimmed glasses that nearly covered her face. "I guess I just didn't hear you."

"Guess not." The photographer shot her another disgruntled

look as he pushed past her, nearly toppling her from the narrow stage area.

Glancing around, Brynn saw that most of the press was crowding around. Which meant Gregory was probably ready to address them. Her heart thumping so hard she could scarcely hear above its rapid rush, she eased forward a bit, finding herself directly next to the speaker's box. Closing her eyes, she made a quick, fervent plea.

And was rewarded by Gregory MacKenzie's dazzling smile. Of course, it was directed past her at the news media; still, she could almost reach out and touch that perfect smile, those flawless cover-model features.

Then he spoke. It was the first time she'd actually heard him talk. Once Brynn had volunteered, she'd assumed she would meet Gregory, but instead she had been assigned to a committee under a minor director's command. Now, though, she would have her chance.

Enthralled, she clutched the framed clipping she intended to casually hand to him during their introduction. He would be touched by her consideration and sensitivity. So touched that he would make sure he knew just how to contact her after the charity auction they were working on, and then—

"Excuse me." One of the committee members passed behind Brynn, pushing her forward next to Gregory.

Glancing up, Brynn caught the flash of the camera as she angled her head toward him. In an instant, she realized she'd just become part of Gregory's photo op. Thrilled, she turned with a dazzling smile as another flash went off, and then dozens more. When the photographers slowed down, Brynn gulped back her nervousness, hoping her smile still dazzled as she looked at Gregory again.

He started forward.

Her heart nearly stopped.

Then he stepped aside, leaving the podium, and was immediately caught up in the crowd. Brynn stared at him hopelessly. Her golden opportunity had been lost.

One photographer stayed behind to reload his camera. Brynn started to leave but then realized he was the one who'd taken most of the pictures of her with Gregory. Seeing that he'd nearly finished changing his film, she scrambled off the podium.

"Sir, excuse me?"

The photographer glanced at her without much interest, once he'd realized she wasn't anyone important. "Yes?"

"You took pictures of Mr. MacKenzie that I believe I was in."

"So?"

She slid two fingers behind her back. "As historian of the auction I need to collect all the pictures I can for our records. Could I get duplicates of everything you took today? I... We'll be happy to pay for them."

He spared her a brief glance. "I think the newspaper can cough up a few extras for charity." He pulled out a rumpled card from his jacket. "Just give me a call—I took about two rolls."

Brynn held fast to the card. "Thank you so much! I can't tell you how much this means to me...us."

"Sure, lady. Money goes to the children's hospital. Gregory MacKenzie might be a corporate stuffed shirt, but he knows how to raise the dough."

Brynn stiffened, but he didn't seem to notice as he ambled away. Her affront faded as she clutched the card. She was going to have pictures of herself and Gregory. That in itself was a dream come true.

BUT BRYNN FOUND THAT her dream needed something more. True to his word, the photographer had given her a complete set of the pictures, yet she longed for them to have more meaning than an image of two strangers sharing the same podium.

Brynn stepped away from her drawing board where she was working on the comic strip, *Stephanie*, that she drew. She picked up the stack of pictures, looked at them once more, then tossed them down on a copy of *Brides* magazine she'd bought as research for *Stephanie*. As one photograph slid across the magazine it landed in a position that made it look as though Brynn's face was above the wedding gown on the cover.

Chuckling, she lined the picture up more carefully so that her head completely covered the model's face. It really did look like a fragmented page from what could be her own wedding album.

Flashbulbs ignited so quickly in her mind that they could have come straight from one of her own cartoon strips. Brynn glanced sideways at her drawing table to make certain they hadn't.

Her own wedding album... A ridiculous idea. So silly it wasn't even worth a thought. So ludicrous a sane person wouldn't even have let it enter her mind. So absurd it was laughable. Still... Her own wedding album. One she could share with Gregory.

Even without his cooperation.

It could be done. Computer-enhanced photos could place people anywhere—including the dream wedding she'd fantasized about.

Brynn traced the outline of Gregory's face on the picture. She'd planned to speak to him the day after the auction on the jogging path, but he hadn't been jogging since the charity event. She guessed he was out of the country again. His position at an international manufacturing firm took him away often—she knew that from the frequent mentions in the papers. But when he got back, nothing was going to stand in her way. She'd gazed from afar for too long. And her elaborate plan to meet him had fizzled. It was time for the direct approach.

But first... She picked up the magazine and positioned her picture above the bride on the cover. She had a wedding album to create.

Chapter One

Brynn leafed through the morning paper, absently dividing her breakfast between her pets. While her cat, Snookems, preferred protein, the fussy feline did like to nibble on a bite of bagel liberally covered in cream cheese. Lancelot, her small, mixed-breed terrier, wasn't as particular, although he loved fruit, eagerly accepting bites of strawberries and bananas. Bossy, her parrot, aptly named because of his commandeering attitude, pecked at the bagel, while muttering a mixture of offbeat slang and sailors' curses.

Brynn shook her head, correcting Bossy's ill manners while knowing he was a lost cause. She didn't have many guests, and luckily those few didn't mind his off-color remarks.

All three of the creatures for various reasons had been practically unadoptable, which was why they'd wound up in her home. It was a good thing she only volunteered twice a month at the shelter, otherwise she would have had to invest in a farm…or possibly a zoo.

Turning another page of the newspaper, she dropped the rest of the strawberries on Lancelot's head. He didn't mind, eagerly chasing the berries as they rolled across the kitchen floor. But Brynn didn't notice. Her gaze was riveted on Gregory's picture and the shocking caption beneath it: Prominent Local Business Executive Kidnapped in South American Coup.

Quickly reading the article, Brynn learned that Gregory had

been taken captive while negotiating arrangements to build another plant for his firm. Details were sketchy, but the situation
sounded grim. More than one American had been detained, as
firms tried to capitalize on uncertain governments and cheap
labor. Apparently the terrorists were holding Gregory for ransom—not out of any political motives, but rather financial ones.

No wonder Gregory hadn't been on the jogging paths lately.
While she'd been agonizing over introducing herself, he'd
been— Well, who knew what he'd been going through. Brynn
shuddered at the possibilities. She'd been gifted or cursed—
depending on how she looked at it on any given day—with an
overactive imagination. It provided the grist for her comic strip,
but in situations like these she could practically feel whatever
discomfort he was experiencing.

Disregarding the alarm that rang reminding her to read the
collection of notes tacked around the apartment, Brynn stared
at the newspaper until the last shrill echoes of the clock faded
away. A scribbled message reminding her to reset the alarm
fluttered to the floor unnoticed.

After rereading the article nearly a dozen times, she carefully
clipped it out. Retrieving the wedding album she'd pored over
countless times, she opened its cover. The clever photographer
she'd chosen had done an extraordinary job using his computer
to create images of herself and Gregory in appropriate wedding
attire and poses.

The pictures were so realistic that even she had to remind
herself they weren't authentic. She'd known from drawing her
own strip that the capacity of computer technology to change
photos was nothing short of remarkable. And these pictures
were even a cut above her expectations. People who either
didn't have the funds for original wedding photos or who
wanted to utilize ones from a previous marriage were turning
to computer enhancement. Brynn wondered how many former
spouses would be appalled to see someone else's face smiling
from their photos. But it was being done more and more. The

photographer hadn't even questioned Brynn's request, assuming the photos were for both her and Gregory.

To the unknowing, the pictures appeared to be the genuine article. And in her dreams they were. She knew her wedding album would seem silly—even ridiculous—to anyone else, but it was her indulgence, a bit of harmless fantasy. With nothing substantial of Gregory's to hold on to, the album was her only link to the relationship she hoped would materialize.

Lancelot pushed his moist nose beneath her hand, begging to be petted. She obliged, picking up his sturdy little body to cuddle. "Do you suppose Gregory is all right?" she asked him, a slight hitch in her voice.

Instantly empathetic, Lancelot licked her hand.

Snookems, sensing her distress, moved closer as well, arching toward Brynn's knees and winding her fluffy tail around her legs. Only Bossy continued his muttering.

Another alarm clock, set in case she forgot to heed the first one, now shrilled. But she ignored it, too.

"I don't guess we'll really know, guys. Who's going to keep us updated on Gregory?" She sighed. "Nobody, I suppose."

Brynn searched her memory for contacts she'd made during the auction, but she'd been her usual shy, reserved self, especially since she'd been thinking of Gregory the whole time. "Nope," she said aloud. "No help there. I guess we'll just find out with the rest of the world."

BRYNN SAT AT HER DRAWING table, doing her best to concentrate on the strip, but her gaze kept wandering to the wedding album that rested on the coffee table. Giving in to the urge yet again, she abandoned her work to study the photos.

She had some time before the strip was due, but she needed to fill her mind with something other than worry about Gregory. And yet she couldn't resist leafing through the album. Each morning since his disappearance, she'd risen early, opening the paper the moment it arrived, searching for any news about him. There had been an occasional update, all indicating nothing had changed.

Brynn tried to tell herself that no news was good news, but it was getting to be a thin platitude. Hearing Lancelot growl suddenly, she paused, listening as well. The doorbell rang and her apartment erupted in sound as Lancelot raced to the door, barking madly. Snookems took up her position in the window seat, proceeding to yowl as usual when Lancelot barked. Bossy launched into a limerick after calling out, "Enter."

Rolling her eyes, Brynn glanced through the peephole, not recognizing the face that peered back, equally close to the door. Startled, she pulled away. "Who is it?"

One word penetrated the chorus of voices that greeted her: "MacKenzie." Could it be news of Gregory? Forgetting logic or rationale, she picked up Lancelot as she whipped open the door. And stared.

Five curious faces stared back at her.

"Hello," Brynn finally managed. "Can I help you?"

"Oh, aren't you sweet?" a middle-aged woman gushed, holding out her hands to grasp Brynn's, forcing her to shift Lancelot, then put him down.

"I'm not sure—"

"You're right, Ruth, she looks delightful," another older woman agreed. "And we're taking her by surprise."

"No, that is—" Brynn began.

"Of course we are," a man interrupted, although in a weak voice. "We haven't properly introduced ourselves. We're the MacKenzies—Gregory's family."

Struck dumb, Brynn could only stare. Had something happened to him? And how had they known about her? "But, how... I mean—" Brynn tried to recover some sort of poise. "Please come in, won't you?"

The ladies filed in first, then a girl of about fourteen or so, a boy who looked to be about nine, and finally the man with the weak-sounding voice.

"I'm Ruth MacKenzie," the first woman began. "And this is my husband, Frank."

He solemnly held out a thin hand and Brynn shook it carefully, feeling its fragility.

As she released his hand, Ruth was already steering her toward the others. "This is Frank's sister, Miranda."

"I'm glad to finally meet you, Brynn," Miranda greeted her. "But I'm sorry we barged in on you like this."

"No, it's fine, really—"

"And this is Heather," Ruth continued without pausing. "She's Gregory's sister. But then of course you know that. Gregory must have told you about everyone."

Oh, yeah.

The teenager didn't hold out her hand; instead she gave Brynn an artless teenage smile. "Hi!"

"Hi," Brynn replied, captivated by the darling girl.

"And this is Andy," Ruth continued. "Gregory's brother. There I go again. You probably don't really need the introductions, much less my explanations of how we're related."

Not much. "Hey, Andy," Brynn ventured, never certain how to interact with children.

"How come you live in half a house?" he asked.

She laughed as Ruth gave him a look meant to quash his questioning. "It's okay." Brynn gestured toward the high ceilings, old-fashioned intricate molding, bay windows, and original wood floors. "As you can see, it's an old house and the owner split it into two apartments."

"Doesn't look much like an apartment," Andy replied. "On TV they always look all new and white."

Brynn laughed again, enjoying his candor. "That's why I liked this one. It was different."

"Yeah," he agreed, bending over to pet Snookems before wandering across the room in the direction of her drawing board.

Brynn glanced around at the circle of expectant faces. "Oh,

and I'm Brynn Magee, but I guess you know that." They all smiled widely at her and she returned the smile uncertainly. "But, I'm not quite sure *how* you know that."

"Your photographer was kind enough to send us copies of the wedding pictures after he read about Gregory's abduction. He thought we'd want our own set of photos. We were surprised but thrilled, of course!" A tear sparkled in Ruth's eyes and her voice trembled.

Frank patted his wife's arm, taking over the explanation. "As you can see, Ruth has quite a way with words and she talked the photographer into giving us your name and address."

"And we wanted to meet the young woman who'd finally captured Gregory's heart," Miranda concluded.

Brynn stared at them as the blood drained from her face. They all thought— Here they were, worried about Gregory's disappearance and now they believed she was his secret bride. What had she done?

"We know you and Gregory must have planned to surprise us and we're sorry we ruined it, but with Gregory's kidnapping, it seemed more important that we all come together at this time. I'm sure neither of you anticipated this twist."

You can say that again. Brynn took a deep breath.

Ruth leaned forward. "I can't wait to ask. How did you and Gregory meet?"

Brynn's lips opened, but no sound emerged.

"And why did you two keep the wedding such a secret?" Ruth continued. "I'm guessing you eloped, but I'm dying to know—"

"Ruth!" Miranda admonished her. "Clearly she's too upset about Gregory to go into all that now."

Ruth took Brynn's hands. "I'm so sorry. My mouth is like a runaway train. We can talk about all that another time. I know that all you're thinking about now is Gregory."

"Have you heard any news?" Brynn managed to ask.

Frank frowned. "Communications are terrible in South America. The State Department doesn't think it was politically motivated since Gregory was there strictly on Drake Chemical business. Unlike some places, they are desperate for the revenue generated by an American business concern, so they're welcoming the new plant with open arms."

"Then why did they kidnap him?"

"Best we've learned is they think they can force Drake Chemical to pay heavily for his return," Frank replied.

Brynn looked at him in alarm. "And do you think they will pay?"

"The CEO assures us they'll cooperate completely. They value Gregory, too."

Brynn tried to imagine Gregory held by third world terrorists, but it was still too much to absorb. "Do you know where they're holding him?"

Looking even more ashen, Frank shook his head. "The State Department assumes they've taken him far from the hotel his meetings were to be held in. But wherever they're hiding him, none of our government's operatives can find him."

"But the State Department told us the kidnappers would keep Gregory alive—it's in their best interest," Ruth added. Concern creased her features as she looked at her husband. "And we know they're right."

"I would feel it if something had happened to him," Frank said quietly. He glanced at Brynn. "Of course you would, too."

Helplessly, Brynn glanced between the MacKenzies.

"Where were you when Gregory was kidnapped?" Ruth asked, twisting again to look at Brynn.

She glanced between Gregory's parents. "Here?" she answered tentatively.

"Of course she was here, Ruth," Miranda intervened. "No man in his right mind would take a new bride to the jungles of South America."

"Rain forests," Frank corrected mildly.

"You know what I mean!" Miranda retorted before turning to Brynn. "Thank goodness Gregory had the sense to leave you in civilization!"

"Well…"

"Whatever the reason, we're grateful, Brynn," Ruth added, dashing at a tear in her eye.

"And we need to support each other," Frank said. "Times like this call for families to come together. Do you have family here in Salt Lake?"

"No. There's just my mother and she lives in Chicago, but—"

"We're family now, dear," Ruth spoke, her lips quivering even as they pushed into a smile—one that seemed to hover perpetually on her kind face. "And you have us."

Before Brynn could reply, Ruth pulled her forward in a huge hug. Helplessly she was enveloped by each family member.

Never having encountered such an outpouring of loving welcome, Brynn was speechless.

"Hey guys! Look! Brynn draws comics!" Andy called out from her drawing board.

"Really?" Heather questioned, turning to Brynn. "Real comics? In the newspaper?"

Uncomfortable with praise, Brynn shrugged, downplaying the cartoon. "I draw a strip."

Heather had moved over to the drawing board as well. "It's *Stephanie*," she shrieked. "My favorite!"

"Mine, too," Andy insisted, not to be outdone.

"We all read it," Ruth chimed in.

"I never miss it," Miranda added. "I can't wait to see what new scrape Stephanie's gotten herself into!"

Brynn felt a blush begin. While she loved hearing that people read her strip, she never knew quite what to say. "Sometimes I feel that way, too, when I start to draw it."

They all laughed appreciatively and Brynn relaxed a fraction.

"Then you work at home?" Frank asked.

"Yes, it's great. I get to be my own boss." She pushed at her oversize glasses. "And I don't have to go to an office."

"You could work in your jammies if you wanted to," Miranda guessed.

"When it snows, I often do," Brynn admitted.

"You don't have to go to an office at all?" Ruth questioned.

"No. I send my work by courier to the publisher." She gestured toward her drafting table. "So this is it."

A new light was twinkling in Ruth's eyes. "So, your work is completely portable? You can do it wherever you want?"

"Luckily, yes. I've finished more than one strip while I've been traveling."

Ruth clapped her hands together. "That's perfect!"

Brynn felt the first stirrings of premonition a shade too late. "What do you mean?"

Ruth turned to the rest of her family, sharing a smile with them. "Then you *can* come home with us!"

Brynn could only stare.

"Family should be together at a time like this," Miranda added. "And we'd so hoped you'd be able to come home with us, but we didn't know what other commitments you had in the city."

"But now that we know you don't have other family here and you don't have to be at an office…" Frank added.

"I can't possibly leave," Brynn began desperately. "I have to be in my studio to work…." Glancing around, she searched frantically for excuses. "And I couldn't possibly impose."

They all laughed as though she'd made a huge joke.

"Since the ski resort has more than a hundred rooms, we can probably squeeze you in *somehow*," Frank replied.

Ski resort? "But I have to get my work to the courier," Brynn protested. "So you see—"

"Even though it's not ski season yet, we have enough off-season visitors to send the shuttle down real often. That's not a problem."

"And I have my pets." She seized on that excuse, feeling inspired that she'd remembered her little brood.

"With thousands of acres of land, a few pets aren't a problem."

"You don't understand. They're really difficult at times. Snookems is nearly blind. Bossy has a terrible mouth. And Lancelot is only sociable with me. He was abused by his former owner and I've just gotten him to trust me. He's unfriendly and aggressive toward strangers." As she spoke, Brynn glanced across the room, seeing that Heather was gently petting Lancelot who was loving it. "Most of the time, anyway."

Heather met her eyes. "If you come home with us, it'd be like having part of Gregory there."

Brynn could see the distress on the girl's face; she had been badly shaken by her brother's kidnapping. Glancing at the rest of the family, Brynn saw similar reactions. While they were bearing up under the pain, they were all equally affected. Knowing they were struggling to maintain optimistic, happy attitudes for her benefit made the ache in her heart that much stronger. But deceiving them would only make that worse. "I'm so sorry, but I—"

Ruth tugged on her arm, dragging her away. "Could I get a glass of water, my dear?"

"Certainly." Brynn glanced once more at the expectant faces and then pushed through the swing door into the small kitchen, Ruth tagging right behind her.

She reached for a glass but Ruth stilled her arm. "The water was just an excuse. You can see that everyone's just holding together by a thread."

Brynn nodded, the truth bubbling on her tongue, churning in her stomach as she tried to think of how to best confess it.

"And I want to tell you about Frank's health."

When Ruth's lips began to quiver, Brynn instantly took her hands. "His health?"

Ruth took a deep breath. "Frank had a triple bypass recently and he's still not well. When word came of Gregory's disappearance—" she put two fingers against her lips to stop their trembling "—I thought we might lose Frank, as well. That's why it's so important that you come with us. If he had something of Gregory's to hold on to, to keep Frank's hope alive..." Ruth smiled then—a tremulous lifting of her lips. "And nothing would be better than Gregory's perfect bride. As soon as we received the album and saw that you two had been married, it brought Frank out of his downward spiral. So you see how important you are...how important it is that you come home with us."

"Brynn! Where's your suitcase?" Miranda's voice carried into the kitchen, startling them both, prompting Brynn into action.

She pushed open the kitchen door. "But I didn't say I could leave, and..." Her voice trailed off as she met their expectant faces, her gaze lingering on Frank's pale countenance.

Ruth went to stand beside her husband, her eyes pleading with Brynn, silently reminding her of his precarious health.

"Like I said, I have the pets...."

Heather scooped up Lancelot. "I've got the dog and Andy can take Snookems. There's plenty of room in the van for your bird and drawing board, too. We brought the resort bus. Please, Brynn?"

Meeting their faces one more time, lingering on Frank's shaky expression and Ruth's beseeching one, she crumbled. Knowing she was crazy, her eyelids fluttered shut briefly. As Brynn opened them, she managed a smile. "I suppose I could come for a while."

A general whoop echoed throughout the room. Miranda took the bird's cage from its stand, looking around for the cover as Frank started to clear her drawing table. Andy was collecting the dog leash from the hook by the door as Heather searched in the hall closet Brynn had indicated for a suitcase.

Ruth smiled widely. "Just until Gregory comes home."

Brynn whipped her head around to see them all smiling and nodding in agreement, realizing she'd just arranged for the final take in her wedding album.

Chapter Two

The drive northward was far more magnificent than Brynn had
expected. Early fall had carpeted the canyons with color—not
only brilliant autumn reds and oranges. Gold, crimson, purple
and sienna leaped from nature's wildest palette. As they
climbed in altitude, snowcapped summits rose above the timber
line and aspen leaves trembled against spruce's dark green.
Wildly soaring mountain peaks competed with plunging canyons. It was a land of contrasts—stark and beautiful.

Through the open window she could smell the Douglas firs,
mountain lupine and the unmistakable novelty of clean, fresh
air. Beyond each crest was another discovery, a newly unfolding panorama.

Unable to tell the MacKenzies that she didn't know which
ski resort they spoke of, Brynn had no idea they planned to
travel so far northward, away from the multitude of ski resorts
that were closely situated to Salt Lake City, most within half
an hour to an hour from the city. Instead they passed even the
well-known northern resorts—Snowbasin, Powder Mountain,
Nordic Valley—as they continued driving.

She hadn't expected to see the rush of Logan River and the
mountain streams, or to experience sensory overload from more
colors than she believed existed in even the most daring artist's
imagination. It was a true feast for the senses.

Baffled, Brynn could only take in the scenery as she tried to guess where in the world they were going. Vaguely she knew that Sun Valley was to the north in Idaho, and wondered if that was their ultimate destination.

Heather and Andy had kept up a steady stream of conversation, each positioned on either side of her.

Bossy continued adding more than his two cents' worth— Brynn figured he was up to at least a ten-dollar bill by now. She couldn't help wondering what the MacKenzies thought of her bird's salty language. But they seldom stopped talking, all wanting to tell her about Gregory, the family, the resort, and just about anything else that popped into their minds.

Used to a quiet, solitary life, Brynn was fairly overwhelmed by it all, but found herself charmed rather than annoyed. She was touched that they were so eager to include her. She couldn't help but wonder if these bizarre circumstances would bring her and Gregory together at last.

Gregory would be thin when he came back after his ordeal, realizing that life was shorter than he'd ever imagined. Realizing that it wouldn't be complete without the woman he loved by his side. Realizing that Brynn was that woman—not some shallow socialite, but a genuine woman; one who appreciated the sensitive side he kept hidden. One who—

"Brynn. Brynn," Heather repeated. "We're here. This is the road that leads to our place."

Jerked back to reality, Brynn stared ahead at the road that appeared to climb the mountain. Swallowing, she gulped back her apprehension and smiled at the girl. "I can't wait to see everything."

The road, a daunting course of switchbacks, wound upward, but Brynn found herself nearly hanging out the window in anticipation rather than fear. As Ruth navigated the turns, it was clear she'd had a great deal of experience driving the challenging road.

"Do tourists ever get intimidated by the approach?" Brynn finally asked, staring downward at a steep canyon drop-off.

Miranda chuckled. "Most of our guests prefer to take the shuttle. There's not much need for a rental car when you spend all your time on the slopes in the winter, or hiking in the off-season."

Brynn listened as she watched the panorama unfold. Each bend took them to more brilliant foliage, more exquisite views. When the bus cornered one particularly narrow bit of road, the vista that suddenly opened up was so incredible, Brynn blinked to see if it was real. While she was well acquainted with the eye-popping scenery throughout the state, this particular view looked as through it stretched out endlessly. "It must be wonderful to see this every day," she breathed, caught up in the wonder.

Frank chuckled. "I'll be glad to hear you say that in the winter when we're under a ton of snow."

Winter! Surely they didn't think she was staying until then. She only planned to stay a few days at the most.

But the road was leading to a wide-open space. An exquisitely carved sign indicated the resort entrance. Everyone in the van began talking at the same time and Brynn wondered how any of them could follow what was being said. She couldn't have wedged in a protest with an industrial-strength shoehorn.

The bus bumped over a bit of rough road, then sped on toward the sprawling lodge that dominated the mountaintop. Brynn was briefly reminded of the mystical headquarters of the gods, looming over the rest of the world. Was this Zeus's second home?

Tall spruce towered over the imposing redwood-and-stone structure, making it, too, look as though it had been lifted from a postcard. Entranced, Brynn climbed quietly from the bus as the others chattered, everyone grabbing pieces of her luggage and life as they prepared to go inside. Lancelot strained on his leash as Bossy warned them that "Last call" was in effect.

The place literally took her breath away. It was the sort of resort that awed, welcomed, charmed and made you feel as though you'd just stepped into the postcard, as well. Far larger than she'd expected, Eagle Point was impressive and then some. Somehow she'd envisioned a quaint family lodge—not this prosperous-looking resort.

Suitcases, birdcage, drafting table and supplies scattered about her, Brynn supposed she must look like one of the Beverly Hillbillies come to stay. Only Granny and Jethro were missing from the tableau.

As a tall, lean man unfolded his body from the glider near the massive double entry doors, she wondered if Jethro, too, was about to make an appearance.

"Matt!" Ruth called out, obviously delighted. "You're home!"

Wondering who Matt was, Brynn tugged gently on Lancelot's leash so that the dog wouldn't growl or jump at him. Brynn guessed that Lancelot's former abusive owner had been a man, since the dog was most agitated around men.

But Matt didn't rush his approach. In fact, he only took a few steps forward, meeting his family partway. While the others crowded around him, he answered their questions, but his gaze never left Brynn. Uncomfortable beneath his scrutiny, she awkwardly dug the toes of her sandals into the soft grass.

As the babble died down a bit, Matt gestured toward her and Ruth jumped on the opportunity. "Of course, Matt, you haven't met the newest member of the family."

Brynn grimaced at Ruth's choice of words. But Matt didn't seem to notice, allowing his mother to think she was in control as she tugged his tall body in Brynn's direction.

"I got so caught up in Matt's update about Gregory that I nearly forgot you were standing there," Ruth babbled. "Matt just got back from Washington—trying to find out more about what's being done to find Gregory." Tears threatened, then Ruth smiled. "But I didn't mean to leave you out. Brynn, this is Gregory's brother, Matt."

Another brother. Why couldn't Gregory have been an or-

phan? She tried to ignore the fact that Matt was sizing her up as she greeted him. "I'm pleased to meet you. I...I've heard so many nice things about you."

His eyebrows rose. "Not from Gregory you didn't."

Brynn sucked in a deep breath, not certain it was relief she felt. So the jig was up. "Well—"

"Gregory never has anything 'nice' to say about me," Matt continued, his scrutiny not pausing. "Unfortunately, he didn't have anything to say about you, either. So, you're a complete mystery."

Brynn managed to smile, barely. "Perhaps I exaggerated. Maybe...'nice' isn't the right word."

"Perhaps," he agreed. "But you're still a mystery."

Brynn willed herself not to flush. "So are all of you," she responded, not without a touch of irony.

"But then normally the family gets the chance to meet the new bride *before* the ceremony's a done deal."

"Well...uh...yes..." she stuttered.

Ruth playfully swatted her tall son. "That's enough of that. Brynn and Gregory have every right to get married the way they want." Ruth turned sympathetic eyes toward Brynn. "I'll admit I would love to have seen you walk down the aisle, but the important thing is that you two found each other, made a commitment before...before." Her voice wavered and tears were threatening again.

Matt put an arm around his mother and she smiled bravely. "Look at me, starting off again and today such a special day. We've brought home a part of our family and I *know* Gregory will join us soon."

Brynn looked helplessly between Ruth and Matt.

"Welcome to the family," Matt added slowly. With his free hand, he pushed at his already tousled hair. "We're all pretty stressed about Gregory...."

Brynn waved her hands to stop the flow of words. "Please don't apologize." She didn't think she could stand any more guilt. At this rate she'd be under tons of the uncomfortable emotion soon. "I'm afraid I've made an already difficult situation worse by being here. I'll leave on the next shuttle to the city."

"I won't hear of it!" Ruth declared in a rapidly rising voice.

"Hear of what?" her husband questioned as he rejoined them, his face pale, his breathing uneven.

"Brynn's talking of leaving."

"We won't hear of it," Frank declared, his voice still weak, but his tone filled with conviction. "We've barely gotten you here. You can't leave."

"Leave?" Heather questioned, bending to pet Lancelot as she, too, joined them. "Who's leaving?"

"Brynn says she is," Ruth replied, clearly agitated.

"But why, Brynn?" Heather asked, turning large, hopeful eyes on her. "Don't you like it here?"

"It's not that…. It's just that I'm making things worse for your family and—"

"Of course you're not!" Ruth contradicted her. "Your being here makes things easier." She reached out to enfold Brynn's hand. "We have a link to Gregory through you. And that's very precious to us."

And very bogus, Brynn wanted to add. "But I don't want to trouble you. This isn't a good time for guests—"

"Number one, you're not a guest, you're family," Frank interrupted. "Number two. You keep forgetting our business is guests. Wouldn't have a business without them. So stop worrying."

She'd barely gotten here and she was already sinking fast. There were simply too many things she didn't know, couldn't know about Gregory and his family.

She nearly thumped the side of her head. But you'd think she could remember they were at a ski resort since the mammoth buildings surrounded her, not to mention the ski lifts dotting the mountainsides. Feeling as she often did when lost in her daydreams, Brynn wished she wasn't always one step out of pace.

Heather picked up Bossy's cage. "I'll take this in and show you to your room. Mom picked out the best one for you this morning."

Ruth had been very sure of her persuasive powers, Brynn acknowledged silently. "Thank you. I wouldn't mind freshening up."

Matt grasped her suitcases, looking skeptically at the dog and cat.

"They'll follow," Brynn told him. "They're not used to being outside and I'm afraid they'd get hopelessly lost."

"We're used to dogs at the resort," Matt replied, not mentioning the cat.

The omission worried her. "Snookems won't get into anything. She doesn't have much sight left, so she sticks pretty close."

"Just what I wanted to hear," he muttered.

"I knew I shouldn't have come with the pets and all—"

"Don't start that again," Matt warned. "You don't want to see Act Two if you get Mother stirred up."

"He's right," Heather agreed tactlessly. "Mom'll come unglued."

"And the meltdown's not always pleasant," Matt added as they left the stone floor of the spacious lobby and ascended the stairs. "She's on the edge already. Won't take much to push her over."

Brynn bit down on her lower lip, considering. The MacKenzies were lovely people and she didn't want to contribute to Ruth's breakdown. Still, when they discovered the truth, the meltdown would be on a nuclear scale. Obviously the best plan was to make her stay brief, leave behind good feelings, and escape before Gregory returned. And then when he did come back and discovered how noble she'd been, he'd be grateful.

Grateful and more, because his eyes would finally be opened. He would see her as she really was, rather than—

"This is your room," Matt told her, shouldering open the door.

Brynn shook off her daydreams and followed him, trailed by Heather, Lancelot and Snookems. Their mini-parade came to a halt when Matt lifted the heavy suitcases onto the luggage rack near the door as though they were weightless.

The effortless bunching of his considerable muscles led Brynn to believe that this MacKenzie brother must be one who used his brawn instead of his brain. Probably a ski bum, one of those dedicated only to the slopes, rather than pursuing important goals or a career. And having a resort in the family was a cushy way to indulge that habit.

"I'll have someone bring up your drafting table and supplies," he added, his gaze lingering just a fraction longer than necessary.

Brynn had an absurd desire to check her wild hair and see just how many curls were tangled about her face. Instead, she pushed at her heavy glasses, glad for their camouflage. "Thank you. I'll be needing them."

Heather cooed at Bossy, who turned his beak to one side as though wondering if the girl had taken leave of her senses. "Take it off, baby. Take it all off."

Laughing at his words, Heather wagged her finger at the mischievous bird.

Matt didn't look as amused. "Unusual thing for a bird to say."

"He's had a rather colorful past, I'm afraid. Hanging out in bars and strip joints didn't do much for his manners," Brynn explained.

Matt's eyebrow rose. "I see."

But it was clear he didn't. "But you don't understand. I mean—"

"None of my concern where you take your bird."

"But I didn't—"

His gaze flicked over her again, then toward his younger sister to emphasize Heather's presence. "But it's not something I think we ought to talk about now." He shook his head. "You're sure not like the girl I thought Gregory would choose. He was always into sophisticated society beauties."

Brynn blanched in spite of herself.

"I didn't mean that the way it came out," he said quickly, reluctantly meeting her gaze. He was clearly floundering for an explanation. "Just that you don't look like a high-powered career woman, or a debutante."

She swallowed the hurt, realizing he hadn't intended for the words to cause pain. "You're right, I'm not. I don't have much in common with those beauties."

He had the grace to flush with embarrassment. "That wasn't a commentary on your looks. You look just fine. I meant you aren't Gregory's usual type. And that's to your advantage."

"Just fine." The way she'd describe an average meal, a cooling cup of coffee, or a day filled with neither sunshine nor rain. Hardly a glowing accolade.

Still, it wasn't Matt MacKenzie's responsibility to find her attractive, or impressive, or challenging. And clearly he didn't. As she shut the door behind him and his younger sister, she wondered why that bothered her so much.

Chapter Three

Although she spent far too long studying the album of wedding pictures, Brynn still wasn't all that late getting ready for breakfast, having risen early. It was the only thing she didn't need an alarm clock for. Rising on time was far easier than remembering appointments and the other distractions of life. Normally she depended on several alarm clocks, enough sticky notes to save a rain forest, and endless recorded messages to remember obligations beyond drawing and delivering her strip. And still she tended to forget many of them.

But she hadn't needed any of those devices to remember to look at the wedding album this morning. She'd felt an urgent need to reconnect with the pictures in the book, to remind herself why she was here putting on a show for Gregory's family. As was her habit, Brynn traced the contours of his face, then flipped through to her favorite pages, smiling at the ones that pleased her the most.

Finally shutting the album, Brynn hugged it close before placing it on the dresser in a prominent spot. Knowing she should make an appearance for breakfast, and realizing she was later than she'd expected, Brynn hurried out of her room. Still, she was unable to resist learning more about her surroundings. Once downstairs, Brynn took her time finding the dining room.

In the confusion of arriving the previous afternoon, she hadn't had the time or opportunity to really look at the interior of the lodge. Now she saw that log-planked walls of the spacious lobby led to other wings that widened and rose above the main area. Discreet signs indicated that dining rooms and banquet halls were close by.

Huge picture windows allowed the mountains and far-reaching views to come inside. Tastefully, the MacKenzies hadn't given in to the formerly faddish rage of decorating in a Southwestern motif. The true Western style, interspersed with striking antiques and traditional pieces, was far more intriguing.

Comfortable, overstuffed leather chairs invited her to sink into their depths. Grouped to take advantage of the imposing river-rock fireplace, more chairs, covered in tasteful, warm-colored fabric, flanked it on each side, and long, deep-seated couches faced them.

Tables of heavy wood burl offered a place to rest a book or hot drink and ottomans offered equally pleasing spots to rest tired feet. Tall indoor trees soared toward the atriumlike ceiling. Skylights crisscrossed the roof, meeting the floor-to-ceiling windows. Except for the reflections of the sun glinting off the polished glass, it looked as though the lobby were set outdoors beneath the pines.

What a magical place to grow up in, she decided, thinking of all the towns and cities she'd lived in during her childhood and adolescence, how eventually they had all blended into one faceless, anonymous lump.

But her mother had been restless, unable to settle long in any one place, always sure that she'd find that elusive "greener grass." Brynn didn't think that grass existed for Charlene Magee, but she'd never voiced that opinion—not that her mother would have listened.

What must it feel like to have always lived in one sturdy home? Lived there long enough to memorize the scenery, to have the landmarks branded in your consciousness for all time. No wonder Gregory was such a sensitive, far-thinking man. He'd taken this solid background and used it as a launching pad into an equally solid career, one that had brought him success and recognition.

Recognition that had gotten him kidnapped.

Trying not to think of that, or how he was faring, Brynn thought instead of the weeks and months of jogging along the same paths, the serious concentration he put into that task, as well.

She'd often dreamed of approaching him—jogging casually alongside him and introducing herself—and of course, his response. He would begin with a casual invitation to coffee...then dinner...and before long they'd be inseparable. He would wonder how he could have jogged past her so many times before asking her out. They would laugh together over his timing; then the laughter would give way to passion as they realized why they truly belonged together. And...

"Brynn. *Brynn!* Are you all right?" Miranda MacKenzie reached out one hand to gently tap her arm.

"I'm sorry. Just thinking, I guess. About how beautiful the lodge is... And about Gregory."

"It's painful for us all, my dear." Flagrantly dyed blond hair bobbed as Miranda nodded her head. Ten years older than her brother Frank, she was holding on to the last of her middle age with a vengeance. Carefully applied makeup hid many of those years, as did her sharp, intelligent eyes and agile movements. Now that gaze met Brynn's. "But he's a sharp boy. Always was. Always figuring angles, coming up with answers no one else does. If anyone can get out of a sticky wicket, it's our Gregory."

Brynn listened to this new information about him, eager as always to gather more details. "Really?"

Miranda tipped her head, studying Brynn. "But surely you already know that. Gregory is a fairly open book—if you can find the index. He likes to put on airs as though he's part of an old Eastern family rather than an equally respectable Western one, but I've never let that dissuade me. And gauging from what I've seen, I doubt you do, either.''

Brynn remembered to shake her head and pretend that this was old news. "No, of course not. I'm sure— I mean, I know that Gregory is very proud of his heritage.''

Miranda looked puzzled again. "Usually not so that it shows. But I expect he let you beneath the layers since he married you. It would be horrific to keep up a pretense like that for long.''

"Absolutely," Brynn agreed with conviction. *Nothing less than horrific.* "I thought I smelled waffles....''

"Oh, I'm sorry. I forgot you hadn't eaten. There are waffles, omelets, french toast, you name it—it's all good. We have a minibrunch during the week, and on weekends it lasts till three in the afternoon, and we serve up everything but the woodwork. And there are times I wouldn't swear we hadn't thrown in a two-by-four, as well. But the guests love it.'' She took Brynn's arm. "The dining room's this way. And everyone's dying to meet you.''

Brynn gulped. "Gregory has more family?''

Miranda chuckled. "Not exactly. I was referring to the staff—but they're just like family. I think Dustin's the only one who actually met you when he brought up your drafting table. The others wanted to meet you as well, but Ruth insisted that you be given your rest and some privacy. Now I think your time's up!''

It was hard to take offense at Miranda's cheerful manner or words. So she was going to be the center of attention. Inwardly, Brynn cringed, hating just such situations. It was one of the reasons she loved her chosen field; she didn't have to deal with many attention-getting predicaments since it was Stephanie's face that graced the funny papers. Smoothing her hands down the soft fabric of her long skirt, Brynn hoped for some composure.

But composure flew out the window when the staff surrounded her, introducing themselves, asking her dozens of questions, crowding out any responses she had to make. It was at once overwhelming and heartwarming. As the MacKenzie family had done, the resort staff welcomed her with warmth and affection. It amazed her to think such openness existed outside of sitcoms and fairy tales.

When she finally sat down at a table, she nearly forgot she was there to eat. Instead, she let her dazed senses take in only a portion of what had transpired in the last twenty-four hours.

"You forgot to get a plate—" an amused voice washed over her "—not that one of your new devotees wouldn't be happy to fetch a plate, or fill it with what you want."

Brynn raised startled eyes and focused them on Matt MacKenzie. He sat at a small table next to hers, some sort of ledger spread out in front of him, along with a carafe of coffee and a thick white mug.

"Good morning," she replied cautiously. "Where do I get a plate?"

He gestured toward the buffet cart. "Unless you'd rather have something from the menu, but the brunch has the best of both—the day's specials and the pick of the menu."

"Uhm, thanks." She rose, suddenly self-conscious as she made her way to the cart to join the other guests already lined up for the buffet. Steaming servers held all sorts of wonderful-looking things, while a second smaller tray was filled with ice, cooling sliced fresh fruit, yogurt and cream cheese.

Deciding on a piece of french toast and some berries, Brynn carried her plate back, pausing as she looked between the table she'd chosen and the one Matt dominated. She wasn't certain she wanted to share that small space with him. Turned halfway toward her table, she stopped as Matt spoke.

"Would you care to join me?"

She wavered, wishfully glancing at the safety of her previous table before twisting back to face him. "Sure—uh, I mean, that would be nice. I'll just get my coffee."

But he was already stretching one of his long arms toward the other table, easily reaching her mug. She continued to stare, amazed at the agility of the man. He was so large—not like Gregory, who was a far more pared-down version. Matt's height included long arms and legs and big strong hands, not to mention an athletic build. She cleared her throat and jerked her eyes away, reminding herself that she really didn't care for such a physical sort of man.

"Thank you." Cautiously, she took the seat across from his, wishing he'd chosen a larger table, one where their legs didn't have to be practically touching. Tall herself, she knew that two pairs of long legs would have difficulty not brushing against each other.

"Did you sleep well?" Matt asked, moving his calculator so that her plate and mug fit more easily on the table.

She remembered the night, her initial restlessness, then her dreams about Gregory, how it would be to share his home, his bed. Embarrassed, she cleared her throat, suspecting that spots of color dotted her cheeks. "Yes. The mountain air is very refreshing."

He chuckled. "Most people say it freezes them out the first time they come up here."

"I do live in Salt Lake," she reminded him. "While it's in the valley, it's not exactly the flatlands."

"True, but it's not at the top of a mountain, either."

She smiled. "And it's a beautiful mountain."

For the first time, she saw a genuinely pleased expression cross his face. "It's that and more."

"So you've never had a desire to leave here, explore other ventures?"

Matt lifted one brow. "I *have* dragged myself away on occasion. Even us backwoods boys like to have a taste of the big city now and then."

Wondering if she'd insulted him, Brynn toyed with her french toast. If he enjoyed being a ski bum, why did her comment upset him? "I'm sure most people envy you your free-dom." She gestured toward the book in front of him, guessing he was doing some accounting for the resort. "Even though I'm sure you get roped in to working, as well."

A frown creased his forehead. "On occasion."

She smiled. "I'm a bit of a rebel, myself. That's why I like working out of my apartment. I set my own rules."

"I see."

"And on occasion, I like to get into the city myself," she added, hoping to lay oil on any ruffled feathers.

"I managed to stumble off the mountain myself this week."

She cocked her head, then remembered. "Of course. You went to Washington."

"And it's a funny thing."

"Oh?"

He stared at her. "You haven't asked what I found out about Gregory. Not once."

Brynn swallowed uncomfortably, caught in the web of her own making. "I thought if you had news, you would share it."

"Pretty big assumption."

She clutched her napkin, balling it into a wrinkled wad. "I think I'd better tell you—"

"Brynn! I thought you might be sleeping in!" Ruth greeted her, swooping down to give her a friendly hug. "You're still a touch pale. You're such a fragile thing—we'll have to feed you well until Gregory comes back. I don't want him to think we let you fade away."

"No, really. I'm fine—"

Ruth waved away her protests. "I'm going to bring you a plate of blintzes—full of cream, strawberries, and all kinds of wonderful things. Now don't go away. I'll be right back."

Torn, Brynn stared between Ruth's retreating back and Matt's unrelenting gaze. "Really, no one needs to fuss over me."

"Mother's right. You look as though a good wind would blow you over."

Brynn pushed at her glasses, mortified as always by her image as the tall, skinny kid.

Matt closed the ledger, seeming to sense her unease. "If she gets to be too much for you, just tell her to back off. Mother will smother you to death if you let her—all with good intentions. She and Dad are really glad you're here. They needed some part of Gregory to hang on to. Especially Dad."

"He's the one who looks fragile," she ventured.

"I'm afraid he is," Matt answered shortly. "But don't let him hear you say that."

Ruth was returning with the plate of blintzes. Brynn stared at them in dismay. She'd brought enough food for Brynn and half-a-dozen football players. "This really is too much."

"Just eat what you want," Ruth answered cheerfully, her attention caught by one of the guests who called out to her.

"You want a reprieve? Go to town with her," Matt advised. "She likes to leave early so she has time to cross the border into Idaho and buy a lottery ticket."

"There's a town?" Brynn questioned, always curious.

"Of sorts."

Brynn looked down at the mammoth serving of food. "You're sure she won't insist I eat all this first?" The thought of riding up and down the switchbacks of the winding canyon after eating nearly a mountain of food was unsettling.

"Nope." He tapped the side of his head. "Lottery ticket. Remember?"

"Suddenly I feel a winning streak coming on," Brynn decided.

"If you're really lucky, you won't win seconds," he warned, one lip curling upward in amusement as he glanced at her loaded plate.

Meeting his gaze, she was struck again by his terribly physical good looks. Hair the color of highly polished mahogany was laced with streaks of gold, no doubt from time spent on the slopes. His face—all slashes and angles of features that without their ruggedness would seem nearly too perfect—no doubt drew women in numbers, especially when they focused in on that dent in his chin, the sensuous lips, the dusky eyes.

Reining her thoughts in with an internal snap, she also straightened in her chair. It didn't matter what Matt looked like. At most all he could ever be was a brother-in-law. But he wasn't looking very brotherly at the moment.

Brothers. She had to remember. He was the brother of Gregory—the man who had captured her heart. The man who had been captured.

That thought shocked all others away.

She pushed away the plate, leaving it untouched. "Thanks for the advice. I'd better find a jacket. If your mother comes back, would you tell her I'd like to go to town? And that I won't make her late?"

Not giving him time to more than nod, Brynn rushed away. She was obviously certifiable. Not only was she playing a terrible trick on these people, she was now having unwanted thoughts about Gregory's brother. And Gregory was the one she needed to concentrate on.

Her Mr. Right—the man who would probably be shocked to find her installed in his family home. She needed to retrieve more than her jacket; she needed to recover what was left of her marbles.

BRYNN TOOK IN THE SIGHTS, the people, the small-town atmosphere—and found herself being charmed again. Although she'd lived in many places, her mother's tastes hadn't run to small-town Americana. In fact, Charlene Magee had been rather vocal about what she'd termed "the bumpkin factor." But Brynn really didn't share many of her mother's sensibilities. In fact, there was little they did share.

Ruth MacKenzie, on the other hand, wanted to share everything—including her friends and neighbors. So far, Brynn had been introduced to everyone they'd encountered. Which made traveling more than a dozen yards a time-consuming feat.

But it was a novel experience for her. Never having lived anyplace long enough to form any real friendships, she'd remained terminally shy. Even as an adult, she hadn't been able to conquer that fear, the timidity that prevented the closeness with other people, which she craved. Neighbors had remained strangers and even the number of her acquaintances had been limited. She'd certainly never talked to everyone she met on the street.

But now, Ruth easily paved the way, making it impossible for Brynn not to talk to those they met. Even the assortment of small-town shops seemed welcoming.

Leaving the hardware store, Ruth led them toward a small gift shop. The bell over the glass door tinkled out a welcome, blending with the aroma of freshly brewed cider.

"Ruth!" A woman greeted them. "Did you find out good news?"

"Yes and no," Ruth replied. "On the down side, we don't have any new updates on Gregory. But on the positive side, we brought his bride home. Wilma, meet Brynn."

Smiling self-consciously, Brynn held out a hand and found it swallowed in a surprisingly firm grip.

Wise, steel-blue eyes surrounded by a waterfall of wrinkles, zoned in on Brynn. "Well, well. I never thought that boy would ever settle down. And you're the girl who hooked him."

Ruth laughed. "What makes you think Gregory didn't do the hooking?"

"Because that boy was a chaser. Couldn't sit still for more than two seconds. He wouldn't settle down without a fight. Hell, he'd more likely ask for a recount."

Ruth patted Brynn's arm. "But Brynn's a very special girl."

"So I see," Wilma commented, her gaze skipping over

Brynn's baggy clothing and oversize glasses. "Tell me, how did you and Gregory meet?"

Brynn felt a trace of panic. Surprisingly, no one had asked her any more details, accepting that it troubled her to talk about it. And what would this apparently astute woman believe? Not that it had been love at first sight. What would Stephanie, the heroine of her comic strip, do?

Tell an outrageous tale.

That was easy. It was something Stephanie often did.

But something Brynn had never tried.

She took a deep breath, hoping she wouldn't be hitchhiking back to Salt Lake City if the story fell flat. "Gregory and I were working on a project together." That much was partially true, but she slid her fingers together behind her back as she continued. "And it seems he's not used to women who say no."

Wilma's brows rose.

Brynn smiled as she thought Stephanie might. "At heart, I guess Gregory really is old-fashioned." She barely kept from wincing at the incredulous expressions that flashed across both Wilma's and Ruth's faces. "I mean that *he* wanted to be the one to do the chasing. The women he'd been involved with were all bright and beautiful—but they didn't play hard to get. In fact, they chased him until they caught him. So Gregory wasn't used to someone who not only wouldn't chase him— but kept him at arm's length." Brynn thought briefly of the wedding album she'd had made and squirmed.

"What sort of project were you working on?" Wilma asked.

Brynn thought rapidly. She couldn't say the auction. There was a good chance Ruth knew about that—it had been publicized enough—and she'd know there hadn't been enough time for a courtship, engagement and wedding since the event. "I'm involved in a program to stop the overpopulation of homeless animals and...I headed a drive to get dogs and cats spayed and neutered. We found veterinarians willing to donate their time and facilities and the volunteers coordinated everything. Some on the medical end, some—''

"You met Gregory while you were castrating animals?" Wilma asked, horrified amusement flashing across her face.

"Well, not exactly. Gregory has such a way with animals—"

"He does?" Ruth interrupted, surprised.

"Well, yes... I mean, he's gotten very good with animals. Very good."

"But why was he volunteering before he found this affinity?" Wilma asked, skepticism showing in both her voice and expression.

What would Stephanie say? "I hate to reveal something that Gregory didn't already confide.... But, I guess if you'll keep it to yourselves..."

Ruth and Wilma both nodded eagerly, as did a younger woman who'd edged over from the middle of the shop and now stood, unabashedly listening.

"Gregory was working late...and there was an electrical fire. It started small but the smoke filled the building before anyone was aware of the fire."

"What about the smoke alarms?" Ruth questioned, her maternal protectiveness kicking in.

"There was some problem...but building maintenance got right on that after the fire so it won't happen again," Brynn assured her, reaching for plausible threads in her story. "Anyway, Gregory was so involved in his work that he didn't notice the smoke. The watchman let his dog loose so it wouldn't get burned, but instead the dog found Gregory. He'd passed out from smoke inhalation and if the dog hadn't found him..."

Ruth clutched her throat. "The dog saved his life? No wonder he changed his mind about animals."

"Yes," Brynn confirmed, realizing belatedly that this might not have been the best story to have invented since Ruth was already worried about her son's physical well-being.

"I didn't read about the fire," Wilma mused.

Brynn jerked her attention back to Wilma. "No! Like I said, it was just a small electrical fire with very little damage. Everything was up and running the next day. But it could have been so much worse."

"You know, life's funny," Wilma mused again. "A boy like Gregory never taking to animals much, but then one saves his life. It's as though life was giving him a new lesson. Maybe that's why his eyes were opened enough to see you."

Brynn guessed that was a backhanded compliment at best. Still, the story seemed to have convinced even the doubting Wilma.

"I wonder why Gregory never told us," Ruth pondered aloud.

Yipes. "He probably didn't want to worry you and now I've done that by telling the story. I shouldn't have—"

"No, I'm glad you did. Gregory never was one to confide much—and he doesn't call or get home as often as he used to. So busy now with his important job. But I like knowing that he could change his attitude like that." She squeezed Brynn's hand. "Maybe it means that family and home are becoming more important to him again."

By now three more women had joined their ranks and Brynn could see they were moved by the sentiment about family and home, even though they hadn't heard the complete tale.

At a loss for words, and realizing that this story was already making a lasting false impression, Brynn could only smile as the women surrounded her, offering congratulations and assaulting her with more questions.

"That's when he met you?" a pretty, thirtyish woman introduced as Karen asked. "After he'd changed his attitude?"

Brynn hedged. "I wouldn't say his attitude had *completely* changed."

"Not until he met *you*," another woman named Becky guessed. "He might have had his eyes opened a bit when the dog saved him, but it takes a person—a woman—to make a man really see the light.''

"That's so sweet," one of the other women introduced as Cynthia said, dabbing at her eyes. "A man changing because of the love of a good woman."

Glancing around, Brynn saw that the other women's eyes were starting to fill as well at that splash of sentiment. For a moment she *was* Stephanie. A girl with enough guts to go for her man and to change that man. Her thoughts drifted. And when Gregory came back, things *would* change. He would come to the same realizations that he had in her story.

Blinking, she remembered her audience. "I don't want to give you the wrong impression...." *Right. And who would believe that?*

Wilma waved away her concerns. "Pish. Just because men won't ever give the whole scoop doesn't mean you shouldn't." She reached between the women clustered around the counter and picked up a beautiful white basket filled with bath salts, soaps, candles and lotion. "Here's a little something to say welcome."

Touched, Brynn's hand flew toward her throat. "Oh, I couldn't. It's too much...." *It's so incredibly sweet.*

"When you two get settled...after Gregory comes home—" Wilma cleared her throat "—I'll send you a real wedding gift, but this is for you. You're part of the MacKenzie family now, so you're part of the community, too. And a new friend."

Brynn felt tears threatening, and she couldn't control a slight quivering of her lips. "This is so very...kind of you."

"Now don't you go all maudlin on me," Wilma warned, but without much conviction. "We'll have a regular waterworks going." She turned to Ruth. "Sure can see why Gregory woke up and got some sense when he met this girl."

Seeing how shaken Brynn was, Ruth took her arm. "I hate to break this up, but we have lottery tickets to buy."

"I already told you, *I'm* going to win Power Ball," Wilma

retorted, seeing through Ruth's words. "You bring your new daughter-in-law around often, you hear?"

Ruth nodded, steering Brynn outside. "Let's go get some coffee."

Brynn sniffed. "I thought we were going to get lottery tickets."

Ruth smiled. "They have coffee in Idaho."

Brynn laughed in spite of herself. "You do know how to chase away the maudlin moments."

"Every woman's entitled to them." They walked a few feet closer to the Bronco, then Ruth stopped suddenly. "There's not a special reason you're feeling particularly sentimental?"

It took Brynn a moment to catch her meaning. No, that would be too much. "There's not any special news, if that's what you're thinking."

"I didn't mean to pry. And, heavens, I'm sure you two want to be married awhile before you start your family. I just couldn't help asking...in case Gregory..."

"He's *going* to come home," Brynn assured her fiercely, knowing how unfair it would be to his family for him to not return.

Ruth smiled again. "With all your faith in him, how could he dare do anything else? They say that special love often brings a man through a terrible crisis, when otherwise... Well, let's just say I'm awfully glad he found you."

Brynn swallowed the truth as Ruth hugged her tightly.

Then Ruth opened the door to the Bronco. After they were buckled in, she turned the key and pointed the four-by-four northward. "Now...we're doubling our chances. We've got lottery tickets to buy."

Chapter Four

Matt watched the newest MacKenzie with interest. From his vantage point, he could observe Brynn without her knowledge. Not that he'd planned to study her. He had climbed up onto the ledge to check the footing along the path. While he was still there, Brynn had walked out on the huge rear deck that wound around the back of the lodge. Behind her trailed her faithful companions—the neurotic dog and nearly blind cat.

Staring at her, Matt doubted he could have imagined anyone more different from the kind of woman he thought Gregory would have chosen. He still found it hard to believe. Gregory had always gone for slick and sophisticated—the kind of woman who was an asset; one who could do something for Gregory.

Matt loved his brother, but he also knew him. And Gregory was no bleeding heart. He didn't go for waifish women who looked as though they might bolt at the sight of their own shadows.

Like Brynn.

Although now, alone with her pets, she didn't look so skittish. Still, it didn't seem likely that she traveled in the same circles his brother did. Maybe, being a cartoonist, she was accepted on the A-list as an eccentric.

Her oversize tuniclike blouse, pullover sweater, and long, flowing skirt hid any clue as to her body. He suspected she had one, but you wouldn't know it under those clothes. And Gregory was definitely a body man. In fact, his initial appraisal of women started below the neck. It would be hard to even *find* Brynn's neck.

She laughed—a light silvery sound that danced around her as she played with the dog. What did she call him? Lancelot? What kind of name was that for a dog? Matt hoped she didn't plan to give her children weird names like that. Might as well pin Kick Me signs on them.

The thought of his brother being a father was unsettling. Gregory hadn't had time or energy for anyone except himself for years. When their father's health had deteriorated, Gregory hadn't even considered helping at the resort. As he'd told Matt, it was unfortunate, but he simply didn't have the time.

It was hard to reconcile that attitude with one that could have changed enough for him to marry a woman like Brynn.

As Matt watched, the ill-named dog jumped up at her, his short legs pawing at her knees, trying to get the toy she was holding just out of reach. With a laugh, she tossed it to him, clearly a game they often played since the dog retrieved the toy and then began another tug-of-war with her.

The cat, meanwhile, lay in the shadow of Brynn's feet, apparently content to simply be close by. Matt wondered why she hadn't brought her foulmouthed bird along as well. Then, out of the corner of his eye, he saw the bird waddling through the open doors. Her menagerie was complete.

Matt wondered how Gregory handled her animals. His brother thought all pets were worthless—messy, troublesome, and in the way. Whatever spell Brynn had cast over him had been all-encompassing. And how had she spun this magical hex?

It was difficult to tell much about Brynn with her face hidden behind those mammoth glasses and the wild mop of shiny black hair that almost obscured her features. And any time he got close enough to try and see, she nearly ran. The early-morning light skipped over her face, then gleamed on her hair, unexpectedly casting her in a soft, feminine glow as she continued her carefree laughter.

Matt hadn't seen her in an unguarded mood before. Relaxed, with no one around but her animals, she acted like a different person. Normally she was so stiff she looked like she'd been dipped in starch. He wondered why.

Of course, having all your in-laws thrust on you at once could be pretty intimidating. Especially his family. Still…there was something. Something else, he guessed. Something he couldn't put his finger on.

Seeing her stroll to the other end of the deck, Matt took the opportunity to hike back down the path, catching her unaware as she spun around to throw the dog's toy. Her pale skin was flushed and her huge blue eyes sparkled. For once, her full lips were turned upward in a wide, genuine smile.

Until she spotted him.

Then they formed an "O" of surprise. The dog immediately leaped in front of her, providing a small but determined barrier.

"Hello! I didn't hear you." She gestured toward the dog. "I was playing with Lancelot."

"I know. I was watching." At her puzzled look, he pointed upward. "From the ledge."

She cast her startled gaze upward, apparently surprised to see there was a ledge above. "Oh."

Matt guessed it made her uncomfortable to know he'd been watching. "I climbed up to check the condition of the path. We like to keep our guests in one piece."

"Of course." She pushed at her glasses. "You're sort of a jack-of-all-trades, aren't you? A little bookkeeping, some garden maintenance. I imagine it keeps you from getting bored before the ski season."

He repressed a smile. "You could say that."

She dared a shy smile of her own. "I've never skied myself. But it looks so graceful…and beautiful." Her face pinkened a bit. "But then I guess men don't like to hear something they do being described as beautiful."

Actually, it was unexpectedly affecting. "Skiing is beautiful. It won't cost me my macho image to admit that."

There was a strange expression in her eyes that flickered, then disappeared. Before he could analyze it, she was backing away, ready to flee again if he guessed right.

Anticipating her move, he reached out and caught her arm. Surprised by the unexpected connection, he let his hand linger, his grip tightening briefly. Seeing an answering light in her eyes, he withdrew his hand abruptly. "Why don't we have some coffee?" He saw her scramble for excuses, but he planned to derail them all. "I'll order a carafe out here."

Brynn tried to protest. "I really should walk Lancelot—"

"He's already had quite a run out here on the deck."

"Well, yes, but—"

"Have you had breakfast yet?"

She hesitated. "No, but—"

"You can have a light breakfast out here…or join my mother for a more hearty version in the dining room."

Although there was a crisp chill in the air, they were both dressed warmly and the potbellied stove on the deck warmed the area. He could see the struggle in her eyes. She'd be no poker player; her face was a transparent window.

"Maybe just coffee and a bagel."

He nodded, pulled out his cell phone and ordered breakfast to be served on the rear deck.

"One of the perks of living in a resort," she commented, first twisting her hands, then shoving them into her pockets, then withdrawing them to cross them over her arms.

Matt wondered if she was that nervous around all men or just him.

Brynn fiddled with her hands again. "Do you have any news about Gregory?"

Matt frowned. "I just got off the phone a short time ago.

They found Gregory's rental car abandoned about twenty miles out of the city. It was clean, no prints. But no blood or bullet holes either. That reinforces their theory—the kidnappers are only after money so they're keeping the merchandise in good shape."

"Isn't there anything we can do?"

"I've been to Washington, rattling every connection we have. I want to go to South America but the State Department said that could hurt Gregory's chances. The kidnappers will probably want a clean electronic cash transfer. If we show up on their doorstep, they could get nervous and hurt Gregory."

Brynn nodded. "I see."

Matt laid a hand over hers. "Trust me. We're doing everything we possibly can to get him home. Dad and I have called every contact we know and then some."

"And you think Drake Chemical will pay what they ask?"

"If not, the family will raise the money somehow, even if it means mortgaging Eagle Point," Matt replied grimly.

Brynn's expression softened. "He's lucky to have you."

Glancing up, he caught her gaze. "And you."

Again, distress clouded her features.

Uncertain how to deal with her, Matt reached down to pet the dog. "How'd you like the trip to town?"

She tilted her head to one side as recognition dawned. "You *knew* how it was going to be. You set me up!"

He shrugged, not completely able to hide his grin. "There's nothing quite like a small town."

"It was like throwing new meat to the lions," she dissented. "While everyone was very nice, you could tell they were hungry for something...or someone...different. And they had the scent of my trail from the minute we got to town."

"I didn't actually call ahead and tell everybody to be on the lookout. But you'll find that there's no need. There's an invisible grapevine that works with a mystique of its own. But then,

I guess you won't actually be spending that much time here once Gregory returns.''

She fumbled again with her hands, finally tucking them at her sides. "No, I guess not."

"You're both big-city people. It's where you belong."

She studied him. "But you and Gregory come from the same place. Why is it he's big-city and you're not?"

"Didn't you ask him?"

She pushed at her glasses. "Before he was... Before he disappeared, I hadn't met you. No reason to ask."

Matt studied her for another moment. "Gregory and I never were much alike, didn't want the same things, the same places. He dreamed about leaving for bigger places. I dreamed about making this place bigger."

"This place?" she echoed.

"Eagle Point. The land's plenty big enough, but the resort can be bigger."

"Does your family's land take up quite a few acres?"

So Gregory hadn't thought enough of the family business to even tell her the rudiments. "More than a few. Why don't I show you around today? I have trails to check."

"But I don't want to be any trouble—or to get in the way."

"You're a MacKenzie now. You have a right to be here, to learn about the family legacy."

"Oh." Her voice was very small, very subdued.

"You'll want to wear something rugged, suited to the trails," he continued.

She glanced down at her silky skirt. "This won't do?"

"We'll go part of the way in the truck, part of the way on four-wheelers. It's not a ride to make in a skirt."

"I'm not sure I brought anything appropriate," she demurred. "I guess I won't be able to come along."

"I'll ask Mother to get you something from the gift shop. We have all the basics."

"But I don't want to be any—"

"Trouble. I know. You aren't. You'll want to see where Gregory grew up—learn a little more about his roots. It doesn't sound like he filled you in much."

"Not too much."

Tracy, one of the girls from the kitchen staff, brought out a tray with the light breakfast Matt had ordered.

"I added some fruit and croissants," Tracy told them as she unloaded the tray. "And a little bit of smoked salmon. Oh, and some muffins and Canadian bacon. Those bagels looked kind of lonely by themselves." As she spoke, Tracy placed dishes of whipped honey butter, strawberry preserves, and fresh cream cheese on the table.

"It looks wonderful," Brynn responded graciously.

Tracy beamed. "I can tell you've hardly been eating a thing since— Well, we just want you to be all healthy and rested up."

"Thanks for your concern, Tracy. I don't think I'll go hungry—not with all this delicious food."

After the girl left, Matt looked at Brynn with growing respect. Most of the women Gregory had dated would have thought nothing of haughtily sending the food back. "It was kind of you to not refuse all the extras."

Brynn sighed. "I know it's a plot. I'll be so 'healthy' you won't be able to pry me through the doorway."

Matt tried not to grin. "It's just their way of saying they care."

Brynn lowered her coffee cup. "I know. I just don't know why."

Matt considered her. "Aren't you used to people showing their concern?"

Brynn shrugged and he could see she was uncomfortable. "I'm used to big cities—living where you don't even know your neighbors."

"But your family?"

"Is small," she replied shortly. "We don't have an...extended family like you seem to here. In fact, it's just my mother and me.''

"And Gregory," he reminded her.

She blinked. "Yes, of course. And Gregory."

Matt picked up the plate of bagels. "I don't want to rush you, but we've got a resort to check out."

She accepted a bagel. "I'm really not all that hungry."

"You wouldn't want to hurt Tracy's feelings, would you?"

She lowered the bagel, a smile playing about her lips. "The lure of the outside breakfast was that I didn't have to eat the lumberjack special."

He laughed. "Some lumberjack you'd make." Not asking her permission, he forked a small piece of smoked salmon onto her plate. "And don't worry. I can handle the croissants and Canadian bacon."

Brynn took a muffin and delicately separated it into small pieces. "Lancelot can show that he appreciates the breakfast, as well." The dog still sat protectively at her side.

"I suspect the cat's going to enjoy the salmon," Matt guessed.

She grinned. "Caught red-handed. I really only want half the bagel with just a touch of cream cheese and a bite of the salmon. And I'd hate to hurt Tracy's feelings...."

Matt couldn't resist her grin. "Good excuse for feeding your beasts."

She gave Lancelot a bite of the muffin before glancing up at Matt in surprise. "It just occurred to me that Lancelot isn't growling at you."

"I'm not growling at him, either."

"You don't understand. He always responds that way to men. I don't know why he's behaving differently with you."

The dog pawed at her knee and automatically she fed him another bite of muffin.

"He doesn't seem particularly threatened," Matt observed, wondering why her dog had such a distaste for men. She didn't look like the sort of woman who would have a parade of men in her life.

Brynn stroked the dog's head. "I guess not. Perhaps being away from the city is so different..." She smiled in an abrupt burst of joy. "The unexpected has a way of changing animals, I suppose—and people."

Matt guessed there was a meaning beneath her words. But at the moment he was more fascinated by the transformation in her face. Somewhere beneath those glasses and all that hair, there was more than he'd expected.

But then she seemed to remember something as she drew back in. "You're right. I should finish my breakfast." She plucked the bagel from her plate. "In fact, I'll take it along with me. I have to find something *rugged* to wear."

"I'll talk to Mother about it. She can find something in the gift shop. There's no need to rush your breakfast." But even as he spoke, Matt watched her wrap the bagel in a napkin, along with a bit of the salmon—for the cat, no doubt.

"I do have to get the animals settled in, too," she replied, rising and edging toward the door.

Matt realized there was no stopping her. He wondered if she was part sprite. The thought barely surfaced and she'd disappeared, calling to the cat and dog and offering her arm to the bird. Noah's little helper.

Shaking his head, Matt glanced at all the food left on the table, then back at the spot where Brynn had disappeared. He realized she'd left him a lot to chew on.

BRYNN GLANCED DOUBTFULLY in the mirror atop the oak dresser in her room, wishing for a full-length one so she could see just how the new clothes fit. Ruth MacKenzie had brought jeans that while not tight were certainly more formfitting than the clothes she was accustomed to wearing. And the chambray shirt and cotton-ramie sweater were also very tailored. Feeling like an Eddie Bauer advertisement, she turned again, trying to gauge the allover effect.

But the mirror just wasn't large enough to give her a true picture. If she'd been more adept, she'd have managed to avoid the entire situation, rather than having to decide if the clothes looked all right. But somehow she'd gotten caught up in the conversation with Matt, momentarily forgetting his relation to Gregory. She glanced at the album on the dresser, quickly opening it to the first picture and caressing the familiar face. It wouldn't do to forget again.

The grandfather clock in the wide hallway outside her room chimed the half hour and Brynn realized she was dawdling. It wasn't like her to spend so much time on her appearance. She swiped at her hair, the curls springing back seconds later. Grimacing at her reflection, she grabbed her glasses and looked wistfully at the album, knowing she had no time to indulge herself, reluctantly closing the cover.

She paused at the door to look at her pets. "Okay, guys. Behave." Lancelot thumped his tail, his eyes pleading to be taken. "Next time, Lancelot. I don't think *I* can ride one of those all-terrain vehicle things, so I really don't think I ought to kill us both."

"Later, baby!" Bossy called out, scratching at the water dish in his cage.

"You too, Bossy." Petting both Lancelot and Snookems, she slipped out. Since she hadn't made specific arrangements to meet Matt, she went to the most obvious place—the lobby. But other than the desk clerk and a few guests, it was empty. Mentally, she ticked off the other conspicuous places, then realized she ought to be looking outside instead of inside.

Pushing open the huge double doors that led outside, she spotted Matt with two staffers. His truck was pulled into the wide circular drive and an ATV sat in the bed of the pickup. Swallowing her apprehension, Brynn ventured closer. Matt looked up for a moment, glanced back at the young man he was talking to, then looked again at Brynn.

Nervously she swiped her hands against the legs of her jeans, feeling self-conscious in the tailored clothes. She smiled at him gamely, wishing the tour was already over. Always uncomfortable around men, she didn't relish time spent alone with this one. Had it been Gregory—the man whose face she'd come to know as well as her own—it would be different. He would gently take her hand and walk with her along the paths they had separately jogged for months. Then he would—

"Brynn. *Brynn*," Matt repeated, wondering where she'd slipped off to. When she'd walked outside, it had taken a moment for him to recognize her. His eyes had been riveted by her impossibly long legs, the curve of her slender waist and the unmistakable flare of additional curves. And his gut had responded immediately with an instinctive jolt that didn't feel even a fraction brotherly.

The breeze blew back her hair, long dark strands that curled over her shoulders, revealing her features, obscured only by her gargantuan glasses. Matt had the ridiculous urge to pull them off, to see just what they hid. Instead, he tried again to catch her attention. "Earth to Brynn."

She flushed, apparently embarrassed she'd been caught daydreaming. "I'm sorry. I was thinking about something else."

"It's all right." He gestured at her new clothes. "Looks like you got outfitted for the day."

She ran a hand over the unfamiliar jeans. "Yes... They still seem strange."

"They don't look strange." He'd meant to sound casual, but instead his gaze lingered a fraction too long on her legs, before traveling upward to her face.

Sudden awareness vibrated between them.

But this time the urge to flee he'd seen in her expression combined with something else—something Matt knew he had to be imagining. That spark couldn't be coming from his brother's bride.

Gregory. He had to remember his brother. He was the reason Matt was showing the property to Brynn. He was the reason she was here at all.

"Are you ready, then?" Matt asked gruffly, turning away.

Taken aback by his abrupt tone, she hastened toward the truck. "Yes. I didn't mean to hold you up."

"I know. You don't want to be any trouble."

"Yes, no. I mean, you're right. I don't."

It wasn't her fault she made a simple pair of jeans look more appealing than the best of Victoria's Secret. He muttered a reply as he opened the truck and waited for her to climb inside.

Pulling away from the driveway, Matt couldn't help noticing that she'd perched on the seat like a child taking her first train ride—staring at the sights eagerly. Withholding a sigh, he swallowed his own unreasonable attitude. "You can see one of the closer lifts right over there."

"Oh! And you can walk right out the front door of the lodge and climb on. What a clever idea!"

Her enthusiasm was contagious. While the resort had always meant a lot to him, it wasn't often he found outsiders who shared his enthusiasm. But then she wasn't an outsider, he had to remind himself.

Matt pointed up the sloping mountain. "And there's the alpine slide, one of the off-season activities."

"Do you get many guests when it's not ski season? Is there anything for them to do?"

"We get more guests every year. We've begun advertising as a true four-season resort." His tone turned wry. "And we find a few things for them to do—hiking, backpacking, kayaking—or you can ride the wind via sailboard."

"And that's enough to get people to come way out here?"

"We have trout fishing—three creeks run through Eagle Point. And there's horseback riding, miles of alpine dirt roads and back-country trails for biking, and sailing, golfing. The mountains call to a lot of people. This summer we had a group of ornithologists...."

"Birdwatchers," she mused. "They would love it here, I'm sure."

"There's a forty-nest great blue heron rookery not far from here. They were in birdwatcher heaven."

"Any other specialty groups?"

"Plenty. We get a lot of people who want to explore ghost towns. We take them jeeping to deserted gold mines and old settlements in the high country that have been abandoned a long time ago."

"Really? What's that like?"

He resisted a grin, thinking of his own boyhood memories, and the lure of a ghost town no youngster could resist. "Sometimes there's not much to see besides a lot of tumbleweed. Other times, if you're quiet and listen, you can almost hear the laughter of the old-timers."

"Or the pain," she murmured, not seeming at all skeptical about the existence of ghostly laughter.

"Maybe. I like to think they were happy. It was a simpler time."

She caught his inflection and slanted a grin at him. "Before tourists?"

"Touché."

She smiled, enjoying the talk, enjoying him. "In other words, there are plenty of all-season activities."

He grunted an assent. "Course I didn't tell you about one."

She angled toward him with interest. "What's that?"

"You can go listening."

"'Listening'?" she echoed.

"Yep." He glanced her way, catching her gaze.

"For what?" she asked, eyes wide with interest.

"For bull elk and buck deer forming their harems."

"'Harems'?" she repeated before the meaning sank in. A fiery heat filled her face. "Oh."

He laughed—a rich masculine sound that filled the truck. "Think we have enough variety to interest everyone?"

She fiddled with the unfamiliar denim of her jeans. "Certainly sounds like it."

Her embarrassment was painful to watch and he took pity on her. "Every season needs variety. In the winter we also have snowmobiling, cross-country skiing, ice-skating."

She spotted another ski lift, trying to tame the fire that still blazed in her cheeks. "But skiing's still the big thing, isn't it?"

"It's the main thrust of our business and always will be. We have trails for everyone—from beginner to enough black-diamond runs to snatch your breath away."

Brynn craned her head to see the tops of the majestic mountains, covered in snow year-round. "It must be something to live around this all the time. Not that I don't see mountains from Salt Lake, but these are so...immediate."

It was an unusual description, but one he felt himself. "Never could see why people would want to live in the city when they're surrounded by mountains. The view would just make you want to escape that much more."

"I don't think I ever felt exactly like escaping." She glanced thoughtfully out the truck window. "But then I wasn't raised here. I guess once this is in your blood, you could never live comfortably in the city."

"Gregory manages."

Her head jerked back toward him, then away again. "Yes, of course."

"But then you know that."

She didn't meet his gaze, instead turning to stare again out the window. "Of course. I...tend to get swept up in new experiences, the sights, the sounds. I have a...rather active imagination."

"Is that why you became a cartoonist?" he asked, easily navigating the well-known road.

Her face screwed into a mask of concentration. "That's not a simple question. I've always loved drawing, even painting. And I fell in love with my first comic strip as soon as I could read. I loved all the daring, better-than-real-life things the characters got away with. I used to wish I could be like my favorites."

"Sort of an alter ego."

"Not many people understand that," Brynn exclaimed, surprised. Then she laughed—a small, embarrassed sound. "So, I drifted toward art school, got an internship with Marvel, then got a break being a colorist for an established cartoonist."

"And how was *Stephanie* born?"

She tilted her head. "Funny you should phrase it like that. Most people think it's just an impersonal drawing. Stick figures with bubbles for thoughts—characters with no more spirit than pieces of fruit in a still life."

Matt studied the waifish sprite next to him. "But *Stephanie*'s more to you than that?"

She nodded. "The day she popped into my brain, she was doing something outrageous—and there she was—full-blown, bursting to get on the paper."

"And she's been doing the outrageous ever since."

Brynn looked at him in surprise. "You read the strip?"

"Who doesn't?"

Again she looked shy, embarrassed. "Oh, well, I wouldn't say—"

"You know it's a successful cartoon?"

"It does okay."

He couldn't help raising his eyebrows. *Okay?* It was a nationally syndicated comic strip, one that had its own line of merchandise. Yet, she seemed uncomfortable with the praise, or possibly her success.

Since he wasn't comfortable with people probing at his motives or feelings, either, to change the subject he pointed at the mountains she'd admired. "These are the Wellsvilles—the steepest mountains in America."

Properly impressed, she gazed upward. "They all seem overwhelming. But I thought these were the Rockies."

"The Wellsvilles are part of the Rockies." The truck navigated a sharp turn and Brynn stared downward at a sheer cliff that plunged from the narrow precipice into a canyon that looked as though it was miles wide and equally deep.

"They're certainly something," she commented in an unnaturally high voice, her eyes wide as she calculated the small distance between the truck and the yawning depths of the canyon.

"In the next valley there's a turquoise gem filled with water—Bear Lake. In the summer when you crest the summit before the valley, and the sun hits the water, you'd swear something that clear and pure aqua has to be fake. You look for the chlorine and the pumps."

"How does it stay like that?"

"It's a prehistoric formation. Beneath the surface are the peaks of an ancient mountain range, so it's incredibly deep."

"And incredibly clear," Brynn murmured. "I'd love to see it some time."

The truck easily took the next precarious turn. "Until then you can see the Bear River. It runs through our property."

"I love all the icy mountain streams," she confessed. "They're so pristine they don't look real. Just like the first time I saw a mountain sunset. It looked like something a painter or postcard artist dreamed up—so beautiful it wasn't believable."

Matt felt admiration flare. "I guess I don't think about how people not living here see it for the first time." He laughed wryly. "Even though we put out brochures describing it in great detail."

"It's not always easy to see something you're so close to."

His gaze flickered to one side. "You're right about that." Seeing the cutoff on the road, he turned, gravel crunching beneath the truck's wide tires. "This is where we get out."

He'd barely spoken when the alarm on her watch buzzed.

"Bus to catch?" he questioned, his brow raised in surprise.

Embarrassed, she quickly turned off the alarm. "I set alarms to remind myself when I need to do something."

"Forgetful, are you?"

"Guess you could say that. I set alarms so I'll look at the notes I've written to remind myself to do certain things."

He glanced over her thoroughly. "I don't see any notes."

Warmed beneath his scrutiny, she had to clear her throat. "I didn't bring the note."

"Anything important?"

"I don't think so."

"You don't *think* so?"

She shrugged, knowing other people found her forgetfulness and disorganization hard to understand. "It was probably to remind myself to finish the strips in time for the shuttle driver to take them to the express office."

"Should we skip the ride so you can make your deadline?"

Brynn considered, then decided it was the chicken's way out. Besides, her conscience needed the relief of telling the truth when possible. "No. Actually, tomorrow's shuttle will be better. Then I'll have more time to go over the final product."

He studied her for just a moment before exiting the truck.

Brynn waited as Matt opened her door, silently appreciating the mannerly gesture, especially in the rugged surroundings. But she watched him unload the four-wheeler with trepidation. Never the athletic sort, she felt gangly and awkward doing anything other than the simplest things. She'd been relieved to see only one ATV, and assumed that meant he would be driving. She fervently hoped that Matt did all the steering and the only thing she had to do was hold on. For dear life, she reminded herself.

"Do these all-terrain vehicles hurt the ecology of the land?" It was a desperate ploy.

"Obviously people impact the environment, but as long as we only leave footprints and not destruction, we're not disturbing the balance."

"Uh-huh." No help there. "Is there much to riding one of these things?" she asked, hoping to sound casual, knowing she failed miserably.

His gaze settled on her for a moment. "Nothing to worry about. Just hang on."

Brynn couldn't prevent a sigh of relief.

"They're pretty harmless," Matt continued.

Meeting his gaze, she saw that he had sensed her anxiety. "I'm sure they are. I've just never been on one."

He grinned suddenly, changing tactics. "Then you don't know what you've been missing."

Incredibly, his excitement was contagious. She found her fear fading as he held out a tanned, strong hand. Tentatively she accepted his grip and climbed on the vehicle behind him, far to the rear, at the edge of the seat. As she searched for a place to hold on, Matt twisted around.

"Unless you plan to fly off when we hit the first rock, you'd better move up and hold on."

Gingerly she scooted forward. "To what?"

"Me."

"Oh." With great care she touched two fingers from each hand to his waist.

He shook his head, then reached out and took both her hands, clamping them firmly around his waist. She gulped, feeling hard muscle beneath the denim covering his lean hips, trying to ignore the fact that she was pressed into the ungiving line of his back. But before she could assimilate the sensations, they were moving.

Expecting to be terrified, instead she was exhilarated as they traveled down the mountainside, the breeze hitting her cheeks, flattening Matt's shirt to his skin, sending her unexpected laughter into the trees.

Expertly, he drove the trail and Brynn could understand the appeal of these freedom machines, easily forging a path where on-the-road vehicles dared not go.

On her own, Brynn would never have ventured into something this out of the ordinary, this different from her normal, safe life. Which was why it felt all that much more exciting.

Closing her eyes for a moment, she tried to recapture the days before the MacKenzies had whisked her away—the sameness, the loneliness. Now each moment was filled with something new.

Matt turned just then, flashing his even-toothed white smile. And suddenly she focused more on how handsome Matt was than on the thrill of this new experience. He had eyes like a cougar, she realized—green with enough gold flecks to give an air of mystery to his Marlboro-man looks. Suddenly the pit in her stomach had nothing to do with the lingering traces of fear from riding the four-wheeler. It was a far different kind of fear.

"We're on a snowmobiling trail," he shouted above the wind. "Farther up it's still covered in snow, and in winter this part will be, too."

Brynn jerked her attention away from his magnetic pull to look again at the wilderness. It was hard to imagine the blanket of snow to come while juniper and lupine scented the air and columbine, Jacob's ladder, sego lilies and wild roses scattered amid the knee-high wild grass, poking their scarlet, fragile pink, ivory and amethyst heads skyward.

"But it's so wonderful right now," she shouted back.

His grin widened. "Enough to bring in tourists?"

"I was young and foolish when I thought that," she replied with a grin of her own, not knowing where her sudden daring sprang from. For a moment she'd imagined what Stephanie would have done in the circumstances. But Brynn didn't think she was brave enough to insist on driving the ATV as Stephanie would have done.

Matt threw his head back and laughed, a husky, richly masculine sound that warmed something deep inside. Brynn hadn't felt anything like that since the first time she saw Gregory on the jogging paths, when he'd brushed by so closely she'd nearly tripped. He'd said, "Excuse me," and her heart had nearly stopped. That was when she'd known that Gregory was the one.

Gregory!

She'd nearly forgotten him in the heady rush of new awakenings. Closing her eyes, she pictured the wedding album, Gregory's strong face, his assertive manner, the many things she admired about him...the many things she'd fantasized about him and the life they would have together.

Without realizing it, Brynn loosened her grip. The four-wheeler hit a bump and she flew up, slamming into Matt's back, nearly unseating him. Definitely unseating her daydreams.

He reached back to steady her, grazing her breasts as he grasped her arm.

Brynn froze.

When Matt didn't immediately release her arm, she felt her heart begin to gallop, racing with the growing pit in her stomach to see which would knock her flat first.

She tried desperately to guess what Stephanie would do. And knew without a doubt that Stephanie had never encountered a man like Matt.

And neither had she.

Chapter Five

Matt reread the fax, translating the bureaucratic double-talk. They didn't know anything more about Gregory. To all intents, he'd disappeared off the face of the earth. But Matt suspected that very image was strategy—to force his brother's firm to give in to their demands when they were presented.

Yet, Matt couldn't stop the unwanted thought that maybe something more drastic had happened to Gregory. Even though they hadn't been as close since his brother had moved to the city, there was still a strong connection. That connection told him Gregory was alive. And no doubt kicking and screaming that he was being deprived of his espresso, penthouse apartment, and Armani suits.

Yet the fax burned in his hand. It wasn't the sort of news his parents needed—especially his father. Frank MacKenzie's precarious health had worsened considerably with Gregory's disappearance. Even though his father tried to hide it, Matt could see that the daily strain was stealing his energy and what remained of his health.

And although Ruth MacKenzie made quite a show of keeping a brave, upbeat appearance, Matt could see that she was doing so only for her family's sake. Fearful over her husband's worsening health, worried about Heather's and Andy's reactions, Ruth was determined to be a pillar of strength. But Matt could see the cracks in that pillar.

His younger siblings were worried, too. Fourteen-year-old Heather, who'd always worshiped everything about her oldest brother, had been hit especially hard. Her constant laughter had diminished, along with the groups of kids that had always hung out at Eagle Point. Now only her closest friends came to visit and even those were quiet visits. And Andy spent far more time in his room than he ever had before—a highly unnatural state for a nine-year-old.

Remarkably, the one thing that glued his family together and gave them hope was Brynn.

Despite how ill-suited she seemed to be for Gregory, Brynn was the embodiment of the hope all the MacKenzies had mustered.

Yet Matt still wondered. The more he learned about her convinced him that she and Gregory were more likely to share a shuttle to Mars than a marriage.

She couldn't be any more different than his success-driven brother. Yet, he could see why any man would be drawn to her.

That elusive, elfin quality of hers, hidden behind all the barriers she erected, was a challenge—the kind of challenge he guessed had pushed Gregory into making an uncharacteristic move.

Matt's thoughts returned to how Brynn had looked in the jeans, his reaction when he'd accidentally brushed her breasts. Neither feeling had been the least bit brotherly. And with the fax still in his hand, Matt felt a pang of disloyalty so strong he winced.

Walking out of the office area, he heard a babble of voices, mostly feminine. But at Eagle Point, there could be any number of reasons for a gathering—not that his mother's friends always needed one.

As he rounded the corner into the lobby he spotted his aunt Miranda in the middle of a group of nearly a dozen women. But all the attention was focused elsewhere. On Brynn.

Folding his arms, Matt leaned against the antique sideboard, watching. And listening.

Miranda tried to get the group under control. "I'm sorry. I forgot about our quilting day. But what with the excitement about Gregory and then Brynn coming, I just lost track of the days."

The babble broke out again and Miranda clapped her hands together. "I'm getting the feeling that you'd all rather talk to Brynn than quilt, anyway."

Wilma, owner of the gift shop, smiled unabashedly. "Word got around about how these two met...."

Matt's ears pricked up. That was a story he'd like to hear.

"And everyone just can't believe how you've changed Gregory," Wilma continued, her attention turned toward Brynn.

"I wouldn't say *changed*," Brynn tried to protest.

Becky, a woman who looked younger than her forty years, spoke up. "We'd love to see your wedding album." She smiled wistfully. "Ruth told us the pictures were wonderful."

Brynn tried to demur again, but they wouldn't hear of it.

"We really want to see the pictures," Wilma nearly pleaded.

"Please," Karen chimed in. Brynn recognized her as well from town, along with Jean, a woman who sat by her side. "I just love wedding pictures."

"We all do," Jean agreed. "Lord knows why, when marriage comes along with it, but I guess we're just saps about the romance thing." A recent divorcée, Jean held little stock in love and marriage these days.

"Actually, I'm not sure just where I put the album," Brynn evaded, her conscience prickling since she knew exactly where it was—prominently displayed as the centerpiece of her room. She spent every spare moment studying the pictures, dreaming of her reunion—rather, her meeting—with Gregory.

"I've got the album the photographer sent us," Ruth volunteered. "And I know just where it is."

As she disappeared, Brynn wished for some sort of escape

hatch. Instead, the ladies crowded around closer. It was gratifying that they were so welcoming since it was something she'd never before experienced. But Brynn knew she was an impostor, that the person they were inviting into their fold didn't exist; and that made their welcome bittersweet.

In what seemed like seconds, Ruth returned with the wedding album. Knowing she was sunk, Brynn took a seat in the middle of the long, leather couch. Miranda sat next to her and, glancing up, Brynn caught her encouraging look. Sensing a sympathetic, possibly even kindred spirit, Brynn was grateful for her presence.

Then Ruth opened the album, sighing as she traced her fingers over the first picture, her eyes fixed on Gregory's clear, confident expression.

Brynn felt a new spurt of guilt. Was this too cruel? Should she just confess everything now, tell these kind people the truth?

"I'm so glad you two found each other," Ruth murmured. "I always worried about Gregory.... But, now, I know at least he found the right partner in life." With visible effort, she brightened. "The pictures are wonderful, ladies. But I'll let Brynn take you through them."

Ruth closed the album before passing it along. Miranda accepted the album from her sister-in-law and gave Brynn an encouraging pat as she handed her the book. Brynn took a deep breath, remembering all the scenarios she had created in her mind since she'd had the album made. She had told the photographer that she wanted to create an album since she and Gregory had eloped.

Of course, Brynn could hardly confide that she'd chosen the casual wedding photos because the more formal ones required group—especially family—sittings. This way there were no gaps where parents and siblings should be, where the best man and maid of honor would be missed.

Brynn wondered how she would explain this odd choice, the

casual poses. Then an unbidden thought popped into her head. What would her strip's heroine do? Fearless Stephanie wouldn't let a bunch of curious women intimidate her. No, she'd invent a story that would make her "wedding" seem like the ideal ceremony, one all these hard-core romantics would sigh over.

She'd had a huge selection of computer-enhanced locations to choose from—everything from the nondescript to the wildly exotic. The images were taken from genuine photos and the resulting pictures of the bride and groom looked equally genuine.

For Brynn, the choice of locations had been easy. All of her life she'd dreamed of the land of her ancestors. The stories of Ireland that her grandmother Magee had told her as a child had never been forgotten. Losing her grandmother when she'd been only ten years old had been the most traumatic event of her young life. But while her loving presence was gone, her stories had never been forgotten.

And Brynn had imagined a wedding set somewhere between the green fields and windswept moors of Ireland. Amid thatched cottages and stone-cobbled roads. For a moment, Brynn stared down at the album that she had lovingly studied for so many hours.

Clearing her throat, she opened the first page. "As you all know, Gregory and I eloped."

Matt settled in to listen, anticipating the details. But just then one of the clerks caught his attention, needing his decision on a tour reservation, a group that wanted to book nearly the entire lodge.

While Matt was diverted, several heads nodded and Brynn tried to regain Stephanie's courage.

"A lot of people don't understand why a couple elopes— the magic, the spirit of romance that captures them."

The heads that nodded were now sighing.

Brynn held up the album, showing them the first page—just

her face and Gregory's in cutout ovals. "And I wanted a record of our courtship, so that's the kind of album we have. It's not traditional, but it tells our story. And this is us when we first met."

There was a chorus of oohs and aahs.

Taking a deep breath, Brynn turned the page. She and Gregory were aloft in a balloon that soared over the mountains in Park City. "And this is...when Gregory proposed." A bit of impish Stephanie crept in. "He knew I wasn't likely to refuse at those heights."

Laughter greeted her words, and emboldened, Brynn turned the next page, warming to the dream wedding she'd always wanted.

She and Gregory stood in the forefront of the picture, but an ancient stone church dominated the background. "This is the place we chose to exchange our vows."

"Where is that?" Wilma asked. "Doesn't look like any place I'm familiar with."

Brynn smiled. "It's in Ireland."

"Ireland?" Wilma questioned along with most of the other women. Matt turned back at that moment and the expression on his face echoed the others' sentiments. "Why did you get married in Ireland?" Wilma asked, as though Brynn had named a colony on Mars or perhaps one of the "Star Trek" destinations.

Brynn called on Stephanie's courage and her grandmother's memories. "Because it's always been so special to me. As a Magee, I grew up hearing stories about the home of my ancestors from my grandmother." She warmed to the tale. "And I'd dreamed about the land—from muddy mountainside sheep trails to old country roads that wound through the forests. I wanted to explore the west coast from Shannon to the Killarney Lakes to the Kerry Way Trail." Her voice unintentionally softened. "To see every inch of County Cork from the wild mountain lands of the west—to the great castles—to the tiny villages sheltered by the mountains and caressed by the seas." Brynn halted, embarrassed by her rush of poetic wanderings. Clearing her throat, she averted her head, staring at the album rather than her rapt audience as she tried to make her tone matter-of-fact. "Gregory knew that and was happy to go there."

Turning the page, the next picture was of the beautiful Irish countryside where the church stood. She and Gregory were silhouetted against the misty lowlands.

"It looks kind of remote," Miranda noticed.

"It is," Brynn agreed. "It's on the way to Brandon's Cottage in the Macgillycuddy Reeks mountains. This little country town's just a tiny place—this is the only church."

"Not an easy place to have a formal wedding. That would have been a difficult place to invite guests if you hadn't eloped," Ruth noticed, a new light shining in her eyes.

"Absolutely," Brynn agreed. "Miranda was right. It's extremely remote. Not the sort of place you'd hop off a plane and whiz to the nearest Hyatt."

"Doesn't seem like Gregory's sort of thing," Wilma commented. "I thought he'd go for a big society splash."

"Which isn't my sort of thing," Brynn answered, knowing it was true. She would hate to be the center of a huge, highly orchestrated wedding.

"You *have* changed that man," Wilma said with a laugh.

Knowing it would do no good to argue, Brynn turned the pages. The next photo was the first one of them in full bridal dress. She couldn't help lingering on this picture as she always did. The computer image of the dress she'd chosen was no less than a wonder. Exquisite Irish lace, a breathtaking headdress that for once made it look as though her dark hair was not completely wild, it was a wedding ensemble that had hovered in her imagination for years. A few quick sketches on her part, which were then translated by the computer, had made it a reality.

Now the oohs and aahs filled the lobby.

"I've never seen anything so beautiful," Wilma breathed, her own romantic nature peeking through. "It's as though the lace was spun by elves."

The other women chimed in with soft exclamations of delight.

"It's exquisite," Becky uttered through a dreamy sigh.

"You make a gorgeous couple," Cynthia offered.

"Even a cynic like me recognizes true love," Jean agreed.

Touched by their support, Brynn managed to smile as she turned the next pages.

Pictures of her walking hand in hand with Gregory through the countryside; a tiny country inn that she told them had been their honeymoon spot; arm in arm in front of Ross Castle. Then an evocative picture of them standing on the edge of the Cliffs of Moher on the Atlantic coast. Waves crashed against the rocks, sending spray upward, just beyond the happy-looking couple.

It was, all in all, a romantic, heart-softening book of memories. Seeing the damp eyes of the women who surrounded her, Brynn could tell they had been affected by the pictures. And for a moment it all seemed real—the courtship, the wedding, her relationship with Gregory, the new friends she was making.

From the corner of one misty eye, she spotted Matt. He lounged on the sidelines, but one look at his face told her he'd heard everything. In that same instant, her stomach clenched as she realized he hadn't bought the story.

As the women crowded around her, Brynn took temporary refuge in the shield they provided. She guessed that by morning, she had better come up with some answers he would believe.

Chapter Six

Having learned Brynn's habits, Matt staked out the patio. It was late afternoon and as he'd expected, she and her pets strolled outside.

"Give us a kiss," Bossy ordered as the nearly sightless Snookems bumped into the high-handed bird.

Lancelot barked, but it was hard to tell whether in agreement or contradiction.

What a menagerie, he thought. He had learned the history of the odd trio from his younger siblings. He watched as Brynn paused at the table, seeing her eyes widen first at the assortment of pastries, finger sandwiches, and a pot of fragrant, newly brewed tea. Then they nearly doubled in size when she spotted the wedding album.

Her hand reached out to touch the cover, as though not certain whether to trust her eyes. "Have you heard news about Gregory?" Trepidation colored her tone, she wondered if this was his way of cushioning a blow.

But Matt shook his head. "Nothing like that. I called about an hour ago. Still nothing."

She gestured to the elaborate spread. "What's all this?"

"I thought we could go through the album," Matt announced from the corner of the patio, seeing her head jerk upward in surprise. "Too many women around earlier for me to get a good look."

She pulled her hand back as though the pictures might burn. "I'm sure you've seen them before."

"I got a glance. But not with the narration."

"There's not that much to tell," she evaded.

"From what I heard, there was plenty."

"Well, I…"

He gestured toward the spread on the table. "And with your Irish background, I thought you might like afternoon tea."

Brynn looked at him, not certain whether he was being thoughtful or simply mocking her story. Nor was she certain whether it was Stephanie's fire or her own she felt rekindling. "Actually, I love tea. And the animals would love a snack."

Matt felt the quick prick of her subtle needling. Snacks fit not for her, but for her own little zoo. He didn't let the aim of her well-placed barb show. Instead, he shrugged. "Everyone…and everything…gets hungry."

Nervously she glanced around as though looking for an escape route. But he didn't plan to let that happen. He knew his brother, and the tale she'd just told about their wedding defied everything Gregory embodied.

Matt pulled out one of the two chairs at the table.

Brynn didn't look pleased, but she sat down.

Taking the other chair, Matt sat close enough to see the album clearly.

Brynn reached for the teapot. "Tea?"

"It probably won't kill me," he acknowledged. When her brows lifted, he shrugged sweater-clad shoulders. "Nothing like a hot drink to take away the late-afternoon chill."

She poured the tea, taking an inordinately long time to fill the two cups.

"Sugar?" she asked.

"No, thanks." He saw her pick up the lemon. "No lemon either."

She passed the tiered plate. "Sandwich?"

At this rate, they'd get to the album in about eight hours.

He picked out a few of the sissy, bite-size sandwiches and before she could retrieve the server, he took some pastries as well, hoping to shorten her drawn-out, stalling actions.

As she replaced the server, he opened the album. The first picture was benign enough. Simple individual portraits.

Then he turned to the photo of the country church. "Ireland, huh?"

"Yes," she answered shortly.

"I can't believe Gregory would agree to such a remote area."

"It's a beautiful spot," she insisted.

"I can see that." Glancing more closely at the photo he could see it was true. "It's just not Gregory's sort of place."

"It's mine," she retorted.

"Uh-huh." And when had Gregory ever bent to another person's wishes so completely? "How'd you ever talk Gregory into eloping? I can't believe he'd give up a networking opportunity like that. Gregory always took self-promotion seriously. That's what made him a corporate vice-president before he was thirty. He could have gotten a lot of miles out of a big splashy wedding in the city."

"That's not the kind of wedding we wanted," she protested stubbornly.

"We? Doesn't look like the kind of wedding Gregory would want. The only time he goes anywhere that remote, it's because his company has business there, like the South American deal that got him kidnapped. I don't remember hearing that there's a plant being built in the British Isles."

"The place isn't important," she replied tightly.

"No, but who you invite is. Gregory has been dedicated to his career since he graduated from business school. Why else does anyone go to Harvard School of Business?"

Brynn's expression was defensive. "Perhaps because you want to be the best at what you do."

"Exactly. And for Gregory that means networking. Constantly. And photo ops. What better combination than a high-profile wedding? One he could parlay into a spread in *Town and Country*. I can't believe Gregory would give up an opportunity like that.''

Two bright spots of color dotted her cheeks and her brilliant blue eyes were lit with a fevered intensity. "When you're in love, people compromise. And they do things simply because they love you. It doesn't have to make sense, or fall into predictable patterns. That's not what love's about."

Matt fiddled with the unwanted cup of tea, quieted by her fervent declaration. Apparently love could change even Gregory. "So you had your dream wedding?"

Her color didn't fade. Instead she clutched the teacup closer. "Yes. Even though it doesn't meet with your approval."

He pushed frustrated fingers through his hair. From her wounded expression, it was clear his questions had hurt her, and that hadn't been his intent. He'd only wanted to discover why nothing about Brynn and her relationship with Gregory made sense. He still had dozens of questions, and an unresolved feeling that he couldn't identify.

But he sensed it was time to back off. The last thing he needed was his brother's bride in tears. "Actually, a casual wedding would meet my approval—it suits me. I never have seen the reason to fill a church with so many people that the bride and groom nearly get lost in the crush. But, then, I don't think much like Gregory."

She took a sandwich, then lowered it to her plate without tasting it. "I suspected it might upset your family that we...that there wasn't a big wedding for them to see."

"As long as it's what makes you and Gregory happy, I don't think anybody cares about missing the show." He thought for a moment. "It might have bothered my mother—you know how they are about sentimental stuff." A sudden thought struck him. "What about your family? Weren't they upset about missing the wedding?"

Brynn felt a sudden constriction. Her mother wouldn't be upset to miss her wedding. Even the real thing. She cleared her throat. "It's just my mother, and she's very...understanding."

"You're lucky, then. I thought the mother-of-the-bride thing was a pretty big deal."

Brynn thought of her mother who tried to pretend she didn't have a twenty-six-year-old daughter because it brought her age into view. "We're not a real traditional family, so she wasn't that surprised by my choice." Brynn wondered why she hadn't been struck by lightning with all the lies she'd been telling. While she got caught up in Stephanie's daring, she was also caught in a mounting dose of guilt.

"You always do the unusual?" he asked, enjoying the soft play of emotions crossing her face. He had the urge to reach out and remove her glasses, to see her huge eyes without the barrier of oversize lenses and heavy rims, to monitor their reactions.

She pushed at those glasses, ducking her head a bit. "I'm not sure you could say that."

"No? You don't consider eloping to an isolated spot in Ireland unusual?"

"I guess that depends on your idea of unusual," she replied.

"Coming from a long line of Magees, I'm surprised you didn't fill the church with relatives."

"As I said, my family's small. The only true Magee I knew was my grandmother." Brynn's voice softened as truth overtook fantasy. "She was wonderful...kind, always having lots of time for me, telling me incredible stories, encouraging my dreams—even my silly daydreams."

"Your father died young, then?"

She paused. "No. He and my mother divorced when I was very young. He moved to Australia and we didn't see him, or hear from him. But, my grandmother Magee insisted on taking care of me. I think she felt guilty because my father disappeared and she tried to make it up to me."

"Sounds like you were close."

"Very. She was everything to me. And her stories opened up a whole world for me." Lost for a moment in those memories, Brynn forgot that she was sharing her most private thoughts with him—thoughts she hadn't shared with anyone else.

"Having divorced parents isn't unusual anymore. Sounds like you had a stable home life."

Brynn laughed at the irony. Moving constantly from city to city, as her mother searched for an inexplicable happiness that constantly eluded her, had been anything but stable.

Shy to begin with, Brynn hadn't lived anywhere long enough to form friendships. And that timidity had remained with her through adulthood, leaving her no confidantes for all the thoughts and emotions she had. As she had when she was a child, Brynn still turned to daydreams as her way of coping, a way of playing out her thoughts and desires. But that would change when Gregory returned. He would listen patiently to all her hopes and dreams. He would be friend, confidant...lover.

"Brynn," Matt repeated, wondering where he'd lost her. "You were telling me about your home life."

Jerked back to reality, rather than answering Matt's question, she picked up the teapot. "More tea?"

He pointed to his still-full cup. "I'm not sure where you'd pour it."

"Oh, I guess I wasn't thinking," she replied, flustered. Daydreaming again. It had often made her look and feel foolish.

"You looked like you were a few galaxies away," he commented, not telling her that he'd enjoyed the unguarded expression, the dreamy look on her face. Since she hadn't noticed, he'd taken the opportunity to study her translucent ivory skin— a true stamp of her Irish ancestry, along with her shiny black hair and remarkable blue eyes. Eyes that he suspected reflected the color of the Irish skies. Catching himself, Matt realized his thoughts were taking a distinctly unbrotherly turn.

Brynn drew her fingers over the rim of her cup. "I...I tend to have an overactive imagination—which helps me in drawing the strip—but it also takes me on flights of fancy."

"Looked like a nice trip."

For a moment her eyes met his. Even with her glasses between them he could see a new awareness—one he realized he shouldn't be seeing; one that neither of them should be feeling.

Her smile was a quick, darting thing, a brief quiver. "I think Lancelot deserves a treat, don't you?" Blindly she turned in the dog's direction. "How about a sandwich, boy?"

Lancelot politely accepted the offer, gently taking part of the tiny sandwich she tore in half.

Watching her jittery movements, Matt wondered if her thoughts had also taken an unexpected turn. He shook his head. That was impossible. She'd just told him how much she loved Gregory, had fiercely defended their unusual elopement. He must have imagined that glint in her eye. It was too bad he hadn't imagined his own.

MIRANDA AND BRYNN DUG through the trunks in the attic, searching for costume ideas for the upcoming Octoberfest.

"Sorry I roped you into this." Miranda spoke from the bottom of an ancient steamer trunk, her voice muffled. "But this morning's telegram about Gregory put me in a good mood. I know there's not any *new* news, but he's alive and they've convinced Matt not to go off half-cocked—at least for now."

Brynn nodded. "That's how I felt and maybe next time there'll be real news. I just wish I could *do* something."

Miranda shook out an ostrich feather duster. "You are."

Brynn picked up a dusty book. "This isn't exactly what I meant, but actually, I like doing this. It's kind of fun. We never had an attic. It's like a treasure trove."

Miranda laughed. "Or a junk pile." She pulled out another bowler hat and set it aside, muttering. "Can't ever have enough of these." Then she glanced at Brynn. "Never had an attic, did you?"

"No. We always lived in apartments. That's why I like my place in Salt Lake. Since it's a converted house it's not so much like an apartment."

"Most young people like slick high-rises. Gregory does. So whose place were you planning to settle in?"

Brynn scrabbled for an answer. This was getting to be a difficult game. "Well, we hadn't exactly decided yet. Maybe neither place," she fabricated. "A new place that's both of ours."

"One you can make your own." Miranda nodded. "That's wise. That way no one's too territorial. Course, you might have a time finding a place that'll take your pets."

An image of the picket fence she'd always dreamed of popped into Brynn's mind. "Perhaps a house, where no one else sets the rules."

"A house?" Miranda's brows rose. "I thought Gregory only wanted a condo. No snow to shovel, no grass to cut."

No yard for children to play in. Brynn shrugged away the disloyal thought. "Well, we all change."

"Change? Heavens, that boy's gone through a complete transformation." Miranda patted her blond, lacquered hair.

Brynn turned to another trunk. "There's so much interesting stuff in here. So many memories."

Miranda picked up a dusty scrapbook. "That's for sure. None of us seems to be able to throw anything away. The MacKenzies' history could fill the library, but I suspect the guests would rather have the latest bestsellers."

"They're foolish, then. This is all so real." Brynn's words hit her as she spoke. It *was* all so real, with one glaring exception—herself.

"'Real' doesn't always translate into 'interesting,'" Miranda noted wryly. "I do have an idea, though. We could put a few of your bound strip books in the library, perhaps autographed ones. Maybe put a few Stephanie mugs in the gift shop. Once they know you're part of the MacKenzie family, the guests will eat it up.''

Such a permanent reminder of her presence at once both pleased and unnerved her. Brynn didn't want to damage the resort's reputation by perpetuating a fraud. "I'll have to check with my distributor."

"Of course. It's all business these days." Miranda took out a ruffled blouse and held it up to the light. "Somewhere, there's a skirt that goes with this."

Brynn searched through her trunk. "Look! Lederhosen! Who wears these?"

"Frank always has. I don't know, though. He's lost so much weight since he's been sick, he might not want to this year." Miranda laughed. "And of course my handsome nephew shows off his good-looking legs in a pair."

"Gregory does?" Brynn asked in delight.

"Why, no." A small frown creased Miranda's forehead. "I was talking about Matt. Gregory wouldn't be caught dead in those. When we can talk him into coming to Octoberfest, he looks like a page out of the L.L. Bean catalog."

"Oh, of course. I...I thought maybe he just got into the spirit of the day—and did something uncharacteristic. That's how I'd feel."

"But I think you're more daring. Don't get me wrong. I love Gregory. Since he was Frank's first child, he was my first nephew and there's something special about that. Since I don't have children of my own, I've always interfered with Frank and Ruth's. Luckily, they don't mind." Miranda laughed. "Or if they do, they don't tell me. So, I kind of feel like their kids are partly mine. And, despite how different we are, I'm close to Gregory. Close enough to know it's important to him to stay within the guidelines. As a child, he never even drew outside the lines in his coloring books."

Brynn digested this, not sure quite how it fit into her picture of Gregory. "No one's ever called me daring before."

"That's because I don't think even you know it." Miranda pulled out another skirt and blouse. "This should look good on you. You're tall and delicate enough for it."

Delicate. No one had ever termed her build that way. She'd always thought she was simply too skinny. "A rack of bones," as the unkind teenage boys had once called her. "If you say so."

They continued their exploration and Miranda shook her head. "We may be here till Christmas."

Brynn lifted up an ancient hatbox, then set it aside. "Miranda, why does everyone call Gregory by his full name instead of Greg? I mean, you don't use Matt's full name."

Miranda didn't look up. "I guess because Gregory's always been a *Gregory.* Never occurred to anyone that he'd be anything else. And Matt. Well, he's always been Matt. Unaffected, unpretentious."

Brynn frowned briefly at the implication. Surely his own family didn't consider Gregory to be pretentious.

But Miranda was making an excited noise as she lifted out tissue-wrapped packages, handling them carefully. "If there are any treasures up here, we've just found them." She untied the string that was tied around the top parcel. As she folded the tissue back, her mood became nearly reverent. Then she lifted up what seemed to be yards and yards of material. It was a dress, an incredible-looking dress.

"It's beautiful!" Brynn exclaimed, reaching out to touch the delicate ice-blue silk.

"I always thought so," Miranda replied in a far more subdued voice than usual.

"Then it's yours?"

Miranda ran one hand over the iridescent folds of silk. "It was. I suppose in a way it still is."

"Was it for a special occasion?"

"Yes. For the Harvest Ball that's at the beginning of the festival. But I never wore it."

Brynn sensed currents of sadness. "I'm sorry. I'm sure you would have looked beautiful in it. I'm sure you still would."

Miranda's lips trembled for a moment. "You *are* a truly sweet girl." Her hand strayed toward the wrinkles that had etched an irreversible path over her face. Wise, often cagey eyes now looked sad. "But I'm afraid my day's past."

Impulsively, Brynn reached out to cover the older woman's hand. "I don't believe that. Sometimes life has a way of surprising us. And I don't think we can ever stop trusting in love…or that our soul mate exists. Sometimes the path is just a little rockier for us than we'd like, but it's still a path."

"How can anyone as young as you have collected all that wisdom? If I didn't know better, I'd guess your path was rocky, and definitely filled with soul-searching."

"I think a lot," Brynn admitted. "Internalizing is what they call it, I believe. I suppose it came from being an only child, with just one parent."

"It sounds lonely," Miranda surmised accurately.

Brynn shrugged away the sympathy she heard. "I'm sure it sounds worse than it was. I simply became a daydreamer—and that's not such a bad thing."

Miranda studied her face. "No, I don't suppose it is. Whatever shaped you made you a compassionate person and that is always a good thing."

Brynn swallowed at the catch in her throat, unused to visible displays of emotion. She must have been right about Gregory, his sensitivity and depth. He would have to possess those qualities, coming from such a giving, caring family. "Thank you." This time she didn't duck her head at the compliment as she was accustomed to doing. Instead she smiled, realizing how very much she was growing to like Miranda.

"You're welcome. Now, shall we keep digging?"

Brynn bent toward the nearest trunk.

"Wait!" Miranda's voice took on a note of excitement.

Startled by the sudden change in Miranda, Brynn abandoned the trunk. "What is it?"

"The dress." Miranda retrieved the blue silk and held it up.

"You're going to wear it after all?"

"No. But you are."

Brynn stared between Miranda and the beautiful dress. "Oh, no, I couldn't."

"I thought you liked it."

"I do. It's gorgeous. Too gorgeous. It would make me stand out. People would notice."

"Notice? Child, you'd be the belle of the ball."

"And the center of attention," Brynn agreed glumly.

"And this isn't a good thing?"

"Not for me. I'm not comfortable in situations like that. In fact, I like nothing better than to be a wallflower."

Miranda stared at her. "I truly can't imagine how you and Gregory wound up together. That boy thrives in the spotlight. And if you're going to be a successful wife for him, you'll have to get used to it."

Brynn's stomach clenched. "But just because Gregory likes the spotlight doesn't mean—"

"Who do you think he'll be sharing that spotlight with?"

Brynn was stumped for an answer. "Still, I couldn't wear anything that gorgeous and... Well..."

Miranda held the low-cut bodice up higher. Although tasteful, it exposed more skin than Brynn had ever dreamed of showing. Nearly backless, it was a dream of a dress. And with vintage styles still imprinting the fashion scene, Brynn knew it would be a knockout. But certainly not the sort of thing she'd choose to wear. It was simply too beautiful. Too attention catching.

Her lips curled in a knowing manner, Miranda cocked her head. "Gorgeous and...daring?"

Brynn nodded.

"Then it sounds like it just suits you."

"I never said I was daring. You did."

Miranda lifted her brows. "But you just said that at something like the festival you'd do something uncharacteristic—just like you thought Gregory might."

Caught. In a trap of her own making. "But that dress is special to you," she protested. "Too special to be worn by someone else."

"Not just someone," Miranda reminded her. "By family. I'll have someone bring this trunk to your room."

Before Brynn could answer, Miranda tugged her toward the full-length antique cheval mirror that rested in one corner of the attic. Once in front of the mirror, Miranda held the dress up to Brynn. Of their own accord, Brynn's hands moved to hold the dress in place.

Miranda pulled Brynn's long hair upward, partially fashioning it into an upswept style. "Yes. Up on your head with lots of loose curls." Then she frowned at Brynn. "How well can you see without your glasses?"

"So-so," Brynn mumbled.

"What?"

"I need them to read," Brynn admitted.

"Then whyever do you wear them all the time?"

"It's just easier that way. I have clear glass in the top of the lenses so I don't have to take my glasses off and on all the time."

Miranda shook her head in disbelief. "Why a lovely young thing like you would want to hide behind those glasses is beyond me. But after you have on this dress, it won't be a problem."

"It won't?"

"Nope. 'Cause you won't be wearing them."

Brynn felt a clutch of panic. The glasses were her security blanket, her guard against anyone crashing through carefully constructed defenses. "I'm not sure that's such a good idea."

"I am," Miranda replied firmly. "And I've been walking that path a good deal longer than you have."

So she had. There was nothing like being rebutted by her own words, but Brynn felt she had to make one last, if hopeless plea. "Are we sure we're talking about the same path?"

Miranda grinned, a thousand-watt smile. "Absolutely, my dear. Absolutely."

Chapter Seven

Brynn finished the last of her lunch, glad that Miranda was out with friends. Not that she wasn't growing very fond of the older woman, but she'd been afraid that Miranda would decide to start a complete makeover. She pushed at the familiar security of her glasses for reassurance, before glancing at her dining companions. Even though Matt was at her table, she sat closest to Ruth and Frank, who had entertained her throughout lunch with stories about Gregory as a child.

Matt had been preoccupied, scribbling in a leather portfolio while they'd driven down memory lane. But the reminiscing seemed to perk up both Ruth and Frank.

That morning the family had spent hours on the phone, trying to learn news about Gregory. Ransom demands had been made. The MacKenzies were ready to pay if Drake Chemical hesitated. To their frustration, the State Department had insisted that they continue negotiations for the moment. Not wanting to set a precedent of a quick cash payoff which could encourage future abductions, the State Department refused to let Drake Chemical pay immediately. Frank and Matt, angered and frustrated, wanted to bypass the system, but that was impossible.

As Frank and Ruth rose, Frank patted Matt on the shoulder. "You have the bids for the new chair lift under control?"

Matt nodded. "Just working out some more cost projections." He glanced at his watch. "But they'll have to wait. I need to check Plum Ridge. If we don't get the new lifts installed next season, we may have to overhaul the quads."

Brynn listened to their exchange with interest, surprised that Matt was so familiar with the business side of Eagle Point. True, he'd grown up here, but this sounded like the nuts and bolts of the organization, not bookkeeping and outdoor maintenance.

"It's an ambitious plan, son." Frank looked at the same time both admiring and skeptical. "But you're right about checking out Plum Ridge. I should be going with you—"

"Don't worry about it, Dad. You know it's my favorite spot. And I plan to take some more measurements. The new lift has to have more room than the quads."

"Then you'll definitely need a spotter—I should go."

"Frank, let's don't have this argument again," Ruth intervened. "You have no business trotting up a mountain. If Matt needs some help, I'm sure he could..." Her gaze landed on Brynn. "If Brynn wouldn't mind, she could go along as spotter."

Brynn caught the pleading look in Ruth's eyes and knew she couldn't refuse. "Of course. I'm not sure I'll be much help—"

"You'll do great," Ruth interjected. "Right, Matt?"

He shrugged, only a hint of a smile tugging at his lips as he looked pointedly between his parents. "You don't have us fooled. You're just trying to get rid of everyone so you two can be alone."

That brought a smile to Frank's face, along with relief on Ruth's.

"Always said you were a bright boy," Frank agreed.

Matt wagged his eyebrows at his father. "You know what they say about the acorn...."

"That it's a good thing for the oak tree that you're around," Frank replied.

Brynn watched as the affection flowed between them, nearly

stunned by the links that bound this family. No wonder they had such strength and happiness.

"Too bad neither the tree nor the nut noticed that we're surrounded by an army of employees. We'll hardly be alone," Ruth teased.

Matt tsked. "The more you protest..."

Ruth took Frank's arm. "Your son's impossible."

Frank leaned toward his wife, kissing her cheek as Matt turned to Brynn. "We'll need to leave in a few minutes."

"Sure." She cleared her throat. "I'll be ready."

Was this how normal families worked?

"Matt, Tracy wants you to look at the catering budget and sales schedule as soon as you can," Ruth inserted, her hand sliding into Frank's grasp. "She needs your approval before booking that teachers' retreat. It's the same weekend as the dental associates' conference. She's jiggled some banquet-room arrangements and she wants to make sure you approve."

Brynn stared between Ruth and Matt. Why did they need *his* approval? Before she could stop herself, Brynn blurted out that same question.

Ruth glanced at her in surprise. "Because he's the director."

"Of banquets?"

Ruth shook her head. "Of Eagle Point and everything that's connected to it."

"Oh." Brynn glanced at Matt, silently asking for an explanation. But he only grinned.

Together they exited the dining room and Brynn waited until Ruth and Frank were out of hearing distance. "Why didn't you tell me?" she hissed.

"You didn't ask."

"You let me assume that you just did odd jobs around here."

Matt shook his head. "You came to that conclusion on your own."

"You still could have told me," she insisted, remembering

that she'd pigeonholed him as a party-loving jock who lived for the winter slopes.

"And spoil all your fun?" His grin widened. "Besides, I tried to correct your impression—you were even more convinced that I was the handyman."

"You could have tried harder," she insisted, uncomfortably recalling that she'd summed him up as a ski bum.

"You could have been more open-minded," he countered.

True, but she wasn't admitting that to him. "I'll meet you out front in ten minutes, if that's all right."

"Don't want to fight this one to the death?"

She rolled her eyes. "Is ten minutes all right?"

"Sure. Then I can gather my tool belt before we leave."

"You plan to get a lot of mileage out of this, don't you?"

He lifted one brow. "Think I can?"

"I think you liked playing with my head. Do you do that with everyone who comes here?"

"Only the ones who marry my brother," he retorted.

Since she knew that was a brief list of one, Brynn didn't have a reply. Their eyes met, the flare of that unwanted connection glaring between them, then receding as Gregory was forgotten. Awareness was a live, pulsing animal, one that breathed between them and rumbled with awakening desire.

"I'll meet you out front," he said finally, jerking away his gaze. "Bring a jacket."

She nodded, wondering if Matt could be as rattled as she was. He knew that she'd already learned that the altitude demanded being prepared for unexpected drops in temperature. Purposely, she didn't look at him as she ran up the stairs.

It was longer than they'd initially agreed before she and Matt were driving away from the lodge. Matt had delayed their departure, allowing some of the tension to dissipate. It was neither a companionable silence, nor a completely uncomfortable one as they rode along for some time, the cab filled with the music of a CD Matt had popped in.

"I need to stop in town at the printing company before we head to Plum Ridge," Matt told her as they descended the mountain. "I have to approve some new brochures."

"That might have been hard to pass off as part of the handyman's duties," she couldn't resist replying, hoping to dissolve the remaining tension.

"You'd probably have decided that I was the copy clerk, as well."

Brynn leveled him with her closest imitation of an intimidating glare.

But he looked mildly amused. "The detour will make us later than I expected. Is that going to play havoc with your work schedule?"

"No," Brynn replied, wishing she could quash her nervousness at being alone with him. Somehow, in the lodge, she felt protected, surrounded by family and staff. Then the unexpected flashes of awareness between them were daring moments she could experiment with. Not to mention that it was easier to escape him there than in a confined, moving truck. "I got a lot done on my strip this morning so I've got some free time."

He glanced at her briefly. "Good. Most of our printing's done in Salt Lake but these flyers are just for the locals—we're having a dance to celebrate the fall colors festival."

"The Harvest Ball," she replied.

He looked at her in surprise. "You know about that?"

"Miranda mentioned it." Brynn fiddled with her hands. "I was...helping her look for some costumes."

"'Costumes'?"

"She said they were for Octoberfest."

Matt nodded his head. "Time's flying. That's next month, but everything's in place. Except the family's costumes apparently."

Brynn felt an impish force nudge her. Apparently Stephanie was rubbing off on her. "I hear you wear lederhosen to the Octoberfest."

Matt straightened a bit self-consciously. "Oh?"

That imp was gaining ground. "Miranda told me how good you look in them."

He straightened even more. "Miranda's having fun pulling your leg." He glanced at his own muscular thighs covered in respectable denim. "But it's gotten to be a family custom. Ah, the joy of relatives."

"You'd miss your relatives if you didn't have them."

He caught her eye for a moment. "I guess we learned that the hard way when Gregory was kidnapped."

The impact of his words struck her when she met his gaze. For a moment she'd forgotten all about Gregory. How was that possible?

"I didn't mean Gregory," she tried to explain, realizing how insensitive she must have sounded. "I was referring to the rest of your family."

"I know. After all, you'd miss Gregory just as much as we would if he didn't come back." Matt looked back at the road, purposely avoiding her gaze. "Maybe more."

Swallowing, she nodded, content to let the music fill the silence again as they drove into Gallagher. They'd barely passed the general store when the alarm on her watch buzzed.

Matt turned toward her, cocking an inquisitive brow.

"Don't worry. I got my strip to the driver early today. I just forgot to turn off the alarm."

"You sure it's nothing else?"

She searched her mind, but came up blank. "I don't think so."

He tipped his head back unexpectedly and laughed—that rich male sound she savored. "You're something, Brynn."

She wasn't sure if that was good or not, but she didn't comment as he pulled next to the curb on the main street. After parking, Matt automatically walked around to her door and opened it. Brynn hadn't expected to go inside with him, but she appreciated his automatic assumption that she would.

Once inside, she met the proprietor, Earl Carouthers, the secretary, Susan, and the two shop technicians, Danny and Bill. Brynn learned that Carouthers handled the printing for all the merchants in the area, including those in the other small interconnecting communities in the valley.

By the time Matt had concluded his business, Brynn had been offered coffee, chatted with the employees, learned the latest town gossip, and tried unsuccessfully to squelch the latest version of one of her fabrications. She wondered if this was how Paul Bunyan had gotten his start.

Even so, their casual acceptance, the cozy friendliness of the town—it all charmed her. Feeling like a corny commercial for a Mayberry reunion, she ate up every hokey moment. Half expecting to run into Andy, Aunt Bea, Barney or Goober, she was pleased when Matt led her toward the post office as well.

Once Brynn was sure she hadn't been sucked into a Norman Rockwell picture, she roamed around the small, rural post office that was tucked next to an old-fashioned hardware store. Matt told her the town's Victorian-style buildings had been built between 1880 and 1900. Well kept and tidy, they lined the town's main streets, adding to the nostalgic aura.

Rich in history, Gallagher, named for Gallagher MacKenzie, had begun as a trading post. Over the years it had burned to the ground twice. And at one time it had evolved into a booming mine town that later went bust, nearly becoming one of the hundreds of ghost towns that dotted the West. Yet each time the town had regrouped, rebuilt, the spirit of Gallagher MacKenzie urging it on.

With enough agriculture in place, the local farmers and ranchers had kept the town alive. Now Eagle Point brought in enough visitors to provide a steady tourist trade. Not as much as Matt envisioned, but enough to keep the town alive.

Brynn had learned a little of the town's history from the various MacKenzies. But when Frank spoke about Gallagher he grew nostalgic, almost sad. He'd muttered something about

Gallagher's quaint sameness, how he wasn't sure he was going to like the changes. Brynn had wondered about those changes, but they'd never been explained.

Reaching out to touch an ancient postal scale on the counter, Brynn was surprised to hear her name called from the doorway. Turning around, she saw Wilma, Donna, Jean and Karen. They were all outfitted in jogging suits and tennis shoes.

"We were just talking about you," Wilma greeted.

Brynn smiled. "Most people won't come right out and admit that."

Wilma waved her hand dismissively. "You're new grist for the mill, dear."

"You've got us all remembering how our own husbands proposed," Karen added.

"Actually, I was thinking about your comic strip," Jean dissented.

Relieved, Brynn turned her attention to the one person who didn't seem to be enthralled with her love life. "Really? Do you get a chance to read it once in a while?"

"Nope," Jean replied, then grinned. "I read it every day. And every day I wonder how you come up with so many ideas. I doubt I'd think of enough to last a week."

"You'd be surprised. Although sometimes it's easier than others," she admitted. "My mind isn't always fertile ground."

"Mine would reek of fertilizer," Jean replied drolly.

Brynn laughed. "I'm afraid mine does at times, too."

Wilma shook her head. "Then where *do* you get your ideas when you run dry?"

Brynn thought of the times she'd brainstormed for new strip ideas by combining Goobers, nachos, housework and a Jane Fonda workout video. But she knew that wasn't the glamorous answer they were looking for. "Actually, sometimes I turn to real life."

"Really…" Jean mused.

"Do you use people you know?" Donna asked.

"Occasionally," Brynn replied cautiously.

"Did Gregory inspire any of your strips?" Karen asked, obviously the true romantic of the group.

Brynn's sleeping imp stretched and yawned. "Actually, do you remember when Stephanie's boyfriend took her up in the hot-air balloon?"

Jean laughed. "And she trapped him inside, giving him a choice between proposing and jumping?"

"Exactly. That was based on real life."

"Of course!" Karen exclaimed. "Because Gregory took you up in a hot-air balloon to propose!"

"I didn't hear this part," Cynthia protested.

Wilma quickly filled her in.

"And did you give Gregory the same choice?" Cynthia questioned, torn between being scandalized and excited.

"Of course she did," Jean answered with airy unconcern.

Brynn laughed at that absurdity, her gaze skipping upward, halting suddenly. Matt stood at a counter not far from them, ostensibly putting stamps on some envelopes. Uneasily, she wondered just how long he'd been standing there.

Matt's lips tightened and Brynn's stomach took a queasy turn.

"Of course, not everything's based on real life," she rushed to add. "And the strip's exaggerated."

"I don't know. Your relationship with Gregory sounds pretty exciting without embellishment," Jean commented as she winked.

"I thought you were the cynic," Brynn tried again, watching Matt out of the corner of her eye.

Jean shrugged. "Most of the time. But even skeptics like me have their moments."

Matt lifted his head at that moment and Brynn met his gaze. Now *there* was a skeptic. "Well, ladies, I think Matt's ready to go, so..."

They all turned to him with a few feminine squeals and

giggles, and enough chatter to fill their corner of the post office. Apparently, simply being a single man was enough to cause a stir, Brynn realized. That and being so good-looking he'd turn heads anyplace he went. Matt responded graciously, complimenting and charming them each in turn. Only Jean lingered, her expression clearly indicating she'd rather stay—as long as Matt remained.

Brynn watched them both intently, trying to see if the woman's interest was reciprocated. But Matt put his hand at the base of Brynn's back, leading her away from Jean. Brynn resisted the urge to look over her shoulder and see what expression remained on Jean's face.

But in a moment they were out on the sidewalk. Matt nodded to and greeted friends and neighbors as they walked back to the truck, stopping only to buy them both soft drinks from an ancient machine in front of the drugstore. He was so casual, Brynn relaxed her guard, deciding she'd imagined the look on his face.

Once inside the truck, she relaxed further as they rolled down the road, the autumn breeze riffling her hair. Lifting the soda can to her lips, she took a deep swallow.

Matt broke the quiet, staring ahead as the truck picked up speed and he shifted gears. "Tell me, how'd Gregory manage to propose in a hot-air balloon when he's terrified of heights?"

Spluttering, Brynn all but spat out her cola. The rest of the liquid went down the wrong pipe. Choking and coughing, she gulped for air.

Matt flicked a glance in her direction. "Something I said?"

It took her a few moments to get her voice back, longer to regain her equilibrium. "Ah...no." She held up her can as a weak defense. "It went down the wrong way."

"And Gregory? He didn't bail out of the balloon when it got ten feet off the ground?"

Brynn looked desperately out the window, wishing she could bail out herself. Urgently recalling Stephanie's ingenious ways.

"Well... You see... Gregory wanted to overcome his fear of heights. It's something he was really working on. First we'd go to the Club at the Top in the Hilton and work on sitting next to the windows." Her brain scrambled frantically, trying to think of something other than a mountain they could have climbed. "Then we'd go to Lagoon and ride the sky tram across the park."

"Lagoon?" Matt asked incredulously. "Gregory didn't even like 'mini-Disneyland' when he was a kid."

"We didn't go for the amusement factor," she insisted, wondering when that lightning was going to get her. "Just for the practice of being up that high."

She dared a glance at him. He was definitely skeptical.

"And then..." She paused. Was her voice getting higher with every lie? "We rode the ski lift at Snowbird to have lunch at the top."

The look that crossed Matt's face wasn't promising.

"I guess that's what made him decide to propose in the balloon," she concluded, knowing how lame her story sounded. "Because he'd been working so hard at conquering his fear of heights."

The silence wasn't thick; it was impenetrable.

Brynn fiddled with the can in her hands, nearly lifted it to take another swallow, reconsidered and decided it wasn't worth choking to death to lift the oppressive gloom.

But when Matt did speak, she jumped as his voice broke the quiet. "So Gregory overcame his fear of heights?"

Brynn pushed at her glasses. "Not completely. But then I guess no one ever totally conquers a fear like that." She resolutely studied the passing scenery, concentrating as though there would be a quiz.

"Sounds like Gregory did a lot of things he never had before."

"Like I said, love..." She glanced up, meeting Matt's gaze. There was something there—that same something she'd seen before. Whatever it was, she couldn't complete the thought, couldn't put the words between them again.

"Changes people," he finished for her. "So you said."

Brynn had the urge to tell him the truth, to explain why she'd carried out the charade, how it had seemed like the right thing to do, but how she now realized it had to stop.

"I guess it's a good thing it can change people." This time Matt didn't meet her gaze. "Otherwise you and Gregory wouldn't be married. And right now, you're what's keeping Dad going. The others, too." His hands tightened around the steering wheel, his knuckles whitening. "If it's all the same to you, I'll leave the measuring for another day and head back to the lodge, but don't let on to Dad. I don't want him deciding he has to help me."

Brynn's confession died in her throat. What if she told all and Frank took a turn for the worse? She never should have started the whole charade, but ending it now could be even worse.

RESTLESS AFTER HER fluctuating emotions and verbal games of the afternoon, Brynn roamed the lobby, picked up several magazines, then replaced them without reading a single article. Another phone call to the State Department had proved fruitless. Frank, looking pale had retired after learning there was no news of his eldest son. While the scent of the nearly always burning fireplace was usually comforting, even the gentle embers did little to soothe her. Nor had the hot tea, cocoa and spiced cider. Asking for warm milk was just too embarrassing.

Although a satellite dish provided over a hundred channels to choose from, television didn't interest her, either. She kept remembering the look in Matt's eyes, her own response, and the electricity that smoldered between them. It was ridiculous. He was Gregory's brother. Nothing more. And Gregory was the man she loved, the one she dreamed of, the one she wanted to share her future with. Then why did she keep remembering

Matt's long, tall body, his strong hands, his lionlike eyes, the glint of gold where his hair parted naturally. And why had an ugly spurt of envy clawed her when she'd seen Jean's interest in him?

None of it was warranted. None of it made sense. She'd pledged her heart to Gregory. With a start Brynn realized she hadn't opened the wedding album in more than a few days. Actually she couldn't remember exactly when she'd last pored over it. Worrying about that was silly, she tried to dismiss. She'd simply been caught up in her work, the newness of her surroundings...and Matt MacKenzie.

It was stress, she decided. At home, she walked several miles a day, draining away the tension. She simply hadn't had enough exercise. A swim perhaps. In the warm mineral-spring pool, then a relaxing soak in the adjoining hot tub.

Just what the doctor ordered, she decided, heading upstairs. The medicinal benefits of genuine mineral water, relaxation under a blanket of stars, and the quiet of a mountain evening.

Ruth had already provided her with a swimsuit. She'd brought it up, along with several pairs of jeans and an assortment of tops and sweaters. And under the cover of darkness, Brynn knew she could be anonymous and unnoticed, both of which appealed to her.

It didn't take long to change. Brynn glanced at her reflection in shock. The swimsuit was little more than an abbreviated scrap of material. Although she eyed it dubiously, she was driven by her restlessness. Besides, no one would see her in the dark.

Wrapping herself in a thick terry robe, Brynn ventured down the back staircase, glad for the discreet employee exit. Once outside, she felt the chill and shivered briefly in the robe, pulling it close as she continued toward the pool, seeing the steam of the warm water rise into the cool night.

At the edge of the pool, she slipped off her glasses and robe and climbed down the concrete steps, her body sighing at the pleasure of warm bubbling water. She swam laps without counting, pushing her muscles until the relaxation kicked in. Then she flipped onto her back, kicking gently to keep afloat.

The water's healing force worked its magic. Heavy languor invaded her body, weighing down her limbs, eroding her agitation. No longer feeling a need for the space of the oversize pool and relishing the thought of relaxing in even warmer water, Brynn remembered the nearby hot tubs. In addition to the two large ones on the west side of the pool, there was a smaller tub on the opposite side, one she guessed would be empty since it was situated away from the main traffic. Even that smaller tub had built-in benches for relaxation, ones she could stretch out on. Ones that sounded infinitely appealing.

As she pulled herself from the pool, the shock of cool air chilled her skin. Brynn grabbed her glasses, then walked the short distance to the isolated in-ground hot tub and slid into the small confined space, the mineral water bubbling around her as she searched in the dark for the bench. This was the perfect prescription. Brynn couldn't remember feeling more relaxed.

She stumbled a bit, having forgotten that the benches were staggered around the perimeter, then reached out to steady herself. Instead of cement, she connected with a firm wall of muscled flesh.

Her serenity fled as she jerked backward. "I'm sorry. I didn't know anyone else was in here."

A familiar male voice floated toward her along with billows of steam. "It's okay." Then that rich, utterly masculine laugh. She could see Matt's white teeth flash in the dark. "I don't bite—very hard."

Brynn felt awash—literally. Her limited experience with men didn't include hot tubs. What would Stephanie do? Gulping, Brynn attempted for her character's flip voice. "And how do I know you've had your shots?"

He didn't reply for a moment and she assumed she'd blown it.

"Guess you'll have to take your chances."

A sliver of moonbeam illuminated his face and Brynn drew in an unexpected breath. Surely it wasn't an invitation she read there. Had her own words or tone been too suggestive?

The sultry heat of the tub pulsed between them. The space was suddenly smaller, unmistakably intimate. And her eyes, accustomed now to the dark, watched the garlands of steam curling around his head. Then her gaze slowly lowered, drifting over his powerful shoulders, the impressive muscles of his broad chest. Her throat dried, she forgot to swallow, and yet she continued to stare.

When she finally raised her eyes back to the level of his, she saw that he was taking an inventory of his own. Feeling every inch the skinny teenager she'd once been, Brynn drew back. As she did, he moved forward, standing in the tub, revealing a lean torso and whipcord-tight abs. Had she thought she wasn't attracted to the physical sort? She truly had been young and foolish.

She scrabbled for her footing, stepping up to the next level and vaulting toward the top. But Matt's voice stopped her.

"Aren't going to leave me out here all alone, are you?"

Was that a mocking edge she'd heard in his words? Or was her overactive imagination going at warp speed? She turned back to him slowly. "You were out here alone before."

"So I was." And at the time he'd thought it was exactly what he wanted. A solitary tub to soak in, to rinse away the unwanted thoughts he'd been having. And then the object of those thoughts had literally fallen into his lap. He should be encouraging her to leave, not inviting her to stay.

Despite the blackness of the night, the quarter moon had provided enough light to clearly see the curves her new tailored clothes had hinted at. Curves that dripped sensuously with a sheen of moisture from the pool. His gaze followed the trickle of water that beaded beneath her chin, then lowered to the lush spill of high breasts, the curve of her tiny waist, the womanly flare of her hips, the shapely long legs—legs he could envision tangling with his own.

He'd never coveted his brother's girlfriends, never competed with him in that arena. And that cooperation had come naturally, without discussion, without problem. He and Gregory had never been attracted to the same type of woman. Matt had easily put his brother's girlfriends in a detached part of his mind, treating them like he would a kid sister.

So why was it that nothing he felt about Brynn was brotherly? While she really didn't seem suited to Gregory, and her stories about him sounded like they belonged in the funny papers, why had he kept challenging their relationship? Pushing her to what? Declare his brother had no claim on her?

Then what? He conveniently moved in for the kill? Having spent the last hour on the phone, fruitlessly trying to find out more information about Gregory, Matt considered that the ultimate betrayal. He should be feeling protective of Brynn, guarding his brother's interests.

Not cultivating his own. His eyes fastened on the betraying pulse at her throat, fluttering wildly out of control, and the agitated rising of her barely contained breasts. And he knew it wasn't a problem he faced alone.

The quarter moon outlined her body, poised to flee, and Matt closed his eyes to the possibilities. Instead, he made his voice deliberately casual. "You're right. I was out here alone. While you're welcome to stay, I think I'll be going in. I have an early date with a ski lift."

"I...I believe I'll be going in, too." Her smile was strained. "I think I've had enough for one night."

Sprinting out of the tub, Brynn paused only long enough to retrieve her robe and belt it around her body. Then she ran. Watching her until she disappeared, Matt spoke into the suddenly empty darkness. "And I've had enough, too."

Chapter Eight

Unable to resist, Brynn dug through the trunk that had been brought down to her room from the attic. She hadn't planned to, but the lure of all those memories drew her. Rising before dawn after a nearly sleepless night, she had plenty of time to kill, not wanting to disturb anyone else.

Unfolding a parasol, Brynn twirled it above her head, imagining the lazy days of summer, women in frilly, pastel dresses, men in seersucker suits. Gregory fit that image perfectly, with his polished good looks and affinity for equally eye-catching clothes. Closing her eyes, she imagined strolling along, arm in arm with him.

But the image wasn't as strong as she would have liked.

Instead, Gregory's likeness faded, was replaced by a stronger, taller man, one whose powerful presence dominated, especially when he effortlessly picked her up, carrying her away to unknown delights.

With a little shake she brought herself back to the present, glancing around to make sure she was still alone. She hated being caught in one of her daydreams. More than that, she hated having Matt take over those dreams, pushing Gregory out.

How had that happened? She'd loved Gregory since the moment she'd first seen him. And reading about him in the papers, learning about his status in and commitment to the community, she'd found him to be an admirable man. His quick smiles on the jogging path told her that he was kind, sensitive—the sort of man she wanted to spend her life with.

So why was Matt threatening to take his place in her fantasies?

Purposely she turned back to the trunk, trying to forget the unwanted visions. Moments later she was lifting out layers of the MacKenzies' past.

A baby's christening dress, delicately embroidered linen handkerchiefs, a hand-crocheted lace collar. Brynn's fingers closed around something heavier, solid-feeling. Pulling the bundle from the trunk, she discovered it was a leather-bound book. Tracing her fingers over the flower-embossed cover, she outlined the word Journal and the date beneath it—some thirty years earlier. She wondered if she dared open the book, to intrude on thoughts put to paper so long ago. Slowly she lifted the cover and stared at the flyleaf. "Journal of Miranda Rose MacKenzie."

Deciding that she would be violating Miranda's privacy, Brynn closed the cover and reached into the trunk to return the journal. As she did, a photograph floated from the book, apparently disturbed when the journal had been opened.

Picking up the photo, she intended to put it back when the faces in the picture caught her attention. One looked like a young Miranda, hand in hand with a handsome man. Their faces reflected happiness and another quality—love.

Curious, Brynn turned the photo over. "Miranda and Neil. Always."

Brynn wondered what had happened to change "always." And what had happened to Neil.

A knock on the door interrupted her musings. Hurriedly replacing the picture, Brynn called out. "Come in."

"Hello, my dear," Ruth greeted her. "I hate to disturb you...." She looked at the tumble of things that had been retrieved from the trunk. "I don't know, on second thought, maybe you'll be glad I did."

Brynn smiled. "I love all this."

Ruth rolled her eyes. "I guess it's good that someone does. But frankly, I can't imagine why." She picked up the christening dress. "Although some things are worth looking at again."

"Gregory's?" Brynn guessed.

Ruth gave the material a little pat, before laying the dress down. "Yes." She firmed lips that had begun to tremble. "Now, before I start crying again I should tell you why I've bothered you."

"You're not bothering—"

"I am, but I have a good reason. First, the State Department said they'll proceed to step two in the negotiations. I'm not sure what that means, but I'm taking it as good news."

Brynn smiled. "My fingers are crossed."

Ruth crossed her own fingers. "Mine, too. Also, Matt plans to go back to Plum Ridge today and Frank's making noises that he should be going. But the thin altitude makes his breathing even more difficult, and he won't take along his portable oxygen tank. At least here I can nag him into using it. I know it's an imposition, but I thought that perhaps since you helped Matt the other day, I could talk you into going again today. More measuring, I believe. If you head downstairs and snag Matt in front of him, I think Frank will assume you set this up the last time you were on the ridge."

"Oh." Another trip alone with Matt. Would her nerves take it? She could hardly tell Ruth they hadn't made it to Plum Ridge the other day. Or why.

"I know taking measurements isn't much fun, but I'm so worried about Frank...."

A picture of his fragile condition flashed through Brynn's mind. "I don't expect to be entertained. Actually...just being here is entertainment in itself." More like a complicated set of entanglements. But ones she needed to get a grip on. Maybe today could be a new beginning—a chance to wipe the slate clean, to see Matt in a proper light.

Ruth's expression relaxed into a loving one. "Gregory certainly found a treasure in you." After enveloping her in a spontaneous hug, Ruth left.

Brynn stared after her. *Treasure?* She had a feeling by the time this charade played itself out, her nerves wouldn't be fit for the junk pile.

PLUM RIDGE ROSE BEYOND the crest of the foothills, eclipsed only by the white-capped peaks of the tallest mountains. Silver-leafed aspens trembled in the soft breeze, while overhead miles of unobstructed blue dipped to meet the wild grass.

To Matt, Plum Ridge was the embodiment of Eagle Point. The land was in his blood, along with his love of the unfettered acres. And that was all wrapped up in his dreams and his family.

Staring at Brynn, he was trying hard to remember that she was family. But in his mind, it was still hard to reconcile. Especially after last night, and the heated dreams that had followed. And knowing nothing had been culminated from those dreams didn't help.

She'd been nervous as they drove to the ridge, clearly not comfortable being alone with him. As soon as they'd parked, Brynn had pulled off her shoes to run through the grass. Even now, she was collecting the last of the wildflowers, exclaiming over everything from the lowly buttercups to the exquisite evening primrose.

Matt remembered Christina, Gregory's last girlfriend. She'd have thought this entire expedition was a waste, not to mention time spent at Eagle Point waiting for word on Gregory. As he recalled, Christina had to be surgically separated from her day planner and then only on rare occasions. Her relationship with Gregory had to be squeezed in between meetings, business trips, late hours. Since Gregory had the same sort of agenda, Matt had wondered how they ever got together.

And then there was Brynn. Seemingly uncomplicated, she was in fact full of layers. But as each layer was exposed, it seemed more impossible that she was his brother's wife.

And even more impossible that he was having so much difficulty remembering the fact that she was.

Shading his eyes from the sun, Matt watched as Brynn studied the magnificent scenery. He knew the landscape was pretty overwhelming—sensory overload to most first-timers. But she couldn't seem to see enough.

He knew they should get started on the measurements, but he hated to begin, enjoying these unguarded moments.

Brynn turned just then, a sudden grin splitting her face. "It's like being on top of the world."

Her enthusiasm was contagious. He closed the distance between them, walking to the edge where she stood. "From here you can see three states."

She looked at him skeptically. "Is this one of those things you tell the gullible city slicker?"

"Nope. You can see Utah, Idaho and Wyoming." He took her arm and turned her toward the north. "Idaho."

"Oh."

"And over there—" when she didn't turn, he put his hands at her waist, turning her toward the east "—is Wyoming." As he spoke, he became intensely aware of where his hands now rested. He had an urge to slide them over the subtle curve of her hips, then up her torso toward her breasts. She'd worn the formfitting jeans again and there was no doubt he liked just how they "fit" her "form." An image of her clad only in the brief bathing suit surfaced and his throat dried.

She was suddenly still beneath his touch. Gone were her usual skittish moves. Very aware of his hold on her, Matt knew he had to either follow his desire or release her.

Cursing silently, Matt dropped his hands. "And of course you can see Utah."

"What?" As she turned to him, he could see a thready pulse beating erratically in the hollow of her throat, nearly matching the whispery quality of her voice—the same betraying pulse he'd seen the night before.

"The three states you can see from here," he replied, realizing his voice was as gruff as hers. He cleared his throat. "And we don't charge extra for the view."

"Good thing," she tried to joke, realizing her experiment had bombed. Apparently there was no way the slate would be wiped clean. "It would take a king's ransom to pay for this view."

Matt took a step back, needing to regain his equilibrium, needing to head far away from the dangerous thoughts that were growing more difficult to control. "More than a king's ransom. It took blood and sweat."

"I'm not sure I understand."

Matt gestured at the surrounding area with a broad sweep of his arm, taking refuge in the familiar. "This is MacKenzie land and it didn't come cheap—and I don't mean in dollars. It's been in our family for generations. Generations of sacrifice, lives lost, hard work."

Brynn studied him, admiring this side of him, his raw, elemental craving for the solid promise of the land. "It means a lot to you, doesn't it?"

He met her gaze directly. "Yes." That one simple word conveyed so much more.

"It's quite a legacy."

Matt thought briefly of Gregory's disdain for the land, wondering how his wife would react to the same heritage. Trying to remember she was in fact Gregory's wife. "And a great responsibility. Each generation has to improve and renew the land."

"And so now it's your turn?" Brynn questioned, seeing the

commitment in his eyes, the steady burn of his dedication; and realizing how much those qualities appealed to her.

"Exactly." He looked out at the land he held so dear, thinking of how difficult it had been to convince his father that it was time for Eagle Point to grow. "And change of any kind doesn't come easy—especially when you're steeped in tradition."

"What changes do you want to make?"

"I like to call them improvements." He couldn't disguise the excitement in his voice. "New ski lifts—six-passenger high-speed detachable chairlifts that'll transport skiers up the mountain at a thousand feet per minute—like the Silverlode in Park City."

"I'm not sure exactly what that means to a ski resort."

"They'll replace the quads—putting us on the cutting edge of technology. And we need more snowmaking equipment— Snow-Cats, additional snow guns. I want the hanging-tower snowmaking guns—again to be on the cutting edge."

Brynn's face was twisted into a question mark. "I don't want to sound stupid, but why do you make snow? Doesn't it just occur naturally?"

Matt laughed, wishing it was that easy. "Skiers expect snow every single day of the season. And nature doesn't always cooperate. So we have to be able to produce it."

"Is it as good as the famous 'greatest snow on the earth' the state's always bragging about?"

"Nothing can match or touch Utah powder, but skiing's big business. Park City has ten million dollars invested in snowmaking equipment—and we have to keep up or take a back seat."

"I guess I just never realized...." Brynn looked boggled at the amount he'd suggested. "But you said there were other improvements, too."

Matt replayed what had been his own internal monologue, representing countless days and nights of planning, calculating, researching, and soul-searching. "I want to expand our ski school, install an indoor pool, build a new fitness center, and enlarge the skating oval so we can bring in big-name figure-skating stars and shows like Sun Valley does."

"Whew! I can't even begin to imagine...."

"And that doesn't include adding new cottages, renovating the lodge, putting hot tubs in all the balcony rooms, and building a four-star restaurant."

"As overwhelming as that sounds, I'm guessing that's not all."

He liked her perceptiveness, her quick understanding. "Right. I want to install more outdoor hot tubs over the natural mineral springs—like our outside pools are."

Their eyes flew together, the previous night demanding to be remembered.

Purposely he kept his voice brisk and businesslike, reminding himself that she was his sister-in-law. Nothing more. "But I want to terrace the hot tubs up the mountainside with a 360-degree view of the mountain peaks by day."

"And," she prompted, adopting his tone.

He grinned, realizing he'd told her more about his plans than anyone except his father, who was still officially the head of Eagle Point, despite Matt's title of director. It was a relief to see his plans reflected in eyes that saw them in a completely new light, without preconceived opinions.

"I want to court investors. Ones who'll build condos in Gallagher. And I'd like to see heli-skiing."

"'Heli-skiing'?" she echoed.

"By helicopter—for strong intermediate or advanced skiers," he replied, envisioning this new resource, one he wanted to develop along with an outside investor. "They ski untouched powder. Guides would show our guests where to find the best bowls and tree skiing they'll ever find at ten thousand vertical feet."

She gasped. "It sounds dangerous—" her lips lifted into an unexpected grin "—but exciting."

"That's why I want it to be developed as part of Eagle Point on a contract basis."

"You might as well spill the rest of it," she suggested.

Once again he admired her quick grasp. "For a world-class ski resort to work, the town needs multimedia entertainment, après-ski—after-ski—clubs, restaurants. I'd like to see more stores and theaters go in—enough diversity so that vacationers who don't want to ski have plenty to do in the winter."

Brynn nibbled at her lower lip. "But wouldn't that change everything? I mean… Right now Gallagher is charming and cozy. What you're describing sounds so cosmopolitan. It would be like, like…"

"Park City? Telluride? Sun Valley?"

"Well, yes, I guess so."

"And all three revitalized the surrounding areas, brought in jobs that were needed, commerce for the existing shops and other businesses."

"I guess so."

Matt knew what she was thinking, had struggled over the same issues. But he also knew that without growth, they risked decline. "We have craftsmen in Gallagher who have clung to the old ways that are literally a dying art. Old-world glass-blowing. Sand-pouring artistry—one of only three artists left in the country is right here in Gallagher. A wood artisan who makes burl bowls from a solid chunk of wood. And we have people who throw pottery on wheels they inherited from their grandparents. Dollmakers, painters, leather crafters. Silver and goldsmiths who make jewelry more unique than you'll find anywhere else. Eagle Point brings a lot of trade to town, but with the kind of expansion I'm talking about, all these crafts-men would have avenues to sell their products and a steady flow of customers to buy them."

Brynn hesitated over the words. "But how would the towns-people feel? Everything would be so different for them."

"Progress and time bring change. The town isn't just like it was when the founders built it. But the changes have made it better—electricity, paved roads, indoor plumbing. Don't you think everyone in Gallagher likes having those things?"

"Well, of course, but—"

Matt voiced the reasoning that had brought him to this decision. "I imagine there was a quite a stir when all of those things were introduced, but the townspeople adjusted. And with the expansion there'd be enough opportunities that their children wouldn't have to leave for the cities. They could find their opportunities right here in Gallagher."

"Are you going to divide up Eagle Point's land? Sell it to developers?"

Territorial instinct sprang into force. "No. That will never be an option. This land will always stay in the family—that's a promise every MacKenzie makes to the following generation. The improvements I want affect the lodge and our business. Selling the land isn't an improvement, it's blasphemy."

Brynn hesitated. "Does everyone in the family feel so strongly about keeping the land?"

Matt's lips firmed, thinking of Gregory's careless lack of concern. His brother wanted to subdivide the land and sell it to the highest bidder. Although Matt felt his soul curdle at the idea of strangers owning their property, Gregory was indifferent to the prospect, seeing only the profit that could be plowed into other businesses. He had used their father's illness as an excuse, saying that it was time to act while the leadership of Eagle Point was uncertain. Luckily Frank MacKenzie had seen through the visionless plans.

And now the responsibility had landed directly on Matt's shoulders. But that was how he wanted it. "No, not everyone cares about the heritage. I guess Gregory didn't tell you, but he's in favor of splitting up the land and selling it off."

Shock filled her huge blue eyes. "That's hard to believe. I can't understand how anyone could give up something so rooted in family. I can scarcely imagine anything passing so solidly from generation to generation." She glanced down for a moment. "All I have from my heritage are my grandmother's stories. Not that they aren't wonderful," she rushed to add. "But, this... This is so tangible...so real."

"To hear you talk it's as though Gregory never even mentioned Eagle Point."

"Of course he *mentioned* it, but nothing was said about selling it off in parcels."

Matt studied her face, seeing what appeared to be genuine concern. More concern than Gregory had ever shown. But, somehow, on this crisp fall day, with its endless sky of unobstructed blue, he didn't want to think or talk about his brother anymore. Because his attraction to Brynn was adding another dimension, a level he knew was even more dangerous.

"Ready to take the measurements?"

She spun around. "I forgot we were here for a reason. I guess I got a little too caught up in the experience. Just tell me what to do."

It was a tempting, if unintentional offer. Instead of immediately starting their task he pointed out a herd of elk in the distance moving from the high country to the low country.

"That's incredible," she murmured, watching the magnificent animals as they swept down from the mountaintop.

Matt walked toward a stand of aspen and rubbed the dark splotches of missing bark. "See these?"

She nodded.

"From the elk. They leave their hoofmarks to show their passing."

"How do you *know* so much?"

He laughed. "You know how to navigate the city, don't you? Where to buy the best groceries, the neighborhoods that are desirable, how the freeways connect? That's the lay of your

land. Here we share it with wild game. Elk, coyotes, porcu-
pines—they're our neighbors.''

She shook her head. "You make it sound easy."

"It is when it's in your blood."

She studied him for a moment, admiring more and more
about him. When his gaze caught hers, she sent him a distracting smile. "It's not in my blood, but I think I can manage to
help take measurements."

Brynn proved to be an able assistant, catching on quickly to
the nuances of measuring for an abstract project still in the
drawing stages.

When she struggled on the last measurement, unable to read
the tape, Matt couldn't resist teasing her. "Those glasses look
powerful enough to see across the canyon."

She flushed, pushing at those same glasses. "They're not for
distance."

"They can't be just for reading," he dismissed. But then her
face flushed suddenly. "Or are they?"

"I'll just get a little closer," she hedged.

She started toward the end of the tape but Matt was faster,
cutting her off en route. She looked around, but behind her was
only the canyon drop-off. Matt could tell she was scrambling
for an escape, but he wasn't giving any quarter.

"Don't you want to get the right measurement?" she asked,
her voice squeaking despite her obvious effort to control it.

"I want to know all kinds of things," he replied, enjoying
the latest change in her expression, the sudden wariness.

"If I were Stephanie, I could tell you something outrageous," she tried to joke, having backed up as far as she could
safely go.

"And as Brynn, don't you know something equally outrageous?"

Her mouth opened, then shut again without making a sound.

Giving in to the urge that had been plaguing him nearly since the first moment they'd met, Matt reached toward her glasses, sliding them forward and then pulling them away.

She blinked for a moment, obviously rattled without the security of the heavy-rimmed protectors—ones she'd worn even into the hot tub.

Huge blue eyes, fringed in remarkably thick, dark lashes were a shock. Although he'd guessed she must be a looker to attract Gregory, and now knew she had a world-class figure, Matt wasn't prepared for the full impact.

Glasses removed, and with the breeze blowing the black curls away from her face, her delicate almost-ethereal features stood in stark relief. Brynn's Irish heritage was painted across her ivory skin as clearly as a well-drawn map of County Cork.

Matt simply couldn't understand why she hid such beauty in every conceivable way. The hairstyle, oversize glasses and baggy clothes all combined into an effective disguise.

He reached out to catch one flyaway curl, feeling its silky texture. While he'd already noticed the luster and wild appeal of her untamed hair, he suspected she purposely kept it that way as yet another layer of camouflage. But why?

And how had the shortsighted Gregory uncovered this treasure?

Without thinking, Matt eased one thumb over the smooth skin of her cheek, discovering another texture of silk.

When Brynn trembled beneath his touch, he spotted the wild, betraying jump at the base of her throat. His gaze zoned in on full, tender lips, bare of lipstick, yet lush with color. Without thinking, he bent his head toward hers, wondering if her mouth would taste as delicious as it looked.

Just a fraction away from her lips, Brynn's watch alarm buzzed, loud and insistent.

Jerking backward, Matt spun away from her, knowing a lit torch wouldn't have singed deeper. What was he thinking? She was his brother's wife!

Clearing his throat, Matt spoke toward the mountain in the

opposite direction, rather than toward her. "You're right, we'd better finish the measuring. The light's tricky. We don't want to lose it."

Her voice was thready, barely more than a whisper. "Of course." She held her hand against the warm spot on her cheek where his fingers had lingered.

But Matt didn't notice. He was too busy putting distance between them as he stalked to the other side of the grassy slope. "You'd better find a way home soon, brother," he muttered.

Chapter Nine

Brynn slowly turned the pages of the wedding album, realizing that nearly a week had passed since she'd opened it. But after her experience a few days earlier with Matt at Plum Ridge, she needed the reinforcement, the connection to Gregory—especially since Frank's call to the State Department that morning had again proved fruitless. Matt intended to fly to D.C. the next day, unwilling to wait for another phone call or fax. And action of any kind helped chase the sickly gray pallor from Frank's face. He was visibly weakening more each day. When Brynn thought about telling the truth and leaving, she only had to look at him to know his health couldn't take the blow.

Why was it that now when she looked at Gregory's picture it was as though she stared at a stranger, someone she didn't know beneath the glib smile and good looks? His eyes didn't tell her anything.

Leafing through the album, Brynn felt as though she was looking at someone else's photos. She could appreciate them, but they didn't speak to her. And once they'd been the only voice in her silent life.

Closing her eyes, Brynn tried to remember the rush of exhilaration that always filled her when she studied the pictures. Not getting anything, instead she focused on remembering Gregory when she'd first met him on the jogging paths. That memory was slightly better, but still faint.

When had this happened? This feeling of distance? Could it just be because Gregory had now been gone for some time? That everything had changed, turned topsy-turvy? Was this a normal reaction that would have happened to anyone?

Or just anyone who'd been spending too much time with Matt MacKenzie?

Matt's face was so much clearer in her mind. But then of course he was closer, too. It was probably some sort of transference, she told herself.

Remembering the look in his eyes when they'd been at Plum Ridge, she knew it wasn't that simple. Her hand strayed toward her cheek, instantly remembering his touch, the warmth of it, and the explosion of feelings he'd ignited.

And she remembered the trail of awareness that had led to that moment on the ridge. It hadn't been just one moment, one look. It had begun when she'd first met him. And it had been escalating ever since.

Brynn wished she had a fraction of Stephanie's impetuous zest for life. To be capricious, daring, and unconcerned about the consequences. But Brynn had always been too practical for such impulsiveness. With a mother who often forgot who was the parent, Brynn had been forced to be responsible, older than her years.

A soft knock on the door interrupted her thoughts, and Brynn was glad for the distraction as she called out, "Come in."

Heather poked a hesitant-looking face around the door. "Mom said I wasn't to disturb you. Am I?"

"Of course not." Brynn smiled. "Come on in."

The girl slipped inside, leaving the door ajar.

Brynn started to close the album but Heather had spotted it. "Please don't put it away. I'd like to see the pictures."

"Certainly." Brynn knew Heather was a sensitive girl and the entire family was worried about her withdrawal. With news of Gregory sporadic and infrequent, Heather had lost weight, paled, and grown far too quiet for a teenager. "I enjoy looking at them over and over, myself."

Heather settled companionably at Brynn's side. "They're such beautiful pictures." She sighed. "So romantic." Her face and voice crumpled. "So tragic."

"I don't think so," Brynn answered firmly, appalled at the girl's dismay. "In fact I look at them in just the opposite way. They're pictures of hope."

Heather glanced up at her, her eyes welling with tears. "You really think so?"

"Absolutely."

"Brynn...do you *really* think Gregory will come home?"

"Yes, Heather, I do."

The girl sniffled as she let out a sigh of relief. "Mom said people who love somebody know—it's in their hearts. I figured since you and Gregory are in love, you're as close as two people can be. And that you must know his heart better than anybody, so if you think he's safe, he must be."

A pang of guilt struck Brynn—fierce, sharp and swift. She *didn't* know Gregory's heart, and to pretend to was a terrible sham. But she couldn't crush this youngster's hope by saying so. Instead, she repeated the belief she'd told herself: "He'll come back. Gregory is always in charge wherever he goes. He's not going to let a few kidnappers get the best of him."

Heather digested this. "I hadn't thought of that. You're right. He never let anybody tell him what to do—not even Mom or Dad. I guess he did when he was little, but I wasn't around then."

Brynn hid her smile. "He's a survivor—just hold on to that thought."

"I will. I don't think I'd be so worried, but Dad's been so sick...." Her throat worked and tears threatened again. "I heard people talking and saying that Dad wouldn't make it. Then when Gregory was kidnapped they said if he didn't come back it would kill Dad. Then I'd lose them both."

Brynn leaned over and wrapped her arms around the girl in a comforting manner. Brynn knew she'd wedged herself into an impossible situation. She shouldn't be continuing this pretense, but unraveling the truth was just as impossible.

"You aren't going to lose either of them, Heather. But you have to have faith in your father and Gregory. If you go around with a long, sad face you'll worry your dad and you know that's not good for him. And I've always heard that prisoners of war sense when people believe they'll come home. They also sense when their families don't have faith, which wears them down, keeps them from being as strong as they need to be. So, you *can* help them both—in very important ways."

"I've felt like there's nothing I could do, Brynn. Nothing that counted."

"Everything you do counts," Brynn answered softly. "You're lucky to have such a close, loving family. Don't ever feel you're being disloyal to Gregory when you're having fun. He'd want you to. He certainly wouldn't want you going around with a long face. He's going to pop in here one day soon and you don't want him to see a bunch of gloomy gusses dragging around, do you?"

Heather smiled. "Gregory would say we were a frightful bore if we acted that way." Her smile faded a bit. "How did you know I felt guilty about having fun?"

"I suspect someone said something to that effect, because you've changed since I first met you. It was after we got back here to the lodge."

Heather nibbled on her lower lip. "Jenny was over when some of the kids came by to see if we wanted to go skating. Jenny said that we couldn't go because of me—that if her brother was being held hostage she couldn't enjoy herself, that she'd spend every single minute thinking about him." Heather shrugged thin shoulders. "So I didn't go, and the kids aren't coming over much 'cause they don't like being around me anymore."

"I'm sure they still like you." Gently Brynn tipped the girl's chin upward. "Just let them know that you'd like to go skating or to a movie, drop some subtle hints about fun things going on here in the lodge, maybe even have some of the kids over for videos and pizza."

"And you're sure it's okay for me to do that?"

"Positive. And when your dad and mom see you having fun, they'll feel better. And you'll be awfully glad you could make that happen."

Heather threw her arms around Brynn. "I'm so glad you're my sister! I always wished for a sister, and you're better than anyone I could have dreamed up."

Tears stung Brynn's eyes. Touched, moved and nearly unnerved, she blinked away the telltale moisture. Too choked up to reply, she settled for smoothing Heather's hair and wishing she truly was part of this special family.

Outside in the hall, Matt walked quietly away, leaving a copy of the latest fax about Gregory at Brynn's door. As moved as the two inside by what he'd heard, he kept on walking, unwilling to let his brother's wife know just how much.

MATT WATCHED ANDY, his youngest sibling, as Andy attacked a man-size stack of pancakes while reading the comics. It was funny, he thought, how different he and his brothers and sister were from each other. Gregory had always wanted something bigger and better; Heather was their sunshine girl; and Andy always took on every event, from eating breakfast to skiing, with the same single-minded diligence.

"Hey, Matt, you coming to my soccer game?"

"Sure, squirt. I've got to find out if my coaching works."

Andy made a face. "You were all-state. Our coach doesn't know half what you do."

"Better not tell him that."

Andy dug into the pancakes, unconcerned. "I already did."

Matt couldn't contain a chuckle. "Guess I'll be real popular at the game."

Andy shrugged. "Wish you were our coach anyway. Then we'd rule."

Matt grinned. "Scary thought."

Andy rolled his eyes and then looked back at the comics.

Ruth smiled between them, then clucked in a mock reproving tone. "Now, now, boys."

But Andy was lifting the newspaper, his face filled with nine-year-old disgust. "Uck, I wonder how come Brynn's making Stephanie act so weird."

"Weird, how?" Ruth asked.

"She doesn't do so much cool stuff."

"She doesn't?" Matt questioned, intrigued.

"Naw. She was always doing really awesome stuff, but now she's...almost *normal*."

Ruth laughed as Matt studied his brother. "She is?"

"Yeah. I liked it better when she was crazier."

Patting her youngest son's hand, Ruth smiled. "Brynn probably has a plan for Stephanie. No telling what she'll be up to next."

Andy brightened. "You think so?"

"I'm sure of it. Now, put it in gear or you're going to be late for school."

"Okay, Mom." His chair scraped across the stone floor as he pushed it back, grabbing his baseball hat from the nearby coat-tree. "See ya."

"Hold it!" Ruth called out. "Didn't you forget something?"

Andy scooted around the table, planting a noisy kiss on Ruth's cheek. "Can we have chocolate-chip cookies after school?"

"Con artist," she replied, playfully tugging the brim of his cap down. "We'll see."

"Don't forget the game, Matt," Andy warned, scooping up his backpack.

"Scout's honor," Matt replied solemnly, holding up one hand.

A whirlwind of energy and movement, Andy was out of the dining room, then bounding down the path that led from the back door toward the shortcut he always took to school.

"Sometimes just watching him wears me out," Ruth commented, pouring them both more coffee.

"Naw, he keeps you young."

She peered at him over the rim of her cup. "You all do."

Matt grinned back at her, glad to see this light side of her again. It had been too long. "We try."

"When you were nine, you not only talked me into baking chocolate-chip cookies for yourself, but enough to sell since you had your own consignment in the gift shop."

"I think you called me 'enterprising,' then."

Ruth lifted her cup. "And I was right. You have wonderful plans for this place."

"I just hope they don't worry Dad too much."

"He has confidence in you, but they are big changes."

"And a big risk," Matt admitted.

"We seldom gain anything without risk."

Matt thought briefly of Brynn, then shoved the thought aside. Instead, he sought to keep his mother's mood light. "Like your lottery tickets?"

She swatted at his hand. "Make fun. But one winning ticket would buy a lot of new ski-lift equipment."

"Not to mention that cruise you've been waiting to take, a few diamonds, maybe a fur..."

"I can see you're going to be impossible, so I'll leave you to your own coffee."

Matt wrapped his fingers around the mug, one side of his mouth tipping upward. "Better hurry if you're going to get your tickets before the deadline."

"A lot you know," Ruth huffed. "They aren't having the draw until Saturday."

Matt's grin was full-blown. "Wouldn't want to wait till it's too late."

"For what?" Brynn asked, coming into the dining room and picking up a mug.

"To become instant millionaires," Matt replied, noticing that her hair looked especially soft, and that the jeans she'd opted to wear still jarred his "alert" mechanism, reminding him of how she filled out a bathing suit. And now that he knew just what she looked like without her glasses, they were no longer a barrier to her beauty.

"Don't pay him any mind, Brynn. When we're rolling in our loot, he'll change his tune."

"You going to town, too?" Matt asked, looking at Brynn.

"Well, I—" Brynn began.

"Excellent idea!" Ruth exclaimed. "Why don't you ride in with me, Brynn? Some of the girls are putting a quilt on today."

Matt saw Brynn grimace at the idea. Deciding he ought to offer an escape since he'd thrown her into the jaws of a possible quilt frenzy, Matt spoke casually. "Unless Brynn would like to see the Alpine Slide close up. I have to check the fence on the terrace behind the slide this morning."

Brynn grabbed at the lifeline. "That sounds really interesting." She turned an apologetic face toward Ruth. "Not that the quilt doesn't..."

Ruth waved her hands, dismissing the notion. "Young people don't get very excited about quilts—and I can understand that. Come to think of it, I didn't, either, when I was your age. Go on to the slide. We won't have that many nice days left."

Brynn looked between them. "It's not time for winter yet."

"Not down in the city, but we'll be getting snow soon," Ruth replied. "You can see we've already had snow up on the peaks. Takes a few storms before enough base builds up for skiing, and it's time for them to begin."

"I guess I didn't think about that. It's just so beautiful outside—the fall foliage, the Indian-summer sunshine—it's hard to believe we're in for storms.''

"You'll believe it when you can't leave the lodge for days unless you're on a snowmobile or wearing snowshoes," Matt told her. "Most people can't stand the isolation."

Brynn shrugged. "It sounds cozy. I love being snowbound in the city as long as I have wood for the fire, hot cocoa and plenty of marshmallows. It's like I have my own little undisturbed world."

Matt glanced at her in surprise. Most city people complained of cabin fever after only a few hours of immobility. An improbable arrow of jealousy nudged him as he wondered if Gregory had ever shared this little world with her.

Deciding he'd rather not know, Matt stood. "We'd better get going before Mom changes her mind and decides she needs someone to help her lug home all those lottery tickets."

Rolling her eyes, Ruth caught Brynn's gaze. "I'm not sure I should leave you to his mercies, but the slide area is beautiful this time of year. Try and enjoy."

RUTH WAS RIGHT, BRYNN decided. The slide area *was* beautiful. Evergreen firs and wild grass provided a backdrop to splotches of crimson and gold, while pumpkin-colored patches of leaves that had surrendered to the ultimate advance of autumn danced across them.

As Brynn bent to inspect a delicate pink bell-like flower, she heard an eerie sound that echoed through the canyon. She glanced up at Matt.

He read her silent question. "Bugling elk. You hear them up in the high country this time of year."

She nodded. "Like the herd we saw on Plum Ridge?"

Only the tic in his jaw revealed any reaction to that day. "Yes. But they're coming down farther now. It seems like civilization but we're surrounded by wild game—deer, wolves, moose, bears, wolverines."

"No bunny rabbits?" she asked in a small voice.

He grinned. "A few. But Bugs and his friends don't hang out in the mountains."

"Too bad," she replied, drawing herself in as though she expected to see a wolf or bear charge through the woods at any moment.

"Don't worry. A lot of people come up here to the slide. All the activity keeps the animals away."

"Uh-huh."

He laughed. "I'm going up that hill to check the fencing." Then he pointed toward some piles of leaves. "The maintenance staff has been raking here this morning, so you're safe."

Relief set in.

"The yard crew will be sacking the leaves before the kids can start jumping in them." Matt spoke like the boss he was, authoritative and in charge. "So, in case you have any ideas—we don't disturb the piles."

His words chased away the relief, replacing it with a slow burn. He'd just implied that she wasn't any more responsible than the kids.

Brynn brushed the dirt from her hands, ignoring the newly picked flowers as she watched Matt walk away. His tone of voice had unleashed an imp so strong that she wondered if Stephanie had climbed out of the frame of her comic strip.

She watched Matt scale the hill and disappear over the top toward the fence. Once he was out of sight, Brynn headed straight for the piles, many of the leaves having fallen recently, splashing their stalwart hues across the grass.

It was a riot of color so sumptuous that Brynn gave in to the urge nudging her—along with a desire to defy Matt's high-handed words. Dropping onto a pile of crisp leaves, she rolled from side to side, kicking them into a small shower of color. The leaves scattered, then floated to the ground.

Standing, Brynn made sure Matt was still out of sight as she brushed away the leaves clinging to her jeans. Remembering how she and her grandmother had once played in the leaves, destroying neatly raked piles, then dancing in the flying fallout, Brynn closed her eyes, imitating those childish moves, inventing new ones.

Afraid Matt would be returning soon, she twirled once more, scuffing the leaves beneath her shoes. While on the one hand she enjoyed defying him, on the other she didn't want to confirm that she was as irresponsible as he'd predicted. Leaves flew into the air. A sharp piquant memory of leaves burning was so clear she could smell the tang, hear the crackle—

"Busted!" Matt shouted directly behind her.

Pivoting, she shrieked before she could stop herself, her flailing arms and legs causing a downpour of leaves that rained over her head and body.

And met laughter that fell from Matt's lips to bounce between them.

"You're too easy," he told her. "A suggestion, one little nudge, and I could tell you were going to hit those leaves in less than ten seconds."

Brynn tried to remain indignant but his laughter was contagious. Her lips twitched, crept upward and then opened as a gust of laughter enveloped her. Brushing at the leaves adhering to her hair, she only succeeded in tangling them further. Still laughing, Matt reached out, fashioning the leaves into a lopsided crown by adding a few more from the pile at his feet.

Touching the makeshift crown, Brynn cocked her head. "Bet you can't make a cape and scepter to go with this." As soon as the words were out of her mouth, Brynn wished she could recall them. Because a devilish gleam lit his eyes, suggesting she would regret the challenge.

"A cape? Full length or just a wrap?" He advanced.

She retreated.

"Actually I'd much rather just stick with the crown. It's a very nice crown." She patted her leaf-decorated hair to prove her point.

"But the outfit's not complete without the cape," he warned.

"You can't possibly get that many leaves to stay on me," she tried again, guessing he planned to drown her with the entire pile.

"Good point." Looking as though he was recalculating, he shot out his arms suddenly, grabbing her around the waist. "It'd be much easier to put you into the cape."

"You wouldn't!" she screeched just as he upended her into the pile of leaves. Spluttering, blowing leaves from her mouth, she scrabbled to surface.

And Matt's reaction was pure laughter. It doubled him over, puffed out his lean cheeks, and brought tears to his eyes.

The spirit of Stephanie, fair play, or her own buried self rose. Grabbing Matt's ankles, she tipped him over before he realized her intent. As he landed in the leaves, she scooped up handfuls of leaves to dunk at him.

But he was fast. Before her well-aimed lobs could get him, he yanked her forward, reburying her in the leaves.

Pushing at the leaves near her head, she grabbed a fistful and shoved them into the open neck of Matt's shirt.

"Ah! Playing dirty, are you?"

Seeing he planned to repay her with far more leaves, Brynn jumped up, started to sprint away and found herself dangling helplessly as Matt grabbed her belt, then filled the back of her shirt with leaves.

"Stop that! Now, Matt!" She laughed, screeched and squirmed as he continued stuffing the leaves until she began to resemble a scarecrow.

"You going to give up?" he asked, not giving her an inch, still stuffing her cotton shirt with leaves.

"Never!" she gasped out, trying to twist away.

The leaves tickled and itched as he continued. When they began filling her sides, she pulled away, only to find herself back on the ground.

"Coward!" she taunted recklessly.

"Glutton for punishment," he retorted, tickling her.

Brynn tried to hold out, but she'd never had any resistance to being tickled. "Uncle!" she finally yelled, her sides aching with laughter.

Lifting her up and settling her back on her feet, Matt wiped his hands together in satisfaction. "A job worth doing is a job worth doing right."

"My sentiments exactly," she replied, turning around and pulling the tails from her blouse, allowing the leaves to fall free. Her back still to him, she cupped her hands and caught some of them.

Spinning quickly, she managed to douse his head with a good-size pile before she took off, not waiting to see the expression on his face when it was free of leaves.

Hearing footsteps pounding behind her, she put some of her earlier ballet training to good use, grateful for once for her mother's insistence on dance lessons. Her long legs stretched out, lithely jumping over crevices, gliding effortlessly over the wild grass.

Like a gazelle, Matt thought, amazed. She looked as though she belonged amid these woods. Gaining on her, he doubled his efforts, reaching out to catch her. Miscalculating the distance and the strength he put into the jump, he tackled her instead.

Hearing a whoosh as they landed, Matt immediately turned her over, certain he'd hurt her. "Brynn, are you all right? I didn't mean to hit you like you're a linebacker for the Cowboys."

When she didn't reply, he smoothed the ebony hair away from her face, absently plucking the errant leaves from silken strands. "Brynn, I'm sorry. I must have knocked the air out of you. I forgot you're just a delicate female."

He saw her glasses sprawled in the grass beside them. Her eyes remained ominously closed, her thick fringe of dark lashes swept over pale, fair skin.

His hands closed over her arms, giving her a little shake. "Wake up, Brynn. God, what have I done?"

Her eyes popped open as though operated by a light switch. "You nearly killed me, that's what you did."

Matt stared for a moment.

Then her lips started to twitch. "Had you going."

"You, you…"

"'Delicate female'?" she suggested.

"Ready to get dunked again?" he threatened.

But her body was shaking with laughter. "Nope," she managed between hiccups of laughter.

Disgusted, he stood and started to walk away, but her feet were faster, quickly scissoring out in front of him. "One trip deserves another," she announced.

But she'd miscalculated his fall. Before she could roll out of his way, he landed on top of her, his chest pressed to her breasts, his hips abrading hers, his legs sprawled intimately over and between hers.

Knowing she should say something, anything, instead her words froze, her mouth open, gasping tiny puffs as her eyes stared into his.

Each point of contact seared and the smoke from the scorching trail clouded her senses.

And took jackhammer swings at his. He should move…roll over…laugh at the absurd situation. Instead he stared, watched as her eyes darkened, read the recognition and felt his own response.

He wanted her. Deep in his gut. Somewhere in his mind. And in every need-filled spot between.

"Brynn." The word was part groan, part plea.

One delicate, long-fingered hand reached up to tousle the leaves from his hair, stilled, then lingered.

Knowing he could get lost in the depth of her incredible blue eyes, he eased one thumb over her cheek, feeling the satin of her skin, imagining the same satin in the breasts that were so close to his touch. The telltale pulse nestled at the junction of her fragile collarbones now leaped out of control, its ragged beat matching the awareness on her face.

A face he'd wondered about. How could he have not seen her beauty from the first instant? How could he have ever imagined that his brother would have missed this treasure?

The unwanted trace of Gregory seeped through. The woman on the ground beneath him, the woman who made him laugh— made him want—didn't belong to him.

For the first time in his life, Matt envied his brother. Wanted what Gregory had. And knew it was one contest he could never win.

Chapter Ten

Brynn loved the air of excitement that filled the lodge. Matt had returned two days earlier from Washington. He had news that negotiations for Gregory's release might begin soon. The State Department promised they would move as quickly and as safely as possible. While nothing positive had been accomplished yet, the family was filled with renewed hope. Brynn shared their excitement, but somewhere during the celebrating she realized that she was more excited for the MacKenzies than for herself.

Disturbed by the sensation, she'd tried to conjure up the excitement she always felt when thinking about Gregory but hadn't been able to. Finally, she'd slipped away from the others.

Pulling out the wedding album to look at his picture, she realized she hadn't opened it in far more than a week. For a time, she'd sat staring at the book, remembering how she'd barely been able to keep her hands off it, knowing why that had changed.

Before she could spend much time considering the shift in her feelings, she'd been drafted into helping prepare for the Harvest Ball. The MacKenzies, with at least a bit of good news about Gregory, were putting their renewed spirits into this fall celebration dance. It had become a celebration of hope, as well. And soon Eagle Point was awash in preparty activity.

Corn husks, stacked hay bales, ornamental gourds, multicolor Indian corn, pumpkins, hurricane lamps, and a few genuine-looking scarecrows populated the lodge and outbuildings. A new coat of lemon wax shone on the furniture, leaving a pleasant tang in the air that combined with the ever-present woodsmoke of the huge river-rock fireplace.

From the kitchen, the aroma of snickerdoodles, gingerbread, and rum-raisin cookies blended with the bubbling scent of caramel for dipping apples and freshly pulled taffy. Jugs of fresh cider were set around the kitchen waiting to be spiced.

Paper lanterns decorated all the paths that led around the lodge and Brynn stood precariously on the top rung of a handyman's ladder hanging more lanterns on the terraced patio. She loved the bustle, the noise of voices calling out to each other, the way the family and staff worked together. Not that they didn't all have their own way of doing things, but tradition ruled. It was an easy feeling, one that made her want to linger over the job, stretching it out.

While she was no expert party decorator, she figured it didn't take a professional to hang lanterns. And when she was done with that task she had a basket of candles to distribute. The lighting for the dance was to be both old-fashioned and subdued—a night, she'd been told, that would resemble dozens that had preceded it.

The lodge was filled to capacity. The traditional celebration was popular with guests, many of whom came back year after year to join in the festivities. And the town considered it their celebration as well. Brynn was reminded of the stories her grandmother used to tell of how villages came together, the spirit they shared.

Driving another nail home, Brynn looked back at the neat row of lanterns she'd tacked up—not a feat of great skill, but she was pleased.

"You grinning about anything in particular?" Matt questioned from somewhere beneath the ladder.

Peering downward, Brynn saw him immediately. His muscled arms were filled with an intriguing load of boxes. In response, she waved her hammer. "Just checking over the lanterns."

"Not much you can do to mess them up," he replied with even humor.

"Thanks a lot." She craned her head backward. "I think they look cheery, waving in the breeze."

He cocked one eyebrow. "They're not the only things waving in the breeze. That ladder looks ready to topple."

She waved her hand airily in dismissal. "It's been perfectly fine."

"You don't want to land on your head."

"That didn't seem to bother you the other day when you dumped me in the leaves." The moment the words were out of her mouth, Brynn froze, remembering just how that day had ended. The painful intensity, the equally painful silence as they'd returned to the lodge.

Matt's hands tightened around the boxes, but he kept his tone light. "I doubt Gregory would appreciate our letting you break your neck."

Brynn lowered herself another rung. "I'm almost done."

Matt shifted the boxes, perching them on a nearby redwood bench. "I'll hold the ladder."

"That's not necessary, I'm steady."

Ignoring her, Matt gripped the ladder with both hands.

Self-conscious now, Brynn hurriedly tacked up the last lantern, then turned and glanced at Matt.

"Is that the last one?" he asked.

She stepped down another rung until they were nearly eye to eye. "That's it."

His gaze didn't leave hers. "Well, then."

Lifting the hammer, Brynn clenched its cold steel. "Yes..."

Matt's gaze slid toward her lips, before it shifted upward. "Yes."

Brynn knew she should say something—anything—but she didn't want to break the moment. Or the connection that lingered between them.

As though silently shaking himself, Matt stepped away abruptly. "I've got things to do."

"Of course," she agreed. "I didn't mean to hold you up." Since she hadn't asked for his help, they both knew she didn't need to offer an explanation, but she felt compelled to fill the awkward silence.

Matt grabbed the heavy boxes as though they were weightless, striding off with them. Though he didn't look back, Brynn kept her gaze riveted on him until he disappeared. But even after he was out of sight, the sensations tripping through her continued—making her wonder, making her question everything. Including herself.

MIRANDA HELD THE NEWLY pressed party dress out to Brynn for the second time. "Surely you're not planning to pass up a dress like this to wear…*that*."

Brynn sniffed, then sighed away her momentary affront as she glanced down at the plain, loose-fitting outfit she'd chosen after her run-in with Matt. "Does it really look that bad?"

Miranda pursed her lips. "I didn't mean to sound insulting. The dress isn't bad. It's just that it doesn't have much shape. And you, my dear, do. But in that dress, nobody would know it. If you were my age, I could see it, but—"

"What do you mean, at your age?" Brynn demanded. "You expect me to wear this—" She stared at the provocative dress Miranda held. Then her eyes narrowed. "Just what are you planning to wear?"

Miranda shrugged. "I hadn't given it much thought."

Brynn stared at the still-attractive, single woman. "Why not?"

"My time's past," Miranda replied. Her fingers stroked the party dress. "I suppose you guessed this dress was special to me and so was the man who was supposed to escort me to the Harvest Ball.'' Her voice started to warble and she took a moment to control it. ''But that didn't happen.''

''Wasn't that…quite some time ago?'' Brynn asked hesitantly.

''Yes. And now I'm a confirmed spinster.''

Brynn's heart went out to the other woman. ''I told you before I didn't believe in that.''

Miranda waved a hand. ''Pish.''

Brynn looked between the dress and Miranda, knowing she could make a sacrifice if it might mean helping Miranda. ''I'll make you a deal. I'll wear the dress—'' Miranda's face broke into the beginning of a grin ''—if you'll wear something just as stunning.''

Miranda's grin dissolved into a grimace. ''I would, but I'm afraid 'stunning' is beyond me.''

Brynn remembered the picture in the journal—Miranda's hopeful young face filled with love. Love that had disappointed her. ''I think you'll look even better than stunning.'' She gently took Miranda's arm. ''Let's go raid your closet.''

''But—''

Brynn uncharacteristically took the lead. ''Come on. I suspect you're holding out on me.''

Miranda grumbled as they walked to her suite of rooms. And once inside, she threw up her hands after pointing out her closet.

But Brynn refused to be discouraged. Even after she'd picked through the first row of clothes and found nothing appropriate. Miranda had a good selection of clothing but nothing with the special flair Brynn was looking for.

Later, almost at the back of the closet, Brynn was nearly ready to admit defeat. She couldn't make a wonderful dress appear just because she believed Miranda deserved to be dressed in one. She reached for one of the last hangers that held an oversize winter coat. Ready to turn away, she automatically pushed the coat aside to look at the last item in the closet. A transparent plastic bag covered golden fabric. Feeling a spurt of excitement, Brynn lifted the covering and found just what she'd been looking for.

The gold silk was a rich yet gentle color that wouldn't seem harsh. Instead it would highlight, soften. The simple lines of the dress gave it luster and style. An off-the-shoulder neckline fed down to elegant dolman sleeves and a classic A-line swirl. It was a garment that flattered, and if Brynn guessed correctly, would make Miranda shine.

Triumphantly, Brynn held it aloft like a trophy as she emerged from the closet.

But she was surprised when Miranda's reaction was a groan. "Not *that*."

Brynn re-examined the dress. "It's beautiful."

"I might as well wear a beacon that says Look at Me!" Miranda complained.

"And why not?"

Miranda planted her hands on her hips. "I should think that would be obvious."

Brynn called on her now close-by imp, wanting Miranda to find her own piece of happiness, even if it meant pushing her into trying new things. "But that's what you wanted me to do."

Miranda's mouth opened, then closed, then opened again. "But you're young!"

"So you're saying that only the young deserve attention."

"Well, no, but—"

Brynn moved in for the kill, knowing she couldn't keep up her uncharacteristic behavior much longer. "Then if you want me to wear the party dress, you'll wear this one."

"But—"

"A deal's a deal." Brynn gestured at the shapeless beige linen she wore. "Unless you'd rather I wore this."

Miranda threw up her hands. "Fine. Guess it won't be the

first time everyone in town thought I looked like a fool.'' She sighed with resignation before her gaze narrowed. "I'll be along shortly to put your hair up and help with your makeup.''

"Makeup?" Brynn repeated nervously, wondering just what she'd started.

"Of course." Miranda smiled slyly, transforming into a cat that had swallowed far more than just the canary. "Without your glasses you'll want a touch of makeup."

Brynn automatically clutched her glasses. "I didn't say I would—"

"Oh, but a deal's a deal," Miranda echoed.

Brynn threw up her own hands. "I guess there's no getting out of this."

Miranda wagged her eyebrows. "Afraid not."

Back in her own room, Brynn stared between her reflection in the mirror and the dress hanging from the closet door. She slipped out of the linen shift doubtfully. While part of her was drawn to the beautiful dress, the other part of her resisted something so obviously eye-catching—especially knowing Miranda planned to add makeup and a new hairstyle to the package.

But for one moment she allowed herself to wonder what Matt's reaction to the dress might be. In the next, she chastised herself for the thought. She should be imagining Gregory's reaction. After all, she was awaiting *his* return.

Shaking her head, she glanced again in the mirror. "You've lost it, girl," she told herself. "Now you're believing your own fables. You're not waiting for Gregory to return. If he does get released, you'd better hightail it back to the city before he gets here."

Her reflection winked back patiently, not saying a word.

"No help from you," she muttered.

A knock sounded on the door, followed by Miranda peeking around inside. "You talking to someone?"

"Only myself."

"I thought you'd be dressed by now," Miranda commented, still out in the hall.

"You can come in," Brynn invited.

But Miranda stalled.

Realizing the reason, Brynn forgot about her own dress. "Let me see!"

Reluctantly, Miranda stepped into the room. The gold dress was a perfect foil for her blond hair and big brown eyes. The muted color softened age lines and enhanced her features. And as Brynn had predicted, Miranda did shine.

"You look absolutely lovely," Brynn declared with conviction.

"You're kind, but—"

"Nothing of the sort," Brynn interrupted. "You positively glow!"

Miranda pinkened a bit. "You have stars in your eyes."

"If I do, you put them there—" Brynn waved to the party dress still hanging on the closet door "—with all your fanciful talk."

Miranda became all efficiency as she swept farther into the room, the folds of her silk dress swirling about her as she brought in her cosmetics case. "We could spend all night complimenting each other. Maybe we should put our dresses to the test and let someone else do the complimenting. But, first, your makeup."

Brynn eyed her warily. "I'm really not used to wearing much…"

"Lucky for you that you're a natural beauty."

Blushing, Brynn ducked her head.

"Even your color's natural." Miranda sighed. "Oh, to be young again."

"What would you do if you *could* turn back the clock?" Brynn asked.

Miranda paused, then smiled softly. "Take more chances. Go after what I really want. Now, no more stalling. Sit at the makeup table and let me do my magic. And off with those glasses!''

When Miranda finished applying the cosmetics, Brynn had to admit she liked the new look. Miranda had used a subtle touch and delicate colors, enhancing rather than changing.

Miranda eyed her critically. ''What do you think?''

''Actually...I like it. Do you think I could learn to do this?''

''Of course you can. You draw a comic strip. Just pretend you're coloring in a new character.''

Brynn laughed. ''I never thought of it like that.''

Miranda scooped up a handful of long, dark hair. ''This is next.''

Gulping, Brynn tried to look cheerful. ''Okay.''

Having come equipped, Miranda pulled a curling iron from her case, along with some rhinestone hair combs. ''We're going to keep it uncomplicated, elegant. You don't want to compete with the simple lines of the dress.''

It didn't take long for Miranda to sweep up Brynn's hair, cleverly fastening it in place on top of her head, then fashioning lots of loose curls to trail over her shoulders.

Fascinated, Brynn watched the transformation. Always having downplayed her wild mane, she'd never considered making it a focal point. Turning her head from side to side, she was secretly delighted as the rhinestones winked back at her.

''Do you like it?'' Miranda asked, sounding as though she already knew the answer.

''It actually looks pretty,'' Brynn responded, amazed.

''It always looks pretty,'' Miranda corrected. ''Now it's striking.'' She stepped back for a moment, obviously pleased with her efforts. ''Now, for the pièce de résistance.''

Slipping the dress from the hanger, she held it out. ''Let's be careful not to muss your hair or makeup.''

The daring neckline and equally low back made the dress easy to slip on. Brynn's first instinct was to cover all the bare skin. But Miranda was fastening the hooks. A second glance had Brynn noticing that the skirt seemed to be made of yards and yards of material.

Hesitantly, Brynn ran one hand over the iridescent folds of silk. It was an incredible-looking dress. Twisting to one side, Brynn was shocked to see that the nearly backless dress revealed even more skin than she'd imagined. Still, it was a dream of a dress. The delicate ice-blue silk was perfect against her fair skin. She couldn't have designed a dress that would have suited her more.

"Still think it's gorgeous?" Miranda asked.

"And daring," Brynn added, uncertain she could pull this off. Could she really walk into a room full of people, knowing they would all be looking at her?

Miranda gently patted her shoulder. "Nervous?"

Brynn nodded, trying to swallow past the sudden knot in her throat.

Sympathy bloomed in Miranda's eyes. "There's no need. Even if you don't believe that you're worthy of the attention, remember you're not walking into a crowd of strangers. Instead of looking at a sea of unknown faces, just pick out all your new friends and remember they're cheering for you."

The knot in Brynn's throat turned into a lump of emotion. "You'll make me cry."

"And ruin my expert makeup job? Oh, no, you don't!" She gave Brynn a gentle hug. "One last thing, though." Miranda turned to the cosmetics case, unearthing a small jewelry box and handing it to Brynn.

"What is it?"

"Open and see," Miranda instructed.

Brynn lifted the lid and stared at emerald-cut diamond earrings, their facets flashing with ice-blue sparks. "Oh, I couldn't."

"Yes, you can." Miranda lifted them from the case and placed them in Brynn's hands. "They were my grandmother's.

And I don't know anyone in the family more suited to wear them.''

Waves of guilt crashed over Brynn. How could she wear the family jewels? It was too much of a mockery. "Really, it's not necessary. I don't need earrings."

"The dress cries out for them. With that neckline, you can't wear anything at your throat. But your earlobes look positively naked. With your hair up, it's no debate. Besides, my grandmother picked the silk for this dress to match the earrings. I think she'd like to know they finally got worn together."

Knowing she couldn't argue and unleash further pain from the past, Brynn shakily donned the earrings. Looking into the mirror, she knew instantly that Miranda was right. They were the perfect touch. "Thank you, Miranda. I feel like a fairy princess."

"You look like one, too."

Impulsively, Brynn hugged her. "Then you must be my fairy godmother."

A soft rush of emotion crossed Miranda's face. "You're a keeper, Brynn. Now, shall we make our grand entrance?"

MATT STOOD IN THE LOBBY, watching it fill, already wishing the evening was over. Unnerved since his encounter with Brynn, he'd been cranky and taking it out on innocent decorations and refreshments. But it beat dumping on employees or guests—both alternatives equally distasteful to him.

Normally he loved the Harvest Ball, which was the official kickoff for Octoberfest. But now all he could think of was the latest fax regarding Gregory's situation. The missive had indicated a measure of hope. And instead of being glad that the brother he loved was one step closer to freedom, all he could think of was that it was also one step closer to Brynn's departure.

Gregory would be grateful they'd taken Brynn to heart, but he'd be equally anxious to sweep her back to their world—a world that didn't include Eagle Point. Or the rest of the MacKenzies—at least, not on a daily basis.

Matt supposed he would see Brynn on holidays—the requisite Thanksgiving and Christmas appearances—provided family celebrations didn't interfere with Gregory's more important plans.

And eventually he'd become Uncle Matt. Good old Uncle Matt.

Hearing a stir in the room, he glanced up and saw his Aunt Miranda descending the staircase. She looked younger, softer and decidedly attractive. Moving forward, he extended his hand as she reached the last step.

"Thank you, my dear." Then she gently withdrew her hand. "You've always been my best fellow. But there's more to come." Miranda stepped aside, directing his attention back toward the staircase.

Matt casually glanced upward, then found his gaze locked in place. He blinked, then stared again.

At the top step, Brynn hesitated, then began her descent.

And as she did, he forgot to breathe. She was a vision, an incredible, magical vision. With each descending step, he fought for air, then surrendered to the inevitable. Some portion of his brain demanded that he remember his brother, but everything else in him refused to listen.

His feet moved of their own accord, carrying him to the base of the stairs, ready to offer his hand when she met him at that last step.

A step that brought them eye to eye, heartbeat to heartbeat.

His brain gauged the absent glasses, the makeup, the elegance of her hair, and then the shimmer of her stunning dress.

Instantly jealous of every other man's eyes on her, Matt knew she was creating testosterone chaos. And he was the prime victim.

Yet her smile was invitingly hesitant, rather than sly. Could it be she didn't realize her effect? The dazzle that began with her sapphire eyes then ricocheted in the diamonds at her ears and the gleam of her striking dress. He was amazed that they weren't surrounded by nuclear fallout simply from her entrance. He knew at that moment that he was little more than ash and dust.

"You look very handsome," she offered, indicating the imported tailored suit he wore.

In his opinion, he could well have been wearing a T-shirt and cutoffs, he felt so far out of her league. He cleared his throat. "You look beautiful, Brynn."

Her eyes widened and he saw shocked surprise before she lowered a sweep of dark, thick lashes. "Thank you. You're very kind."

No. He simply wasn't blind anymore. Had he actually once thought she was too plain to attract his discriminating brother?

Feeling as though he'd been poleaxed, Matt remembered to extend his hand and lead her toward the ballroom. Her hand was soft and delicate within his, the long elegant fingers curling deliciously in his grasp.

The band began to play, but Matt scarcely heard the music. The room itself seemed to fade away. But his father's voice near his ear brought reality back with a snap.

"You look lovely, Brynn." Frank's voice was weak, but sincere.

"Oh, yes, dear. You're positively radiant," Ruth agreed, never far from her husband's side. Her worried glance lit on Frank before she turned the rest of her attention to Brynn. "I love the way young people bring back fashions and make them seem even better the second time around."

Frank's eyes held a puzzled expression. "That dress looks familiar."

Brynn smiled diplomatically, not certain Miranda would want her past paraded out for discussion. "It's like wearing a family heirloom. It seems familiar and special."

Ruth turned to her son. "This is a lovely song. Perhaps you

should ask your aunt to dance. As usual, the women outnumber the men.''

Glancing up, Brynn saw a pained expression cross Matt's face and wondered at the cause—especially since she knew he was very fond of Miranda.

Matt started toward his aunt. At the same time Brynn noticed a handsome, older man approaching Miranda. Impulsively, Brynn reached out to stay Matt's departure. ''I think she may have a dancing partner.''

Ruth and Frank heard and glanced at Miranda, as well.

Ruth, the eternal romantic, sighed. ''This looks promising.''

''If she'll give him a chance,'' Frank muttered.

Ruth met Brynn's eyes. ''Men!''

Since she was hardly an expert on that subject, Brynn wisely chose to only smile. At the same time, she allowed her gaze to dart sideways briefly, taking in Matt's Continental, yet uncultivated look. Having thought of him only as rugged, outdoorsy, and athletic, it hadn't occurred to her that he could look so unaffectedly sophisticated. And both looks were equally appealing.

''Since Miranda has a partner, you young people can dance,'' Ruth urged. ''No sense wasting great music.''

Matt heard his mother's words with a mix of anticipation and dread. Could he hold Brynn in his arms and remember she was now a sister? Why couldn't Gregory have kept to his old habits and chosen an ice queen?

Welcoming the torment, he offered his hand to Brynn. ''Would you like to dance?''

When she nodded, the diamonds on her ears signaled their own fiery reply and elusive glints of captured starlight twinkled in her hair.

Matt held her a respectable distance away. But his arms itched to draw her closer, welcoming her bewitching spell.

Brynn glanced at the other couples, at the filled room, and sensed the good feelings flowing among the people. ''It must be wonderful to claim a tradition like this for your own, to know every year that it will continue on.''

"The harvest is because of the land. And the land guarantees permanence,'' he replied, warmed by the subject closest to his heart, driven to share its importance with her. "As eternal as the mountains guarding it, as diverse as the sky above it.''

Brynn's eyes widened. "You sound almost poetic...as though it's in your soul.''

"That's because it is. Eagle Point's more than the lodge and ski lifts, more than all the improvements I want to add. It's a renewal. A promise that the family and what we stand for goes on.''

Her eyes clouded and he was instantly reminded just where her position in that family was. At whose side she belonged.

"I guess I hadn't thought of it that way,'' she finally replied, lifting troubled eyes to his. "Family's very important to you, isn't it?''

Painfully, unmercifully so. Matt straightened, girding his resolve. "More important than you could know.''

Her huge sapphire eyes shadowed, then glimmered with a suspicious sheen before she glanced away. "That's the way it should be.'' Her smile was tremulous. "The way I always wanted my own family to be.''

"The way you speak of your grandmother I thought your family was important to you.''

"Oh, it is. But my grandmother's gone now.''

"Your mother's alive.''

"So she is.'' Brynn glanced down again. "But I'm sure you'd rather talk about something more interesting than my family dynamics. Like how you get all this to come together.'' She waved her hands around the glittering room. "It's really wonderful.''

"You were part of the process,'' he reminded her.

"So I was.''

A small silence fell between them, brimming with awareness. The music slowed, causing a subtle shifting that brought couples closer together on the dance floor. Eyes met as bodies melded.

The silk of Brynn's dress swirled between her and Matt. As did the complicated tangle of their relationship. Smiles held resolutely in place, they turned around the dance floor, the ache of what could be resonating between them. The truth of what couldn't be, a silent chaperon—one that refused to relinquish its grasp, or ease the longing between them.

Chapter Eleven

Brynn entered the dining room warily, not certain she was prepared to face anyone over breakfast. Emotionally drained, she'd slept in but the restless slumber had only exhausted her more.

She'd considered losing herself in drawing her strip, but she couldn't begin the day with Stephanie's unerring sense of self. Especially since her own sense of self was blurring more each day.

To her relief, the dining room was nearly empty. Only Miranda sat at the table usually occupied by the family.

"Good morning," Brynn greeted her, reaching for a mug, practically inhaling the brew. "I think I need a caffeine transfusion."

Miranda laughed, looking completely rested. And something else. "Perhaps a coffee IV drip would do."

Brynn searched her expression, wondering just what was different. "Any news about Gregory?"

Miranda shook her head. "No, but Matt's been on the phone with the State Department for hours."

Brynn tipped her head, studying Miranda. "You look awfully chipper after a late night."

"Hmm."

Now Brynn was certain something was up. Miranda was never this succinct. "What aren't you telling me?"

"Excuse me?"

"There's something different about you today."

Miranda smiled into her coffee. "Funny. You've known me for two months and you can tell. But Frank and Ruth didn't have a clue."

"Then I'm right! What..." Her eyes narrowed as some of the caffeine crawled through her system and made contact. "Does this have something to do with the handsome man I saw you dancing with?"

A definite glow transfused Miranda's features, even though she tried to make her voice sound innocent. "Edward?"

"I wasn't introduced. Does he live in town? Or is he a guest?"

"A first-timer," Miranda mused. "He heard about our Octoberfest from friends and decided to come this year."

"Are his friends staying, too?"

"No. Funny thing. They all made reservations, then had to cancel at the last minute, but Edward decided to come anyway."

"I'm guessing he's single, then," Brynn offered.

"Widowed. Ten years now."

"Oh." That was hardly a statement she could whoop over, even though it meant he was available. And apparently interested in Miranda.

"He's nice," Miranda said simply.

"There's a lot to be said for nice," Brynn offered, hoping this meant a romance was in the air.

Miranda shook her head. "Don't make more of this than it is. He's simply a guest. Perhaps a lonely one, but still just a guest. He needs someone to talk to. That's usually what people seem to miss the most when they're alone."

Brynn guessed Miranda was an expert on the subject, but suspected she should navigate this field carefully. "Where's he from?"

"California. At least, that's where he lives now. But he isn't too happy living there. Things have changed a lot in the last decade."

"Is he thinking about joining the exodus from California?"

Miranda ran her fingers across the rim of her mug. "He didn't say."

Brynn wondered what he *had* said. "What sort of business is he in?"

"He's retired now, but he owned a public-relations firm. He said he got a buyout offer too lucrative to refuse, so he sold. But I have the feeling he misses it."

"He's quite handsome," Brynn commented, searching for the other woman's reaction.

"I suppose so." Miranda glanced up and saw the disbelieving look on Brynn's face. "Okay, yes, I noticed he's handsome. But as I said, he's simply a guest. I enjoyed talking to him." Her fingers drew a circle on the linen tablecloth. "Very much. But that's all there is to it. You're young and you see romance and stars everywhere." A flicker of sadness touched her expression. "But I learned the hard way that's not true."

"He's not Neil," Brynn said gently.

Surprise etched itself in Miranda's eyes and upraised brows. "How did you know about Neil?"

Embarrassed, Brynn met her eyes. "The trunk you sent to my room. There was a journal in it." Miranda's eyes widened further. "I didn't read it," Brynn rushed to assure her. "Not that I wasn't tempted, but when I started to put it back, a picture fell out."

"Neil," Miranda confirmed.

Brynn nodded.

"Nonetheless, I'm no starstruck girl," Miranda insisted.

"Perhaps that's better. You're wiser now."

"I notice you didn't say older," Miranda retorted with a trace of her normal humor.

"That's relative. If you and someone you meet—perhaps

even Edward—share common interests and concerns, don't you think you'll recognize that better now?"

"Possibly," Miranda admitted in a grudging tone.

Brynn thought of her own daydreams about Gregory, fantasies that no longer seemed real. Dreams that were increasingly difficult to get in touch with. Dreams that had carried her through lonely times, empty times, bringing her life a dimension it lacked. Dreams that had brought her to create a wedding album and inherit a ready-made family. Dreams that were being replaced with a flesh-and-blood man. A solid man who personified the land he loved. A man who made her laugh. A man who made her want. A man very unlike the one she'd pined for, had thought she wanted.

"Brynn. Brynn," Miranda repeated, covering her hand. "I think Scotty may already have beamed you up."

Brynn flushed. "I tend to get lost in my daydreams."

"Sometimes they're a nice place to go."

"And sometimes it's nice to have company," Brynn replied gently. "If you seize the moment."

"Are you suggesting I have a vacation interlude?" Miranda asked, amusement sparkling in her eyes.

"Not exactly," Brynn hedged. "Just because he's a guest doesn't mean it has to end when his visit does."

Miranda's lips tightened. "In my experience, that's the way it works."

Brynn wondered if she could be referring to Neil. Had his family been one of several that Frank had told her about? Families that used to stay entire summers at Eagle Point? And had Neil failed to return for the Harvest Ball? A poignant, sad image rose in Brynn's mind. If so, no wonder Miranda was so afraid to trust.

"Have I lost you to the extraterrestrial regions again?" Miranda questioned, a smile in her eyes.

"Afraid so. I'm really quite hopeless about my daydreams." Brynn fought for courage. She wasn't accustomed to giving anyone advice. "Miranda, have you thought about getting to know Edward? Enjoying the time he does have here? Leaving the door open to other possibilities?"

"Aha! You *are* suggesting an interlude!" While Brynn tried to protest, Miranda waved her explanations aside. "Don't worry. I'd been entertaining the idea myself. He'll be here for a week. And knowing that going in, I'll be prepared."

Brynn stared helplessly at the older woman who deserved so much more. But could she argue? Based on what? Her vast experience with men? Less than half-a-dozen words into that argument would show her own woeful ignorance.

Miranda pushed her chair back. "As they say, time's a-wasting. Don't worry, I'm going into this with my eyes open. You said it yourself. I'm wiser now."

Brynn watched her leave with mixed feelings. While she wanted Miranda to explore this possibility, she also didn't want her to get hurt. Because although Miranda was wiser, she was also vulnerable. And this time she might not recover.

BRYNN GLANCED AROUND at the riot of noise, confusion, and the unmistakable air of a party. Octoberfest was in full swing. Self-consciously, she fingered the full skirt, equally aware of the low neckline of her peasant blouse. Everyone else wore their costumes easily, but Brynn couldn't shed her innate lack of confidence that casually.

Still, she loved the excitement. Townspeople had arrived before dawn, filling the stalls they'd already set up with all kinds of food, desserts and crafts. And of course the beer tasting arena was a focal point of the festival.

Grilled German bratwurst, knockwurst, and weisswurst tinged the air, making her mouth water. Having seen sauerkraut, hot potato salad, and knödel, Brynn knew she would burst trying them all.

And she'd been eyeing the dessert stalls with equal interest. Richly spiced pfeffernusse cookies, strudel made of the flakiest layers of dough, and a multitude of other pastries begged to be tasted.

A Swiss band played, and children ran among the many games, shrieking and carefree in the lofty alpine meadow. The MacKenzies were determined to keep the celebration festive even though they still didn't have any definite news about Gregory. His briefcase had turned up at the local police station near the point of his capture, and the family was determined to see that as a good sign.

Strolling among the festival crowd, Brynn spotted Miranda and Edward West, her gentleman friend. Both were laughing, relaxed, and clearly having fun. As she watched, Edward placed a casual arm around Miranda's waist. Brynn held her breath, but Miranda accepted the gesture, turning to him with a smile. Silently Brynn cheered them on, hoping Miranda could find a bit of happiness.

Although tempted to track her friend's movements, Brynn caved in to her better sense and walked the other way, weaving among the stalls, stopping to admire handmade lace tablecloths and exquisite porcelain dolls. Then her attention was caught by a display of cuckoo clocks. Delighted by the variety of the charming timepieces, she examined several before reluctantly moving on.

As she turned from the booth, she spotted Matt. True to Miranda's predictions he was dressed in traditional lederhosen. Strong, tanned, muscular legs filled the leather suspender-held shorts. Brynn's mouth dried at the sight—especially since he was in charge of the old-fashioned game where contestants used a sledgehammer to slam down a marker, sending it speeding upward to ring the bell and measure the intensity of the swing.

His sleeves were rolled up, his muscles rippling as he demonstrated the sport, encouraging others to join in. Feasting on the sight, Brynn was content to watch, absorb, and appreciate.

Laughing with one of his neighbors, he turned toward her.

Pretending interest in the exhibit of hand-carved pipes, she tried to look as though she hadn't been watching him. When Brynn met his gaze, she waved casually, or at least she hoped she did.

Stealing a glance at him, she saw him turn over the game to one of the lodge employees. A few moments later, he was at her side.

"Nice pipes," he commented. "Thinking of taking up smoking?"

Brynn tried to think of a sensible answer—any answer—and failed. "They're very interesting."

"Uh-huh. Have you ridden the tram yet?"

"No. I didn't realize that was part of the Octoberfest."

"Last chance before ski season," he replied. "You game?"

Having told him she'd fearlessly ridden in a hot-air balloon, she could hardly confess that the tram made her nervous. Instead she steadied her smile. "Sure. Why not?"

"Let's grab something to take along and we can eat at the top."

Her stomach roiled, but she kept her smile in place. "Okay."

Together they picked out a wurst fest of sausages, cheeses, hard rolls and some wicked-looking desserts. One of his employees discreetly stowed their choices in a wicker basket.

As Matt tugged her toward the stalls of local brewers, Brynn tried to ignore the ripple of reaction his touch created. In moments, she was surrounded by a mountain of confusing choices. The vendor's discussion on hops, malts, and grains blurred and Brynn didn't know what to pick.

"Try more than one," Matt encouraged, pointing out the small tasting cups. "They have the beer on tap."

Gamely, she accepted the first glass, sipping through the huge head on the small tumbler. When she took the cup away, she saw a growing smile on Matt's face.

Reaching close, he wiped away the foamy white mustache decorating her upper lip.

As she swallowed the knot in her throat, Brynn tried to remember to smile, despite the play of long, strong fingers that stroked her upper lip, inciting a riot of other suggestions. When neither of them moved, Brynn blinked, then tried to think of something casual and witty to say.

Instead her words emerged as a croak. "I think I've tried enough."

"You have?"

"Uh...yes." She struggled to answer, his touch rendering her brain inoperable. "I'll take the first one."

"Of what?" he asked, his hands still dangerously close to her mouth.

"What what?" she questioned, her mind refusing to cooperate.

"The beer," the vendor bellowed. "Did you like it, miss?"

She jerked backward as though stung. "Yes. Very much. Could I have that kind, please?"

While the vendor retrieved a bottle from the icy barrel, Matt plucked a second bottle from the display, adding it to their basket.

In quiet accord, they got in line for the tram. Heart thudding, Brynn tried to act as though being touched by an exciting man was an everyday occurrence—even though that man was the brother of her supposed husband. The complications of it made her head throb.

Then they were on the tram, the alpine terrain dropping away beneath them. As the view unfolded, Brynn sucked in her breath. Although she'd seen the area, she hadn't viewed it from this vantage point.

"It's magnificent," she breathed, forgetting her nervousness.

Matt's eyes weren't on the breathtaking expanse of mountains. "Yes, it is."

Her heart thudded dangerously in its caged barrier. For an insane moment, Brynn wanted to confess everything, to plead for his understanding. But then her very surroundings struck

her. He believed in permanence, family, the honest tradition of
the land. Brynn could imagine his face if she told him the truth.

Feet dangling in the open air, Brynn opted to enjoy the ride,
the company...and the interlude. Miranda was right. They
wouldn't last forever.

Chapter Twelve

Matt studied the contractor's proposal, loan information from three banks, prospectus folders from potential investors, and his accounting firm's cost projections. No matter which way he sliced it, there would be no expansion without heavily mortgaging Eagle Point.

Suppose he did and revenues fell, or his father needed additional expensive surgery? At one point the possibility of a heart transplant had been discussed. Since their insurance carrier still termed the operation experimental, should Frank need a transplant, it would be costly. And ready cash had to be available.

It was a crushing decision, one that could buoy Eagle Point permanently, or send it into a downward spiral they might never recover from.

And in the midst of the papers he studied was a brief fax—one that outlined the latest round of discussions regarding Gregory's release. Between all the double-talk and posturing was the barest scrap of truth. They knew no more now than a month ago. Matt had really believed he had made progress on this last trip to Washington. Apparently, it had been a pretense intended to mollify the family. However, Matt was feeling anything but mollified these days.

Matt had already made nearly a dozen calls that morning, hoping to uncover more information. And each call had been a dead end. His college friend in the State Department had squeezed every possibility, cashed in every favor, and side-stepped regulations to cull each new piece of information. And still nothing.

In his gut, Matt believed that Gregory would be all right. But logic told him the longer his brother was held, the slimmer his chances were.

Glancing out the huge picture window that dominated his office, Matt remembered earlier times—days when he and Gregory had shared every path; walking side by side through school, sharing childhood hopes, dreams and fears.

Only thirteen months apart, he and Gregory had been like twins, each knowing the other's thoughts. And the sixth sense and intuition of their formative years was still strong. Strong enough that Matt believed he would know instantly if something had happened to Gregory. Something that would keep him from returning…permanently.

But that sixth sense hadn't kicked in. At least not negatively. But as time had passed, Matt wondered if his intuitive connection to Gregory had faded.

As adults, they no longer shared a single vision. Even when they were teenagers that vision had splintered, sending them in different directions. Gregory had been driven toward an Ivy League education rather than a state university as Matt had chosen.

After college Gregory hadn't come home, instead parlaying his Harvard degree and the contacts he'd made there into an astounding corporate springboard. Matt knew Gregory hadn't chosen to live in Salt Lake in order to remain close to the family. Rather, through astute networking, he'd landed a plum job at one of the richest, fastest-growing firms in the country. The fact that their western office was located in Salt Lake had been a coincidence. Gregory would have preferred living in New York City, but as long as his career continued to climb, he would have moved anywhere. Rooted in the land, Matt couldn't understand his brother's disdain and it had pushed them in opposite directions.

Had those directions been so far apart that he and Gregory were no longer closely linked? No longer sharing an intuitive spirit?

Matt didn't want to think so. He hated to even acknowledge the possibility. But there it was. Glaring at him. Mocking him. Questioning him.

What was he doing coveting his brother's wife? Feeling like the bad half of Cain and Abel, Matt finally understood one of the things that drove wedges into families. It was something he'd despised and had assumed would never happen to the MacKenzies.

Even if he said and did nothing, allowing Gregory and Brynn to continue on without any detours, the wedge would be there. Growing deeper and wider. He knew he couldn't watch the two of them without wishing Brynn was his.

Voices rose in the corridor. With ski season approaching, the entire staff was in full gear as preparations got under way. Even from the insulated privacy of his office he could hear the increased hustle.

Yet he was restless.

It was one thing to study documents and papers from the insular security of his office. It was another to make the decision while standing on the very land he risked.

Grabbing his keys from the desk, Matt unhooked his leather jacket from the coat-tree and headed outside. He easily spotted his truck in the parking lot and headed in that direction. As he neared the vehicle, he slowed his steps. Curved hips and long, slim, denim-clad legs were bent over the bed of his truck—distinctive legs that could belong to no one but Brynn, especially since her dog and cat were on the ground at her feet.

He approached quietly. "While I appreciate the view, I can't help wondering what you're doing."

Lancelot growled, then relaxed, his tail wagging. Startled,

Brynn swung the upper part of her body up, her head twisting around to stare at him. "Hi," she offered awkwardly.

"Hi, yourself. Can I help you with something?"

"Bossy decided to go exploring. He's in the back of your truck and he doesn't want to come out."

"He's an unlikely hitchhiker," Matt replied. "And with his mouth he's liable to get us both in trouble."

"You were going somewhere?" she questioned. "Of course, why else would you be in the parking lot?" She leaned back into the bed of the truck, affording him quite a view. Lancelot stretched up on his short hind legs, clearly wanting to help.

Although Matt could have watched Brynn all day, he didn't think his hormones could take it. Walking around to the cab, he opened the door, then reached inside to slide open the air vent in the rear windshield. "If you can get him to jump through here, it'll be easier to catch him."

Brynn narrowed the space the bird was roaming in, forcing him toward the back of the bed. With a squawk, Bossy flew toward the open vent. Pleased, Brynn jumped down from the back of the truck and rushed toward the cab. As she opened the door, Lancelot ran between her legs, jumping into the cab, as well. As Brynn climbed into the cab, Snookems meowed plaintively.

Standing outside, Matt leaned his forehead briefly against the roof of the truck. Then he lowered his head and spoke through the partially opened window, knowing instinctively that he had wanted to seek her out; that it would be easier to make the decision about the resort while she was standing at his side. "Put the cat inside, too, and they can all go for a ride."

"Really?" Brynn asked uncertainly. "They're a handful."

"I could use some company." Matt glanced at the mini menagerie with skepticism. "They weren't quite what I had in mind, but there's plenty of room where we're going."

Brynn scooped up Snookems, then tried to settle all her animals down. Lancelot agreeably curled up on her feet. Snookems chose her lap and Bossy continued to stare at Matt in challenge.

"Sorry about Bossy," she explained. "He's…well…bossy."

"So I see," Matt muttered, starting the truck and putting it in gear.

"Drop dead!" the bird ordered.

Matt resisted a comeback, instead quickly pulling out of the parking lot, ignoring Bossy's continued insults. Knowing the route he wanted to take, Matt quickly maneuvered the back roads of the resort, heading upward. While snow already covered the upper peaks and mountaintops, he knew of one grassy knoll that wouldn't yet be blotted out by early snow. The grass would be yellow, the aspens nearly bare, but he would be able to walk the land, feel the crunch of the earth beneath his boots.

It wouldn't be long now before the major storms started dumping on the mountains. It had begun snowing in September at the highest points, but now the weather would soon blanket the entire mountainside, even dipping into the valleys.

Brynn seemed to sense his mood, quietly petting her animals, stroking the nearly blind cat until she purred contentedly. Even Bossy quieted, although the bird kept his gaze fiercely on Matt.

The four-by-four competently climbed the last dirt road up to the meadow. Although he knew the landscape well, Matt stared at the magnificent backdrop, knowing he couldn't bear to lose this land.

Far above, trickles of crystal-clear water slowly turned to torrents that rushed down the cliffsides. And Matt knew that once he left the truck he could see the falls that water created, plunging down the mountainside, then crashing through a narrow box canyon. It had been a spot he and Gregory had claimed as their own hole-in-the-wall outlaw hideaway as kids. But Gregory had quickly outgrown childish games…and dreams.

After parking, Matt turned to Brynn. "This is where we get out."

"The end of the road. Literally." She glanced around the secluded area as Lancelot and Snookems wandered through the grass, sniffing. Bossy hopped behind them as though marshaling his charges. "We could be the only people in the world up here."

He studied her in surprise. "That's how it usually makes me feel. That's why I like it."

"You running away from someone in particular?" she asked, swallowing a premonition as she spoke.

Matt searched her eyes, but knew he couldn't confront that problem right now. "More a something than a someone." Tucking his hands in his back pockets he walked toward the edge of the meadow.

Brynn followed him. "Problem?"

"I have to decide whether to commit to the entire expansion project."

Puzzled, she cocked her head. "I thought you were already committed to that."

"In theory, absolutely. But I have a lot of things to consider. We'll be tying up all of our liquid assets and Dad might need more surgery. Expensive surgery."

"Can't you set aside funds for that?" she asked. "Ones that aren't figured into the business accounts, ones that can't be touched if anything goes wrong?"

"A medical trust?" Matt asked, wondering why he hadn't thought of it himself.

She shrugged. "I'm not sure about the terminology, but money that's legally separate."

"It might work," he replied slowly.

"You don't sound as though that's all that's worrying you."

"Do you know why this is called Cache Valley?" he asked, not directly answering her.

"No."

"Back when it was first discovered, the only people who lived here besides the Indians were mountain men. It was the land of the Shoshoni and the explorers—Jim Bridger and the other scouts who came after him. It was too cold and desolate for families to think about settling here.'' Matt stared across the wide chasm of the cliff. ''In the late 1820s, 1830, it was the era of the Rocky Mountain Fur Trade. And this area was the crossroads and camping ground for almost every mountain man that ever fought, trapped and traded in the Rocky Mountains.'' Matt gestured toward the unforgiving land. ''It was a rugged life for rugged men. They valued the area because they thought it was a good place to 'cache' or hide their furs and supplies.''

''Cache Valley,'' she murmured. ''It fits.''

''But Gallagher MacKenzie saw more than cold and isolation. It was 1830 and he stood here—in this meadow—looked across that mountain and knew it wouldn't always be a hideaway.''

''He had vision,'' she guessed.

''Incredible vision. It's prime real estate now, but then...'' Matt shook his head at the thought. ''He staked a claim when others passed it by, eager to get to California and the land of milk and honey. Farther than you can see, it's MacKenzie land—and has been for eight generations, almost nine.''

A faraway expression lit Matt's eyes as he continued. ''I told you once it didn't come without a price. It was a harsh place to raise a family. And when the first MacKenzie to think about turning it into a resort took his life savings and built the original ski lift by the dell, everyone thought he was crazy. But he took the risk, defied the odds.'' Matt laughed at the memory—the story told to him since he'd been old enough to sit at his grandfather's knee. ''Who would pay to come up a mountain and then slide halfway down?''

''But they came,'' she said softly.

''Yes, they came and Eagle Point was born. Even though Gallagher MacKenzie didn't predict skiing, instinctively he recognized the value of the land.'' Matt gazed into the distance.

"Eagle Point has the same appeal Telluride does—it's far enough away from civilization for people to feel they've left it behind."

"But most people won't recognize that as an asset," she murmured.

"No." And most people didn't have her astute grasp. "When times have been bad, the family's been faced with parceling off some of the land but they never have. Even during the Depression they hung on when other places gave up and sold out. And during good times when it would have been easier to live comfortably from the profits, the money was reinvested into Eagle Point, always improving it, making it better, ensuring the future of the coming generations."

"Which is why it's so successful today."

"The original lodge is the main core of Eagle Point but it's more than six times its initial size."

Her brows lifted in surprise.

"That doesn't count the cottages, outbuildings, expanded lifts or summer recreations. Each generation has made additions. Additions that didn't come without sacrifice. But we couldn't compete today if that planning hadn't been in place all along."

"And your decision now?"

"I can take Eagle Point into the twenty-first century, make it a true world-class resort, or I could drag it into bankruptcy if I'm wrong."

Brynn probed his expression. "Do you believe in your plans?"

"Yes, but that doesn't mean I'm right."

"And if you don't make the improvements?"

"We can glide along as we have."

She met his eyes. "You told me it was the responsibility of every MacKenzie to ensure the success of the coming generations. Gliding along doesn't sound like it's going to cut it."

"And if I'm wrong?"

Her eyes held his, steady and unblinking. "Taking a risk is your legacy from Gallagher MacKenzie. Suppose he'd let uncertainty sway him?"

"We'd probably be standing in someone else's barn or factory, or the middle of a housing development."

"Or someone else's Telluride?" she suggested gently. "You have the vision, Matt. That's why you're the one who inherited the responsibility. And you have to follow the courage of your convictions."

His face tilted up sharply, his gaze seeking hers. The double meaning of her words struck them both. He wasn't a man who could live with dishonor. And wanting his brother's wife was the worst kind of dishonor he could imagine.

He bit out a muffled curse, then shoved his hands through already tousled hair. "You're right. About everything."

Her heart clenched as she realized what he meant. She may have convinced him to follow his convictions and those same convictions made her strictly off-limits.

The small distance between them seemed to widen in the silence. When he finally looked away from her, she saw his face change and then suddenly he began to run. "Oh, hell."

When he accelerated into a sprint and she saw that he was heading directly for the edge of the meadow that spilled over the cliff, her hand flew to her mouth and her heart lodged somewhere not far behind. "Matt!" She'd intended to shout the word but it came out as a strangled whisper.

Then it looked as though he'd fly off the edge of the cliff, but he slid to a stop, grabbing at something, then rolling backward. Concentrating only on Matt, Brynn hadn't seen anything else.

Racing toward him, she finally recognized the gray fluff cradled in his big hands. Snookems!

As she reached him, she dropped to her knees. "Matt?"

"Your blind beast was about to take her last leap in this world."

"Snookems!" Brynn half scolded, relief filtering the words. Grateful to see that neither of them had come to harm, Brynn started shaking.

"Oh, jeez," Matt groaned. "She's okay. But next time you'd better put her on a lead."

"What if you hadn't been able to stop when you'd gotten to the edge?" she questioned, feeling tears sting her eyes.

"I did. Look, you were right about one thing. I'm a trained athlete. Used to be on the U.S. ski team—remember, it's head-quartered here in Utah. I love to downhill and I'm in heaven when I hit the moguls. And off-season, I four-wheel, play rugby and work out. I wasn't in any danger."

"Still…" Brynn couldn't contain the concern that over-whelmed her. When she'd thought there was a chance he was in danger, she'd felt her heart almost stop. A feeling so intense it still swamped her. A feeling, she realized suddenly, she'd never experienced in worrying about Gregory—a man who was a fantasy, not a man she loved; as she did Matt.

And he *was* the one she loved. With all her heart.

And now he was gently helping her up, still cradling the cat. Lancelot was licking both her hand and then Matt's—an acceptance she'd never expected from the wounded animal. Matt had managed to ensnare them all.

Even Bossy was strutting beside them, his shrill voice cutting through the mountain breeze. "Good job!" the bird kept repeating, interspersed with a colorful injunction on how they'd better get out of Dodge.

Brynn wondered why her newfound realization didn't shout itself to the literal mountaintops as it crowded her in its rush to be free.

Her hand still held solicitously in Matt's, she walked with him back to safety, knowing that that in itself was an irony. She'd never be safe again. Not with her soul committed to a man she could never have.

Chapter Thirteen

Heather and Andy trooped beside Brynn as she walked along the main street of Gallagher. So far they'd gone into every store, examined everything from hair barrettes and earrings to comic books and the newest candy in the drugstore.

Having been promised ice-cream cones, they were now headed for the Hamburger Hut, a place that served old-fashioned custard ice cream. Brynn hadn't known such places still existed. Nor had she ever heard of Andy and Heather's own brand of logic. They needed ice-creams cones now before winter set in. Although the nip of autumn and the approaching winter chilled the air, this was a not-to-be-missed treat.

Ruth had explained the custom, then hesitantly asked Brynn if she would take the kids to town. Frank was having a bad day, Ruth had explained. Having heard nothing about Gregory in the last two days, Frank had gone into a slump. And Ruth didn't want to leave him on his own. Matt had already left earlier and Ruth didn't know when he planned to return. She'd hated asking Brynn but her worry about Frank had overridden any concern about breaching manners.

But Brynn had enjoyed the excursion, delighting in the spontaneous things both kids said. And she was settling cozily into the perfect fit of the town. Like a well-broken-in pair of shoes, it cradled every ill-fitting experience from the past.

Brynn urged the kids along the sidewalk, hoping she could

stand to eat frozen custard in the cool temperatures, but not wanting to miss the unexpected treat.

"How come you live in the city if they don't have good stuff?" Andy asked around a mouthful of bubblegum.

"Well, there are fun things in the city, too."

Andy's face screwed into a skeptical mask. "Doesn't sound like it. Not even any good ice cream."

"We have Häagen-Dazs in the stores," Brynn offered.

Andy wasn't impressed. "Gregory always made living in the city sound good. Guess he didn't want us to know how bad it really is."

Brynn's lips quirked upward, but she valiantly tried to control the grin threatening. "When you're a grown-up, different things are fun."

"Well, you're a grown-up and you like it better here."

So she did. "You sure you're not a midget?"

Andy rolled his eyes.

Seeing this, Heather looked big-sister pained. "Boys."

Which only caused Andy to roll his eyes again. "Like you know anything."

"More than you do," Heather countered.

Fortuitously, they'd arrived at the Hamburger Hut. Not certain how far the squabble could escalate, Brynn issued a silent sigh of relief. "Here we are. Would you guys like some food first?"

"Heck, no," Andy replied without consulting his sister. "I might get too full for ice cream."

"And that would be a crime," Brynn agreed, her own mouth watering at the promise of a creamy cone. They approached the order window and Brynn peeked inside the tiny place, watching the well-orchestrated bustle. A wonderful aroma of freshly cooked burgers and the tang of recently sliced onions and pickles filled the air. The shakes she saw being made looked tempting, too. Another feast for the senses.

A few minutes later, loaded with cones that were two and

three dips high, they sat at one of the small tables scattered outside the Hamburger Hut. Not large enough to have indoor seating, it was a place where teens congregated, children raced to, and adults indulged in.

Briefly, Brynn could remember going to a similar place with her grandmother when she'd been very young. But her mother hadn't the patience or tolerance for such places. Instead, she purchased pints of gourmet ice cream in exotic flavors. Licking her cone, Brynn knew none of those luxuries had tasted nearly as good as Hamburger Hut's custard.

An older couple approached the order window and both Heather and Andy waved to them. Brynn smiled as well and when they'd placed their order, the man and woman walked over.

"Hey, Uncle Mick!" Andy called out.

"Hi, Aunt Lucille," Heather added when they were closer.

"Those look good," Lucille commented as she watched them tackle the cones.

"Aren't you having any?" Andy asked.

"I wish," Lucille answered. "But we have to watch our cholesterol. It was either hamburgers or ice cream. Not both."

Mick made a disgusted face, indicating his feelings about their healthy diet.

"I'd have picked ice cream," Andy replied.

Heather poked him none too subtly.

"He's right," Mick defended, a twinkle in his eyes. "Actually I want both."

"Good thing I'm along to make sure you don't!" Lucille reproved.

"Yeah. Good thing," Mick muttered.

Lucille ignored him, watching Brynn instead. "I don't think we've met."

Before Brynn could speak, Heather jumped in. "This is Brynn. She's our sister now."

The guileless, trusting words cut a new path to Brynn's guilt.

She was beginning to wonder how long she could keep up this charade. The lies and pretense were eating her alive.

"You must be Gregory's wife!" Lucille exclaimed, thawing at the realization. "I thought you were a tourist at first. We just got back to town late last night. We spend the early fall in Denver close to our children—before we have to battle ice and snow. But Ruth told me all about your elopement before the family went to meet you." She pointed to her husband. "I'm Lucille Stratton and this is my husband, Mick." She didn't give Brynn a chance to respond as she continued her monologue. "I'm dying to learn all about you, Brynn. But, first. Is there any news about Gregory?"

Brynn saw the shadows instantly touch both Heather and Andy, the concentration on their ice-cream cones diminishing, the easy laughter in their eyes dimming. "Actually, we're very encouraged. While a definite agreement hasn't been reached, the negotiations are at a very positive stage. Both his firm and the government feel hopeful that they can reach an agreement soon."

Brynn was relieved to see some of the shadows on the children's faces disappear.

"I never doubted it for a minute," Mick replied. "That boy's a fighter." His cheery gaze rested on the children. "Do we know anyone smarter?"

Both children shook their heads.

"Or more ingenious?" he continued.

They shook their heads again.

"Well, then. Is he going to let a few backward rebels stop him?"

"Course not," Andy declared, caught in Mick's enthusiasm. "Gregory always wins."

"He's very clever," Heather added.

"Yes, he is," Lucille agreed, seeming to finally realize that her question had disturbed the children. Bright eyes lit on

Brynn as she tried to shift the topic. "Since we know he's going to be all right, let's hear about you."

"She draws *Stephanie*," Andy added between bites of ice cream.

"*Stephanie?*" Lucille questioned.

"The comic strip," Brynn explained.

"In the newspaper?" Lucille questioned with new interest.

"Sure," Heather replied with pride. "She's famous."

"I wouldn't say that—" Brynn began.

"Brynn's just modest," Heather explained. "She practically saved Gregory's life!"

"What's this?" Mick asked.

"Gregory was in a burning building," Heather began.

Lucille and Mick drew in matching gulps of air. "What?"

"Actually, there was a dog—" Brynn tried again.

"And you saved them both?" Lucille exclaimed.

"That's not—" Brynn started.

"That's why Gregory likes animals now," Andy said as he struggled with his cone, catching a sliding mound of ice cream before it toppled.

"He does?" Lucille queried. "Well, that's unusual for him, but I guess sharing a traumatic experience will do that for you."

"But—"

"And Gregory has quite a way of expressing his gratitude," Mick said with a twinkle. "He marries his lady to the rescue."

"That's not exactly how—"

"And she taught him how to not be afraid of heights," Heather added.

"He can even ride in hot-air balloons now," Andy said.

Brynn fervently hoped that no one put Gregory to this test when he returned.

"You *have* transformed Gregory!" Lucille exclaimed. "His fear of heights is one reason he never wanted to stay here. It's hard to live on top of a mountain when you become sick just coming and going.''

"And sometimes people in the *Stephanie* cartoon are real," Heather added in a rush. "So Gregory has been in them lots."

With a gulp, Brynn realized that small-town gossip traveled swiftly, if not accurately. "Just because—"

"Then you and Gregory have done some of the crazy things in that comic?" Mick nearly roared, clapping his hand down on the weathered wooden table.

Visions of this new and no-doubt-embellished tale rose in Brynn's mind. "There's a lot of fiction to—"

"Sure, you have to spice it up," Mick agreed, still laughing. "But now that I think about it, I can see our Gregory in just those scrapes."

"*Your* Gregory?" Brynn questioned with a sense of foreboding.

"He's our godson," Mick explained.

Lately, Brynn wondered if her foot had been permanently planted in her mouth.

"And we'd hoped he and our daughter Alyson might marry someday," Lucille added.

"Lucille!" Mick shot her a reproving look, but Lucille waved him away.

"Brynn should know our history. Besides, obviously they're not going to get married since Gregory has chosen Brynn." Lucille turned her full attention on Brynn. "Do you know if Gregory told Alyson about your marriage?"

"I...I'm not sure...but perhaps it would be better coming from him," Brynn managed.

Lucille drew her brows together. "I suppose you're right. And it's not like they had an exclusive relationship. Frankly, I don't understand young people today. Alyson told us she needed to explore her options, whatever that means. Personally, I think if she cared about Gregory, she should have concentrated on him." Lucille had the grace to look embarrassed. "That didn't come out just the way I meant."

"Never does," Mick muttered.

"You're a lovely girl," Lucille continued, reaching her hand out to pat Brynn's. At that moment a fat drop of sticky ice cream dropped, hitting Lucille's hand and splattering.

Brynn's unattended cone drooped as she tried to hand Lucille a crumpled paper napkin.

"You keep it," Lucille insisted, pushing the napkin back to Brynn. "Looks like you'll need it more than I will."

At that moment the woman inside the Hamburger Hut called out an order number.

"That'll be us," Mick announced. "We're taking our burgers home—Lucille can't miss *Oprah.*"

"But we'll see you again soon," Lucille inserted, holding her sticky hand awkwardly as though not sure what to do with it. "Now that we're family."

As they walked away, Brynn realized that the "family" was growing at an alarming rate. And turning to her two companions in crime, she realized she'd just added more fodder to the gossip hotline.

A familiar truck pulled up to the curb, parking in front of the Hamburger Hut.

"Matt!" Andy and Heather called out, spotting their older brother.

"Hey, brats," he answered fondly.

They didn't take offense, instead crowding around him. The difference in their ages, Brynn suspected, elevated him beyond mere brother.

"What are we having?" he questioned, crowding Andy as he pretended to take a predatory interest in his ice-cream cone.

"We could be having more ice cream if you'll pay," Andy responded guilelessly as he bit into the cone, quickly finishing the one he was eating.

Matt pulled out a few bills and peeled them off, handing

both to Heather. "Andy, you can order whatever you want, but Heather's in charge of the money. With what's left you can buy something at Brewer's."

Andy let out a whoop. Brewer's was the store they'd lingered in the longest. Carrying everything from bubblegum to hammers, soccer balls to laundry baskets, T-shirts to Nintendo games, it was a kids' paradise.

"And if we don't spend too much here, we'll have more there," Andy translated quickly. "Come on, Heather. Let's forget about the ice cream."

Heather delicately licked at her ice-cream cone, plenty of it remaining since she hadn't demolished hers as Andy had. "When I'm through."

Andy groaned. "How come she's got to carry the money, Matt? She's so *slow!*"

"You'll live," Matt replied without sympathy. "The last time I gave you the money, you brought home ten dollars' worth of live bait and baby mice. Mother nearly skinned us both."

Brynn grinned. She doubted anyone could skin someone as overpowering as Matt, but the vision of Ruth trying to was an amusing one.

"I was lots younger then," Andy protested.

Matt plucked Andy's baseball cap off, turning it around so that it sat at a smart angle. "You're right. You were barely out of the cradle. Must have been at least three months ago."

Heather finished the last of her ice-cream cone. "Come on, Andy. With me holding the money, you can decide first what you really want so we don't spend the money and then wish we hadn't."

Andy grumbled, yet jumped up and walked with his sister down the street.

Seeing that Matt's gaze rested on her, Brynn shored up a smile and tried to act casual. But his words threw her.

"You been trying to avoid me?"

Since that was exactly what she'd done, Brynn didn't know quite how to answer. "Why would I do that?"

"You tell me."

"I've just been busy. My *Stephanie* calendar was due—"

"So late in the year? Aren't the ones for next year already in production?"

"It's one for the following year and I've got a deadline on my greeting cards and—"

"Whoa." He held up his hands. "So, you've got a good store of excuses."

"They're not—"

"I see you've left the glasses off."

Thrown off track, self-consciously she reached to where her glasses normally sat before letting her hand fall away. "Yes."

"Looks good."

Brynn concentrated on her melting ice-cream cone, realizing that between Gregory's godparents and now Matt, she'd only had a few bites of the delicious frozen custard. "Thanks."

Her self-confidence had increased since she'd come to Eagle Point, Brynn realized. And as her self-confidence increased, her need for the protective barrier of her glasses had diminished.

"I see you're traveling practically solo," Matt commented.

Brynn cocked her head. "With Heather and Andy in tow?"

"But without your menagerie."

Brynn tried not to look pained. "As you know, they're hard to travel with. I can handle Lancelot. But you saw how bad Snookems's sight is—the trouble she can get into. And Bossy's just too vocal to take out in public."

"Heather tells me you got him from the shelter where you do volunteer work."

"No one else would take him," Brynn mused. "His repartee isn't what most people are looking for."

"Unlike your lifesaving dog."

Uncomfortably, Brynn recalled how Heather and Andy had stretched and enlarged the truth just a few minutes earlier. She wondered if they'd told Matt that Lancelot was the dog that had dragged Gregory from the burning building.

She wished the kids wouldn't embroider the stories. Brynn didn't need any help in that direction. She was doing fine, fabricating a life for herself and Gregory on her own. She wondered how he would deal with everything she'd told his family and friends—especially since she wouldn't be around to translate and explain.

A babble of feminine voices approached. Glancing up, she saw some familiar faces. Judging from Matt's expression, he didn't welcome the interruption.

"Brynn!" Jean practically squealed. "I'm so glad we ran into you. I just heard the most exciting thing about you."

"You did?" Brynn croaked, dreading the worst.

"I ran into Lucille Stratton," Jean explained, all but clucking her tongue. "She told us how you pulled Gregory from a burning building and saved him. And, that if it wasn't for you, everyone in the building would have perished, including the animals!"

Matt cocked one eyebrow.

Brynn saw his disbelieving expression and cursed her unfortunate meeting with the Strattons. "I'm afraid that she's exaggerated—"

"Lucille said you were modest," Becky added. "She wasn't kidding."

"You're a lot like that courageous character you draw in your comic strip," Jean declared. "I don't know how you do it."

"Me?" Brynn nearly choked. "Like Stephanie?"

"Of course. I could see it right away," Becky told her. "I'm sure you can't make all that stuff up. Part of it must come from real life."

"Like the time she enlisted her boyfriend in the Foreign Legion," Karen breathed in excitement.

"Surely you don't think I—"

"And the time she had a load of manure delivered to her boss's house in the middle of the night and they dumped it in his swimming pool."

"I don't actually work directly for one person, so I couldn't—"

"Or the time that Stephanie ran an ad for a garage sale at her ex-best friend's house starting at six in the morning!" Laughing helplessly, Jean clutched her sides.

"Or when she reported her neighbor to 'America's Most Wanted'!" Becky recalled.

"You must realize how much fiction there is to drawing a strip," Brynn tried desperately, refusing to meet Matt's gaze. "So, you see—"

"And then there was the time Stephanie rerouted her boy-friend's mail to a radio shrink who read it out loud over the air," Karen recalled. "She told him it was a good way for his mother to hear from him."

Brynn shifted uncomfortably. "They say fact is stranger than fiction, but in these cases—"

"No wonder Gregory married you!" Jean enthused. "Your life must be like a never-ending carnival ride."

"You have no idea," Brynn admitted. And this was one carnival ride that was spinning out of control.

Unexpectedly she met Matt's gaze.

And that carnival ride was definitely sending her in circles.

"Ladies, I hate to break this up, but Brynn and I have to get going." Matt unfolded his impressive height from the wooden bench. Not giving her time to agree or disagree, Matt took her arm.

Amid the murmured goodbyes Brynn considered her escape, but doubted she could make it far.

"So, what diabolical plan are you hatching now?" Matt asked as they walked across the street.

She stopped abruptly. "'Plan'?"

"Am I going to see my name in lights? Or spelled out in bikini underwear across the Alpine Slide?"

Brynn started to sputter when she saw the laughter lurking in his eyes. Still, she wasn't sure if he was referring to her comic strip or her outrageous tales. "I thought you didn't approve of Stephanie's antics."

"Maybe not, but it sure as hell was funny."

The absurdity of the situation struck her at the same time, and laughter erupted. Before she could guess what was happening or why the mood had suddenly lightened, Brynn laughed with Matt until she nearly collapsed against him.

Wiping tears from her eyes, she wagged a quivering finger at him. "*You* are a bad influence."

"This from a woman who single-handedly concocts torture between the sexes? Enough to keep every man in America running for cover?"

Her finger wavered, then lowered as another fit of giggles struck her. "I guess I hadn't realized the true power of the pen."

"Worse than a ground-to-air missile," Matt confirmed.

"At the rate gossip inflates and spreads around this town, word will be out by morning that I've declared war on Idaho!"

Matt grinned. "Just think what fun you'll have blowing up all those potatoes."

Their laughter trailed across the street as they convulsed into fit after fit of hilarity. Forgetting the observant group of women, the children shopping nearby, and all the constraints that had fallen between them, they gave in to the mild hysterics of shared nonsense.

And from across the street the ladies watched, nodded, and collectively wondered when the absent husband-and-brother would return. And a few wondered just what Gregory would find when he did.

Chapter Fourteen

Brynn liked this time of day at the lodge, the sun still new in the sky, the crisp early-morning air redolent with the tang of pine, fir and cedar, and sprinkled with the chorus of songbirds that hadn't yet migrated south. She recognized the distinctive birds—MacGillivray's warblers, Frank had told her.

Strolling out on one of the upper wooden decks that angled to one side of the lodge, Brynn clasped a steaming mug of coffee, relishing the warmth, welcoming the rush of caffeine. She leaned against the railing, looking out over the circular drive that led to the parking lot, enjoying her clear view of the front of the lodge.

She had taken to rising early since Matt took advantage of the difference in time zones to call the State Department early each morning. But like too many of the previous mornings, they had no solid news. Impatient with the delays, Matt was talking now about hiring a private investigator and possibly even mercenaries to find Gregory. But Frank was afraid that might endanger Gregory even more.

Even though it was early, there was already plenty of movement. One of the resort's shuttles was loading up departing passengers. Luggage was scattered about and the chatter of guests drifted through the air. Brynn knew that in a few hours there would be another equally excited group—guests just arriving for their visit. She could see the appeal of innkeeping—new faces and old, the constant change, no two days the same.

It was a good life, she realized—especially for people like the MacKenzies. Filled with that contented thought, she glanced down again, her gaze scanning the wide front porch of the lodge. It skipped along, then stopped suddenly.

Miranda and Edward stood at one edge of the porch. And next to him were his suitcase and duffel bag. Unabashedly staring, Brynn watched, hoping the luggage belonged to someone else. But just then the shuttle driver walked up to Edward and he indicated the bags at his feet. Heart in her throat, Brynn watched as Miranda valiantly bade him goodbye.

Certain that Edward would extend his stay since he and Miranda had hit it off so well, Brynn had confidently told Miranda that she was sure this was not to be a short vacation romance. Seeing that he really planned to leave, Brynn fiercely regretted her reckless words and ignorant confidence. As disappointed as she was, Brynn could only imagine how crushed Miranda must feel.

As she watched, Miranda kept a smile fixed on her face. At what cost? Brynn wondered. Had she told Edward how she felt? Or had the past left too deep an imprint for that kind of truth?

Miranda reached out and smoothed his lapel. It was a sweet, loving and most revealing gesture. Then Edward picked up that same hand, kissing it gently.

Now, now he would tell her he was staying, Brynn thought, and instruct the driver to retrieve his bags. But as she watched, Edward briefly touched Miranda's face before turning away and climbing into the van.

Brynn gripped her mug so tightly the coffee sloshed. How could Edward leave? He and Miranda had taken to one another from the moment they'd met. Sure that he was the one who would reverse the Harvest Ball curse for Miranda, Brynn knew he'd built Miranda up to believe it, too.

Brynn watched Miranda as she lifted her hand in a wave. As the van drove off, Miranda took a few steps forward, her hand faltering, then finally dropping to her side. As the vehicle navigated the winding driveway and then finally disappeared down the road, Miranda still watched.

Without the chatter of the departing guests, it was painfully silent. Still, Miranda stood, unmoving in the solitary quiet.

Brynn quashed her urge to rush downstairs, suspecting that Miranda wouldn't appreciate the intrusion.

Had it only been a few days since she'd celebrated her new-found confidence? And what had she done with that confidence? Given bad advice to Miranda, causing her to get hurt. Brynn wanted to kick herself. What made her think she could go from a life of daydreams to dispensing romantic counseling?

A sharp, poignant memory of her wish book—the wedding album—surfaced. Somehow that now seemed like a simpler time, when her choices and ambitions had been so clear. She'd seen Gregory and thought she knew what she'd wanted. Love at first sight had been part of the belief system her romantic nature embraced.

Life in her daydreams hadn't been very realistic. But it had certainly been easier.

TWO WEEKS LATER, BRYNN stared at her drawing board, unable to concentrate on her strip. She wasn't quite sure how to handle the creative block since she'd never had this problem before. She'd always been able to lose herself in Stephanie's world—a world she'd created to be more appealing than her own.

Lancelot stood on his hind legs, pushing his nose beneath her hand. "Ignoring you, aren't I?"

His tail thumped in agreement.

"I guess you could use a walk."

His ears perked up at the familiar word.

"But Snookems doesn't much care for her lead," Brynn warned.

The cat, asleep at her feet, didn't stir.

"Send 'em all to hell in a handbasket!" Bossy ordered.

"Now there's a thought," she muttered. "Okay, guys. Maybe we've got cabin fever." Ridden with guilt about both Miranda and Matt, Brynn had kept a low profile. Having stayed as much to herself as possible to avoid the MacKenzies and the complications she'd caused them, her room had become her refuge. And cabin fever was now a distinct possibility.

Miranda had waved away Brynn's stumbling apologies, assuring her they weren't necessary.

"I'm a big girl, Brynn. I knew what I was getting into. Told you, didn't I? But that's past. Don't give it another thought. I chose to let myself care for Edward. That decision didn't have anything to do with what you said. For all your wisdom, you're still a young woman. My decision was based on a lot more years than you've seen. And I don't regret it. It was an interlude, Brynn—one I'll remember fondly."

Still, the guilt ate at Brynn. And a steady diet of deception had depleted her spirit. Seeing Matt multiplied the guilt. Not to mention the hope she saw on Ruth and Frank's faces, the utter trust on Heather and Andy's. What a mess.

Lancelot whined, his eyes pleading.

"You win. Go get your leash."

Happy to obey, Lancelot trotted to the basket that held his leash. Bringing it to her, he didn't release it immediately, playing the tug-of-war game with the leash that had become their habit. Obliging him for a few minutes, she then clasped his leash in place.

"Didn't get Snookems's leash, too, did you?" she asked Lancelot, who ignored her to chase the trailing leash attached to his collar.

Laughing, she started toward the basket containing her pets' toys and accessories. Glancing down she saw a sticky note nearly beneath her foot. As she picked up the note, she scanned quickly, realizing it was one she'd scribbled late the previous evening when she'd thought of an idea for the strip, but had been too tired to follow through on it. The scrap of paper could have saved her an unproductive morning.

Turning, she planted her hands on her hips as she stared at Lancelot, guessing how the note had wound up on the floor. "You've been on the nightstand again, haven't you?"

Too involved to act chagrined, Lancelot continued to play with his leash. The dog had always loved climbing from the bed to the nightstand, investigating for treats, poking his nose into the pile of papers she kept there. Staying at the resort apparently hadn't changed the habit.

Sighing as she shook her head, Brynn headed again for the basket. And saw another note. "I wonder if I did more last night than I thought," she wondered aloud.

Whirling around, she narrowed her gaze on Lancelot. Part of his heritage had come from longhaired terriers, providing him with a lengthy coat of hair extending from his haunches to his paws. Hair that dragged against the ground, making his coat act like a dust mop. One that operated on four legs. And one that picked up sticky notes as though the animal had been bred for the job.

While the dog played, she followed him, picking up the scattered trail of notes, then drawing him close to pull the remaining ones from his fur. "Ah, Lancelot. Treasures you've been collecting, huh?"

He cocked his head and she couldn't resist his appeal, once again engaging in a game of tug-of-war with him.

Snookems wakened to the noise of their play and stretched sleepily. Brynn patted Lancelot one more time, then retrieved the cat's leash.

"Okay, gorgeous, your turn." Brynn secured the lead to Snookems's collar.

With what little sight she possessed, the cat sent her a baleful glance.

"Sorry, baby, but I couldn't take another close call with

you.'' Petting the cat, she then turned a skeptical gaze on Bossy. ''And you, my friend, had better behave.''

''Ratted out!'' the bird shrieked. ''Ratted out!''

Brynn rolled her eyes. ''Okay, troops. Let's roll.''

Once outside, the animals wanted to run in three different directions. Since Brynn could have cheerfully run off in the fourth direction, she compromised. ''Since Bossy's not on a lead, we'll go his way,'' she told the others.

Head held at a haughty angle, Bossy waddled forward, his clipped wings outstretched. Lancelot charged every bush in their path while Snookems delicately picked up each paw, not seeming to want to muss her long fur.

Her eyes on the trail, Brynn didn't look up as she walked ahead. The trees, now bare of leaves, held new snow. The storms had come, each bringing a new accumulation of white powder—the powder Utah was known for, worldwide.

With Thanksgiving approaching, Eagle Point had gone into advanced preparation mode for the coming ski season. Traditionally the season opened on Thanksgiving weekend, and not a moment was wasted as the entire staff prepared for the on-slaught of eager skiers.

Brynn had wanted to volunteer to help, but the prospect of leaving her sanctuary daunted her. She'd even taken most of her meals in her room, pleading deadlines. Taking to walking her animals early in the morning and late in the evening, she managed to avoid a lot of contact. She hoped it would ease the break so that she could leave. What she was doing simply wasn't right.

No matter what the initial reasons and intentions, she was deceiving a family who had extended their hospitality, opened their home and treated her as one of their own.

Over the past weeks Brynn had deliberately studied the wedding album. And as she did, she found herself staring at the faces of strangers. Even she wasn't the same anymore. And, sadly, Gregory had been and always would be nothing more than a daydream.

Head down, Brynn found her thoughts drifting as she escaped into a daydream of a different sort. She could leave the resort. Gregory would be released, but rather than coming to Eagle Point he would return to Salt Lake, never encountering the wild stories she'd fabricated. And Matt, happy over the return of his brother, would believe that the wedding story had been in everyone's best interests. Instead of being angry, he would be glad that she was free. And he would come after her. The deception would be forgotten; but the feelings that flowed between them wouldn't. No longer would they have to hold back....

Smacking into something firm and unmoving, Brynn's daydream flew out of her head, along with her ski cap. Not having a strong grip on the animals' leads, they, too, went flying.

"What?" she began, then stopped as she met Matt's curious gaze. "Oh, hello. I wasn't expecting anyone."

"Apparently," he replied, picking up her ski cap.

"The animals," she blurted out, uncertain what else to say. "I let go of the leads when you...when I..." She cleared her throat. "I'd better go find them."

As she started away, Matt called out, "Lancelot. Here, boy."

Brynn turned back to him. "He won't come. Especially if a man calls."

She'd scarcely stopped speaking when Lancelot dashed up to them, apparently content to let Matt take his leash.

Brynn stared at her normally predictable dog. Traitor, she thought.

Matt's voice was mild. "I told you before that I don't growl at him. He's a smart dog and knows when it works both ways."

Brynn wondered at his affinity with the animals. Despite his put-upon attitude when dealing with her pets, he was actually very good with them. "I'm guessing there's something you're not telling me."

"Could be all sorts of things," he replied enigmatically.

"I meant about the animals," she retorted, spotting Snookems and reaching for her lead.

Matt shrugged. "I thought you were buried under a ton of work."

"I am. I mean, I just took a quick breather. The animals needed some air, but I do have a mountain of work... deadlines.... It's really frantic."

He smiled. "I think I get the concept. How's it been going?"

"What?"

"The work." One brow quirked upward in question.

"Of course," she replied hurriedly. "I guess I'm just tired from the—"

"Work," he chimed in.

"It has to be done," Brynn explained with more force than necessary.

Matt looked at her quizzically. "Most work does. Mother's been worried about you—says you're not eating enough to keep a bird alive." He shot a glance at Bossy. "But I guess that's a matter of opinion."

Brynn ignored the fact that she had indeed lost weight. "I'm eating plenty. There's no need to worry. After all, I'm a big girl."

"That you are," he murmured.

His gaze warming her, Brynn felt a familiar jolt in her midsection. Why couldn't she have met him under different circumstances? Instead of ones that no daydream could change. "Well, I'd better head to the lodge," she managed. "I have to get back to—"

"Work," he finished for her.

Helplessly she gazed at him for a moment before calling her animals and fleeing back to the lodge.

Matt watched as she disappeared. He'd seen so little of her in the past weeks that she could be the figment of his wishful imagination. The telltale tracks in the snow convinced him otherwise.

But Matt knew what Brynn doing. She was slowly disappearing, distancing herself so that the break wouldn't be as severe when she left. Still, the distance would be there.

And though he still fervently prayed for his brother's safe return, Matt knew that once Gregory was back, that distance would be in place. Permanently.

BRYNN STUMBLED THROUGH the darkened lobby, wondering what was going on. An urgent call from one of the staff members had brought her downstairs. Since the call, apparently either a fuse had blown or the electricity was out. Luckily one of the candlelit sconces in the hallway had illuminated the stairway.

Running her fingers across the wall, she looked for a light switch just in case it had been accidentally turned off.

So far she'd managed to knock down the MacKenzie coat of arms and tip over an oil painting of Gallagher MacKenzie. Brynn figured that at this rate, she could single-handedly destroy the lobby.

Hearing a quiet noise scuttle close by, Brynn hesitated. Was she not alone? A shiver danced down her spine and she turned to investigate.

As she did, the room burst into a kaleidoscope of light, noise and motion.

"Surprise!" a chorus of voices shouted.

Pure shock kept her frozen in place. It wasn't her birthday. Had she intruded on someone else's surprise and ruined it?

But the women were all crowding around her and somewhere in her brain she registered the wording on the banners and decorations. Congratulations?

Ruth and Miranda pushed forward. "It's a bridal shower for you," they explained together. "We thought with an elopement there couldn't have been time for a shower and with your family living far away, we doubted you'd had one afterward, either.''

"Well, no, I haven't," Brynn managed, overwhelmed by the roomful of beaming faces.

"It's one thing to skip the wedding," Ruth told her. "It's another entirely to miss the shower." Then her face beamed. "And with the encouraging fax about Gregory yesterday, we thought we should make up for lost time."

"The guests didn't mind clearing the lobby." Miranda grinned. "For such a good cause—plus we set up a complimentary buffet on the deck."

Pulled to the center of the room, Brynn looked at the beautiful cake that held the place of honor on the buffet table. Her name and Gregory's were twined together beneath double wedding bands. A rush of uncertain emotion choked her. "You *really* shouldn't have done this."

"Pish," Miranda dismissed. "What's the fun of getting married if you can't have the parties?"

"I'm not sure," Brynn admitted, realizing there was little she *was* sure of anymore.

"The ballroom's set up for dinner," Ruth told her, taking her arm. "And your place of honor is at the head of the table."

Brynn clutched Ruth's arm for support. She'd thought the buffet table looked scrumptious, but once inside the ballroom she was staggered by the exquisite formal dinner. Apparently the buffet table was the dessert course.

Throughout the meal, Brynn could only battle her amazement. These wonderful people were far more than she deserved. And they deserved far more than her deception. Yesterday's fax, though reassuring, hadn't provided any real reassurances. The negotiations were proceeding and hopes were high. But Gregory was still in the hands of his captors. They had learned that the kidnappers were low-level South American Government officials. They had known Gregory would be there for negotiations, hoping to build a new plant. They'd taken advantage of a pre-planned meeting to swiftly abduct him. And Brynn didn't believe she could wait out his release.

Even as she graciously dined with her new friends, Brynn thought about what she must do. First, she had to determine if Frank's health was steady. If so, it really was time for her to leave. She simply couldn't continue to lie to the nicest people she'd ever known. Brynn's throat constricted as she thought of leaving these new friends, the cozy town, and her adopted family.

And her heart felt as though a fist had clamped around it as she thought of leaving Matt. When had that feeling become paramount? And what was she to do about it? Confess that she'd lied and deceived him and somewhere in the process, tangled her feelings irretrievably with his?

The dinner drew to a close and the women strolled back into the lobby. A few of them nibbled on the pastries and chocolates lining the buffet. But most of them gathered around an armchair that was surrounded by a huge pile of gifts.

Seeing the presents, Brynn could scarcely stifle her cry of dismay. "You really, *really* shouldn't have done this."

"A shower without gifts is like Christmas without Santa Claus," Ruth told her.

"Or Christmas without gifts," Miranda added in a droll tone, making everyone laugh.

"But this isn't necessary, and—"

"Come on, kiddo," Miranda intervened, taking her arm. "This is your chair—the place of honor, so to speak. And the way you're dragging your feet we won't get those gifts open till next *Christmas*."

More laughter erupted and Brynn allowed herself to be ensconced in the huge leather chair. Meeting several pairs of curious, cheerful eyes, Brynn knew she couldn't stall much longer. Still, her hands moved slowly as she pulled the ribbon and bow from the first package.

"I'll take the bow," Becky offered, her hand out. "I'll make a wreath out of them."

"That sounds nice," Brynn murmured, not caring what happened to the bows.

"The way the bows line up tell you how many children you're going to have," Becky informed her.

Brynn nearly choked. "'Children'?"

"Sure. It sounds silly, but the wreath from my shower was right on."

Brynn turned her eyes heavenward. Where was a good strike of lightning when you needed it?

Ruth's eyes softened. "Children are always a blessing."

Brynn silently agreed. Right now she wished she had one in the lobby screaming its head off to divert all the attention turned on her.

"That package won't open itself," Miranda reminded her.

Brynn peeled back the wrapping paper, revealing an expensive, cream-colored box with a distinctive engraved store emblem. She barely contained her sigh. The hole she was digging for herself could stretch nearly to China.

Removing the lid and lifting back the tissue paper, Brynn saw a beautiful, cream-colored negligee. Tiny, exquisite satin rosebuds decorated the silk bodice. It was both simple and elegant. Nestled in the folds of silk, Brynn spotted a small card and picked it up.

With love, Aunt Miranda

Brynn's eyes misted, because in her heart, the woman had become family, someone for whom she truly cared. Someone she would miss dreadfully.

"Now don't go all maudlin on me," Miranda warned, a suspiciously hoarse note in her voice, as well.

Brynn reached out to hug the older woman. Miranda returned the embrace, then cleared her throat as she patted Brynn's back.

"Now, now, you've got other presents to open."

Brynn brushed away a tear and accepted the next present she was handed. Taking less time with this one, she wished she'd lingered when she saw the contents. An outrageous bit of fluff that could be loosely termed lingerie emerged.

"Let us see!" the women urged her, then broke into a chorus of oohs, aahs, and laughter as they saw the garment.

Hoping it was one of a kind, Brynn opened the next present and saw something so similar it could have been its twin. Gamely she held it up. "This one's red instead of black."

"Can't have too much of either color," Jean told her with a broad wink.

The next two boxes contained flimsy bras and minuscule panties that Brynn doubted she'd ever have the courage to wear. She could just envision herself lying in a hospital emergency room trying to explain them to a stern-looking nurse.

Attempting to maintain a smile, she dived into the next box. At first she was relieved. Sweet-smelling lotion was perfectly normal. As was the matching talc. Pulling out a third bottle, she paused. Body oil. So far, so good. Continuing to read the label, her eyes widened as it proclaimed to be edible and highly delectable.

"Showers are different than in my day," Ruth said with a sigh.

"More interesting now," Miranda observed, handing Brynn another box.

This one contained another provocative gown. Holding it up so that the women could show their appreciation with hoots and a few embarrassed titters, Brynn glanced up herself. And met Matt's smoldering gaze.

For a moment she faltered. Was he imagining her in the gown? Or in his brother's arms?

Before she could more than wonder, he disappeared.

192 The Accidental Mrs. MacKenzie

Prodded by the women, Brynn continued opening gifts, mouthing all the appropriate words, but her thoughts were far away—with the man who'd walked into the room and left with her heart.

Chapter Fifteen

Brynn tossed the ball for Lancelot to chase, watching him bound over the snow-covered ground as though he was used to walking through several feet of snow every day. The animals were so acclimated to Eagle Point that she knew they'd have to readjust to her apartment when they returned.

Brynn had given up the idea of complete reclusion. The MacKenzies simply outmaneuvered her, drawing her out, refusing to let her hibernate completely. And since the shower, Brynn had been awash in mixed emotions. Each time she'd brought up the subject of leaving, she'd been swamped with pleas for her to stay. Ruth had cautioned her about Frank's precarious health; and Matt's silent, watchful gaze left her completely unsettled.

As Brynn glanced upward, the ski lift cycled again. Last-minute checks were all that was left before the season opened. The phone lines were jammed and everyone had been pressed into taking reservation duty. Some were new reservations, some were changes. People anxious to hit the famous powder. When Brynn had left the main building, she'd spotted Ruth in the office taking the switchboard's helm.

While Thanksgiving was a special holiday for all of America, it held exceptional significance for ski resorts. With full bookings and record snowfall, Eagle Point was particularly thankful.

Seeing Andy across the way chasing the dog, Brynn frowned. Lancelot still didn't openly accept everyone. The only person other than Brynn that he'd completely accepted was Matt. For him, the dog would roll over on his back, exposing his vulnerable belly in the ultimate gesture of trust. And Matt, with his easy, consistent ways, had continued to hold that trust.

Lancelot loped toward her, Andy following close behind. As the boy thundered to a stop, Brynn caught his arms, preventing a skid. "Whoa! You'll take the knees out of those new jeans and your mom won't be happy."

Unconcerned, Andy reached over to pat the dog. "He won't ever let me catch him."

Brynn gentled her voice, yet her concern crept through. "I've tried to explain about Lancelot, how he came from an abusive home. It's hard to understand how people can be cruel to animals, but sometimes they are. And because he was mistreated, it's hard for him to trust people."

"He trusts you," Andy replied.

"That's because he's lived me with for quite a while now. He knows what to expect from me."

"But he hasn't known Matt that long and he likes him."

"True," Brynn agreed, equally puzzled. "But Lancelot just seems to know that Matt won't hurt him. And that's surprising, because it was a man who was unkind to him, so Lancelot never likes men."

"Maybe he can tell that Matt was going to be a vet."

"A vet?" Brynn echoed in utter surprise.

"Yeah. Long time ago. He had to decide between running Eagle Point and being a vet. Mom said he used to fill the lodge with stray animals till she thought they were going to have their own animal hospital."

So that was it. "Really?"

"Yeah. He even hid elk in the sleigh barn so they wouldn't get shot during hunting season." Andy's expression turned fierce. "It wasn't dopey. Just 'cause some people like to shoot 'em doesn't mean everybody has to."

Touched both by Andy's devotion to his brother and her discovery of Matt's soft spot for animals, she draped an arm around the child's shoulders. "Of course not. I wish no one ever had to shoot another deer or elk or moose. I'd like to see the woods filled with wild creatures."

Andy looked undecided, not certain whether she was simply humoring him. "Really?"

"Absolutely. That's why I bring home the animals nobody else will have. I guess I hide my own elk in a way. No one wanted a dog that growled at everyone who tried to pet him...or a cat that was going blind.... Or a bird with...well, not always the nicest things to say. And if I hadn't taken them home..."

"They'd shoot 'em?" Andy questioned, horrified.

"Not exactly. But I'm afraid you've got the idea. So, you see, I believe in protecting creatures that can't protect themselves."

"Just like Matt."

She ruffled his hair. "Yeah. Just like Matt."

"Good." His brows grew together in obvious thought. "'Cause we're family now and we should think good stuff about each other."

That hitch was finding a permanent place in her heart. "You're right about that."

"Is your other family like that, too?"

Brynn's eyes flickered shut as she thought about her self-absorbed mother. Always chasing an elusive piece of happiness—and never finding it. "Not exactly," she answered briefly. "But I always think of Stephanie as part of my family."

"Yeah," Andy replied, understanding dawning. Then his brightness dimmed. "But she's acting awful goopy lately."

"'Goopy'?"

"Yeah. She used to be really cool, but now she's all goony over this guy. Before, she would've done something really awesome to him, but now she's acting all *nice*." His intonation indicated "nice" was the worst possible description for his favorite comic character.

"She really seems that different?" Brynn asked, appalled at what was dawning on her.

"I'm not even sure she's Stephanie anymore," he replied, as guileless as he was tactless. "It never used to be a *girls'* comic strip, but now it is."

That term needed no translation. As her own feelings had changed, apparently she'd put Stephanie through a metamorphosis of her own. And now she'd spilled out her own feelings for the entire comic-reading world to see.

Cocky, fearless Stephanie had fallen in love—sweetly and with all her heart. Brynn had created a carbon copy of herself— a woman never before touched by love, charmed by her new prince and totally captivated by him.

And acting completely out of character.

Brynn's lips firmed into a grim line. *Face it*, she told herself. *You've given Stephanie a personality transplant.*

Unable to prevent it, Brynn groaned aloud about the consequences of her own transparent feelings.

"You okay?" Andy questioned. "You don't have a stomachache or something, do you?"

"No. Just a headache thinking about all the work I have to do."

"More dead stuff?"

"Deadlines," she corrected, a touch of humor returning.

He shrugged. "You coming out of your room this time?"

Brynn withheld her groan this time. "Sure."

"Cool. I gotta go inside. I have to stuff envelopes."

Even Andy and Heather had been drafted into service. "See you later, then."

Andy reached down to give Lancelot one more pat. "After he gets to know me better, he'll trust me, too."

With that he was running through the snow, leaving a powdery trail in the crisp air. Brynn knew her creative block had just been smashed open. It was time she got Stephanie back on track. It was a wonder other readers and her publisher hadn't complained. Stephanie had to regain her edge and return to her wacky, tortuous self.

An image of her own leaf-jumping escapade came to mind. With a few twists, Brynn could take that episode and turn it completely to Stephanie's advantage. And restore the star of her strip as the independent woman she was, rather than a transparent carbon copy of herself.

Glancing toward the lodge, Brynn watched Andy disappear, realizing in that moment there could be no more time for Andy to bond with Lancelot, or for her to continue accepting the MacKenzies' hospitality. Andy had opened her eyes. If even her comic strip had dramatically and visibly altered, it was finally time to do what she should have done long ago.

And with Thanksgiving only a few weeks away, Brynn needed to be with her own mother—to prove to herself that she didn't need to "borrow" someone else's family.

And Thanksgiving would be the perfect break. The MacKenzies would have to understand that she should be with her own family for the holiday. With the excitement and rush of the start of the season, her departure wouldn't be as traumatic. The family would be too caught up in attending to the surge of guests. It would be difficult to bid them goodbye. But if she put it off any longer, it would be unbearable.

BRYNN WIPED HER perspiring palms against the jeans she now wore with ease. Collecting her courage she dialed the phone, her never completely quenchable optimism in hand, along with a great deal of need. While she and her mother didn't make it a habit to celebrate holidays together—that simply wasn't in

Charlene Magee's game plan—Brynn needed her mother now. Needed to know that when she walked away from the MacKenzies she would still have someone to reach out to—someone who would care about her.

"Mom!" Brynn spoke in a rush, glad to hear the familiar voice.

"Brynn?"

Great deductive powers, Brynn couldn't help thinking, since her mother had only one child. "Yes, Mom. It's me."

"Is something wrong?"

Brynn closed her eyes and took a deep breath. "No, Mom. But Thanksgiving's just around the corner. I thought we could spend it together. It's not like we have a whole lot of family to gather, but we could still roast a mean turkey and I have Grandma Magee's recipe for Irish whiskey cake—I know how you love it—"

"Brynn."

The tone alone stopped her flow of words. And she waited.

"I...I didn't expect you to call about Thanksgiving. You've been so caught up yourself, lately. And actually... Well, I've made plans to take a ski vacation...."

The irony wasn't lost on Brynn.

"Of course, I'm planning to go to the eastern slopes," Charlene continued.

Of course. Especially since she had a daughter in the western Rockies only minutes from the country's finest ski resorts. But she couldn't give up. Not yet. "I could meet you, Mom."

"Well...Brynn, the truth is I've met someone new."

Brynn had lost count of all the "someone news" her mother had met over the years.

"And Brynn...it would be hard to explain a daughter your age."

"How old is he?"

Charlene stalled, then finally sighed. "Twenty-eight, okay? But he thinks I'm ten years younger than I am, which makes our age difference just a small gap instead of a glaring gorge. But if you show up, he'll know I can't have a daughter your age and be—"

"Mom. It's okay." Brynn clutched the phone a little closer, wishing for the zillionth time that she had the storybook family she'd always dreamed of. "It's last-minute, anyway. Flights would be difficult to get—"

"Impossible," her mother interrupted, hope singing through the phone lines.

That same hope killed Brynn's. "Right. And what do we know about cooking turkeys?"

"Best left to the experts," Charlene agreed with relief. "What else are chefs and restaurants for?"

Cold, lonely holidays. But Brynn didn't share that with her mother. "Exactly. Maybe…maybe I'll try skiing myself this year."

"Well, you're in the right place for it."

A tear squeezed past Brynn's tightly closed eyelids, despite her intention not to cry. If only her mother knew. Or cared. "And I have a ton of work to do. In fact, I'd better go and get on it. Deadlines."

"Of course. We'll talk again. When all this mad rush of holidays is over."

Realizing her mother had just dismissed Christmas along with Thanksgiving, Brynn managed to say goodbye, her hands shaking as she gave in to the tears she couldn't hold back any longer.

Downstairs, Ruth's hands were shaking as well as she hung up the switchboard master line, having overheard Brynn's conversation. Initially, she'd just wanted to break in on the call to tell Brynn that her publisher was holding on another line. Hearing Brynn speaking to her mother about Thanksgiving, Ruth decided it would be best not to interrupt and was about to click off when she heard Charlene's excuse for not spending the holiday with her daughter. Knowing she was shamelessly eavesdropping, she couldn't stop, worried about the girl who had grown so dear to their family.

And now shock battled with a need to protect. How could any mother be so callous? Especially to a girl as sensitive as Brynn? Mindful of everyone's feelings, considerate to a fault, it was hard to believe she came from a mother who possessed neither quality.

Ruth knew she had to convince Brynn that she was needed here at Eagle Point for the holiday. Otherwise, she suspected that Brynn might escape to lick her wounds, unable to deal with such a family-oriented holiday without any family of her own.

As she worried about Brynn, Ruth also thought about Frank's faulty health—the effect her departure would have on him. This past week he'd looked paler. His sleep was uneven, his appetite all but nonexistent. With no real news of Gregory, his spirits were fading. With all the fierce instincts of motherhood, Ruth believed her firstborn was alive, that she would know in an instant if her son had been taken from her. Matt had flown again to Washington, but he had returned frustrated, feeling he hadn't accomplished anything that would help Gregory. Still, Ruth believed.

But Frank had lost two brothers in the Vietnam war—brothers he'd also fiercely believed would return, but not in caskets. It was more difficult for him to cling to hope. And Brynn was their only tangible link with Gregory. If she fled home to Salt Lake, Ruth feared Frank's reaction.

She also feared how Brynn would deal with being alone. Despite her apparently cold mother, Ruth had never seen anyone who needed and treasured the familial connection more than Brynn.

For both their sakes, Ruth had to keep her family together. Frank and Brynn deserved that much. Remembering Charlene Magee's thoughtless words, Ruth knew Brynn deserved far more. And while she was at Eagle Point, she was going to get it.

Chapter Sixteen

Brynn stared around the room that had become her own. Then her gaze rested on the half-filled suitcase. She wished she could pack away the memories and feelings she'd gathered here as easily. Although it was after ten in the evening, she was neither sleepy nor inclined to finish her packing.

Restless, she decided to take a break, knowing she could find cocoa or cider in the huge kitchens. Large enough to handle banquets, yet filled with the cozy comforts of home, the kitchen was always a welcoming place.

At first Brynn had thought it was odd that the family shared the kitchen with guests. It had seemed so impersonal. Now she appreciated the diversity. Not many people's homes were stocked with fresh out-of-season fruit, gourmet meats and cheese, caviar, French pastries, tortes, and fresh seafood. She could nibble on shrimp salad or an exquisite napoleon. And she could also opt for pretzels and cocoa.

Pushing on the swing door at the rear of the kitchen, she was surprised when it didn't move. Since she knew it didn't have a lock, she pushed again.

A muffled but amused voice spoke through the thick wood. "One of us had better stop pushing or we're never going anywhere."

"Matt?" Dropping her hand, she stood back.

"Brynn?"

She waited. When the door didn't move, she stepped forward, then stepped back as quickly. She didn't particularly want the door to crash into her face.

Amusement doubled in Matt's voice. "And if we both stand here staring at the door, waiting for it to move, we won't get anywhere, either."

Despite her troubled mood, Brynn's lips quirked upward.

"Ladies first," he urged.

Cautiously she pushed on the door, poking her head inside. "I didn't mean to create an impasse. I just wanted some cocoa."

"Having trouble getting to sleep?"

She shrugged. "Not exactly. Just restless, I guess."

He met her roving eyes. "I have a better antidote."

Seeing his eyes darken, she felt the sudden, insistent thudding in her chest. "Doing what?"

"A sleigh ride. There's a full moon. And the horses are nipping at the bit to get out. And in a few weeks when the season opens, the sleighs will be full every night."

The idea appealed to her. More than appealed to her. Because when those sleighs were full she wouldn't be at Eagle Point any longer. "I'd like that." She met his warm gaze, his lion-colored eyes. "A lot."

For several long seconds neither of them moved. Before the moment could go further than either of them could live with, Matt stepped back. "I'll get the sleigh ready while you grab a coat. It's cold out."

She tore her gaze away. "Right." Even though she suspected that she wouldn't feel an arctic blast at that moment, Brynn gathered her jacket, scarf, and hat.

Once outside, Matt met her at the porch, taking her arm and leading her to the horsedrawn sleigh. Matt had chosen one of the smaller sleighs, rather than one that could accommodate a group, Brynn noticed. And it was an old-fashioned delight. Long silvery runners, deeply burnished carved wood, and a leather seat with only enough room for two passengers. It was charming…and intimate.

Matt held out his hand, helping her up and onto the seat. Then he joined her, taking the reins.

"I thought the draft horses were for the sleighs," Brynn wondered aloud, referring to the Belgian mares stabled in the barn.

"They are. But you don't need a team for the small sleighs. Put a dozen people in one of the group sleighs and you've got to have a team of drafts or you won't get any farther than the barn.

"This is like the one in 'Jingle Bells'—a 'one-horse open sleigh,'" she realized with pleasure.

"But we're not 'dashing through the snow,'" he warned. "Not at night."

"Are we singing all the way?"

His eyes briefly met hers. "If you like."

Despite the insistent thudding that clamored in her chest, she kept her tone light. "We could go 'o'er the fields, laughing all the way.'"

Matt's lips twitched as he snapped the reins and then clucked to the horse. "Wait'll you hear the 'bells on bobbed tails ring.'"

To her surprise they did. Delighted, she listened to the merry bells that danced in a twinkling accompaniment to the horse's steps. "I thought things like this only existed in storybooks and black-and-white movies."

One brow lifted. "Only black-and-white?"

"Back when romance was alive. Before cable and big-budget films ruined it."

"You like a little dash of Hepburn and Tracy?" he quizzed.

"And lots of Cary Grant," she added. "Back then, romance was bigger even than the stars—the ones in Hollywood *and* the sky."

"Not like today?"

"*Definitely* not like today."

"That has a distinct ring of cynicism."

She shrugged. "It's the truth."

"But a strange attitude for a new bride."

Brynn froze, then cursed her impulsive tongue. "I meant in general."

He probed the open wound. "Then you believe in romance for yourself."

Brynn's eyelids flickered shut. "I'm afraid so."

Matt clicked the reins again, only the bells on the horse's halter breaking the silence as they rode deeper into the remote meadows. It was a still fairyland. Snow like heavy bunched cotton hung on the pine boughs and giant ice cascades sparkled in the moonlight.

Brynn shivered in the bite of the cold air and Matt withdrew a woolen blanket folded into the seat box. Stretching it out, he tucked it over their laps, still expertly driving the horse. It seemed suddenly intimate to share the bulky garment, and to be fitted beneath its heavy folds.

The light from the full moon glittered over newly fallen snow, turning the meadow into a field of diamonds. Gliding through the aspens, beneath the stars, the echo of quiet sounded in the winter hush.

It was like a moment plucked from time—from one of her daydreams. A magical moment that she didn't want to end.

"I don't know where city people go to think," Matt said, finally breaking the silence. "Where do you find quiet like this?"

Brynn acknowledged the exquisite quality of the snow-shrouded landscape, the unique tranquillity. "You don't," she answered truthfully. "You know this is one of kind. That's why you're here."

Matt angled his face toward hers. "You understand."

It wasn't a question. It was an acknowledgement. One that spoke of the unvoiced pull between them.

Matt slowed the horse, stopping at a break that looked down on an icy mountain stream crossed by a wooden suspension bridge. Snow brushed the limbs of overhanging trees and icicles dripped from their branches. The moonlight glinted from both, illuminating the rock-strewn riverbed as the water rushed along its ancient path.

"So much beauty," Brynn breathed, caught up in the spell of their surroundings, and of the man who filled the seat beside her.

Matt turned to her, his expression unguarded, his longing clear for her to read. "Yes."

The simple word hung between them. A shiver, not caused by the cold, tripped through her. Instinctively she brought her bare hands together.

"Where are your gloves?" Matt asked, picking up her hands, warming them between his palms.

Brynn couldn't answer. Overwhelmed by the strength and tenderness of his touch, she wanted nothing more than for it to continue. For him to show her exactly how he felt.

Knowing he couldn't cross the line she had erected with lies, Brynn was trapped. Trapped into a charade that had become meaningless. Trapped into a lifetime sentence of knowing that she had to walk away from the man she loved. Or face his censure.

And because of that love, she gently withdrew her hands, unable to cause him to feel guilt. If Gregory didn't return, Brynn couldn't make Matt live with the knowledge that he'd betrayed his brother, not knowing whether he was dead or alive.

Despite the love she held for Matt, Brynn couldn't wish for Gregory's demise, and the pain it would cause all of them. Knowing now how she felt about Matt, she realized how immature and unformed her feelings for Gregory had been. Silly dreams...lonely fantasies.

Whereas this was real—a man who cared for his family,

revered the legacy he'd inherited, guarded his heritage, and protectively warmed her hands beneath the moonlight. It seemed simple to see that now. But more complicated than the worst scenario even her fiction-filled mind could create.

Matt read the reasoning in her eyes. Still he hesitated, then finally picked up the reins, signaling the horse. The sleigh glided over the snow, the whistle of the runners and the jingling of the bells filling the silence that lumbered between them.

TOO MANY LIGHTS WERE ON. The thought struck Matt as they approached the lodge. It seemed that every light in the place was lit and it was nearly midnight. A sudden sense of unease gripped him.

"I wonder what's going on," Brynn questioned as they stopped.

"Something's wrong."

"Gregory?" Brynn murmured.

Their gazes jerked together, twin flares of guilt flickering in their eyes. Matt bolted from the sleigh, hurriedly helping her down. Then they raced across the packed snow toward the wide double doors of the lodge.

One flung open before they reached it. "Thank God you're back!" Miranda cried out.

"Gregory?" Matt questioned, his voice grim.

"No."

Brynn issued a silent prayer of relief.

"It's your father."

Sucking in her breath, Brynn took a step toward Matt, then paused, knowing it wasn't her place to comfort him.

Matt's eyes locked with Miranda's. "Is he…"

"The ambulance took him to the hospital. Your mother's with him. The paramedic says it's another heart attack. I wanted to go, but I couldn't leave Heather and Andy."

"They should be with him." Matt spoke with the authority of the head of the family, a position he hadn't claimed before.

"I wasn't sure." Miranda hesitated.

"I am. If he gets better, they'll just be missing some sleep. If not..." He strengthened his voice. "If not, they need to be there."

From behind Miranda, a worried-looking Heather pushed forward. "Matt? Is that you?"

"Yes, punkin."

Heather rushed to him, seeking the shelter of his comforting embrace.

He smoothed her hair. "It's going to be okay."

"We're so scared," Heather admitted, the words punctuated with a hiccup of tears.

"I know." Matt tucked back her hair as he confronted the tears running down her face. "But you've got to be strong for Dad. Now, where's Andy? He's going to need you, too."

Heather lifted drenched eyes to stare at her brother. "You think so?"

"Absolutely. It's something we pass on. You're his big sister. Go find him and you two get dressed into something warm."

She stumbled toward the stairs, then scampered upward. Matt turned to his aunt, seeing her ashen color. "Let's go into the family room."

The women followed as Matt opened the liquor cabinet, pouring three tumblers of bourbon. He handed them each a glass, then tipped his own, needing the fiery warmth. A cold pit had settled in his stomach, one that even the fine liquor couldn't chase away.

Frank MacKenzie was the backbone of their family. Strong, understanding, a driving force in making Eagle Point what it was today. It had been difficult to watch him grow physically weak, dependent on doctors and hospitals. But it would be more difficult to watch him die.

Matt met Brynn's concerned gaze, read the instant understanding. Believing that certain codes of honor couldn't be bent, not even tampered with, Matt hoped he hadn't tempted fate by wanting Brynn. Surely fate wouldn't have repaid him by striking down his father.

Turning away abruptly, Matt slapped the glass on the bar. "We'll take the van. I'll go collect the kids." He watched as the women's gazes met. "There's no time to waste."

Chapter Seventeen

Brynn hated the antiseptic smell of hospitals. The odor was tied irretrievably to her grandmother's death—the tall, sterile bed she'd lain in. A woman of remarkable spirit, she had shown none of that when she was swamped by machines and IV drips, her will taken over by a troop of white-uniformed doctors and nurses. She'd never come home.

The loss was still there—not as fresh, but still painful. Feeling that, Brynn willed Frank MacKenzie to live, to return to those he loved and who needed him. And with secondary insight, she prayed for Gregory to receive the same fate.

Miranda and Ruth stood together in the hall, clinging to one another outside the intensive care unit as the doctors worked to stabilize Frank.

Buoyed by Matt's trust in her, Heather kept a watchful eye on Andy, finding his favorite candy bar, casually settling him on the couch beside her.

Brynn drank her fourth cup of coffee and swallowed the last bitter dregs. Crushing the paper cup, she walked toward the garbage can. Still restless, she continued to pace. They'd been there for hours. Brynn no longer knew how many. Frank was alive, but his condition was critical.

She'd watched Matt closeted with the doctors, the grim expression that clouded his face. Yet Ruth insisted there still was no diagnosis.

Then Matt had disappeared. Worried, Brynn had finally searched the halls of the hospital, but hadn't found him. She'd casually asked Ruth about him. Distracted, Ruth told Brynn that if she needed Matt, to call his cell phone. He was somewhere in the hospital, in one of the offices. Then she'd returned to her husband's side.

Miranda had patted her hand, telling her not to worry, that Matt was dealing with things. Concerned but not wanting to upset the family, Brynn had staked out a portion of the waiting room, hoping Matt would return soon.

Glancing up, Brynn saw a nurse hovering at the doorway. Fear clutched her.

"Miss Magee?"

"Yes," she managed to choke out, fearing the worst.

"Phone call for you at the nurses' station."

Unable to imagine who would be calling at the hospital, Brynn blindly followed the nurse, picking up the phone she indicated at the critical-care unit.

"Hello?"

"Brynn?" Matt's voice flowed through the wires.

Relief made her sag. "Are you all right?"

"Brynn, did Gregory make out a new will after you got married?"

"What?"

"Did Gregory make out a new will?"

She answered truthfully. "No, but what—"

"I'll get back to you."

A dial tone buzzed in her ear as she stood, listening blankly. Seeing the nurse's curious glance, Brynn replaced the receiver. "Thank you."

Returning to the waiting room, Brynn couldn't settle into a chair, instead continuing to pace as the time dragged. Intermittent announcements over the paging system called for everything from maintenance cleanup to code blue. Still Matt didn't return. Checking with Ruth, Brynn knew there hadn't been any change in Frank's condition.

She'd expected Matt to stand vigil by his father's side, not to disappear. It wasn't like him. Steady, dependable, a man who could head the MacKenzie family, Matt didn't run away from responsibility. He embraced it. So where was he?

Another hour passed. Wearily, she leaned against the wall, her gaze lingering on Heather and Andy who were curled together on the couch, both finally dropping off to sleep.

Hearing footsteps approach, she closed her eyes, hoping they would pass, wishing that would mean that Frank hadn't taken a turn for the worse. But they came closer.

"Brynn?" Matt's hands closed around her shoulders. "Are you okay?"

"Where were you?" she blurted out, terrified and concerned.

He managed a tired smile. "I didn't bolt and run."

"You could've fooled me."

He tucked back a wayward curl of her hair, then glanced at the sleeping children. "Come with me."

"Is—"

"Dad's the same. No change."

She followed him into the hall, to the long bank of tall windows. "I'm sorry. I didn't mean to bite your head off. After all, it's your father who's…who's not well, and—"

He placed two gentle fingers to her lips. "I appreciate the concern, but I need your signature."

For the first time, she noticed the file folder in his hand. She raised confused eyes. "What's this about?"

"Trust papers." When she continued to look confused, he explained. "The medical trust. The one you suggested. I thought it was a good idea, I just didn't know I'd need it so quickly. I placed the order for the new lifts the day we spoke, but I didn't take care of the trust."

"And now?"

"I called our lawyer. He drew up the papers and we ironed

everything out in the nursing director's office. She's an old friend of the family—insisted we use her office.''

Confused, Brynn stared at him. ''What's that got to do with me?''

''There's one hitch in a trust like this.''

''And?''

''The trustee can't be anyone with a financial interest in Eagle Point. And everyone in our family has one. Since Gregory didn't change his will yet, that leaves you. Because officially he's alive—'' only a tick in his jaw betrayed what he left unsaid ''—and hasn't changed his will, you're the only one in the family who doesn't have a financial interest in Eagle Point.'' Matt stared away for a moment. ''And if Gregory doesn't come home, it will take a while to make that legal, probate his estate. Until then, you're an independent agent. That's why you're set up as the trustee.''

''What?'' Shock filled her face and voice.

''The trustee,'' he explained. ''Of Dad's medical trust. They're talking possible transplant. These funds have to stay liquid—no matter what happens at the lodge.''

''You want to make *me* trustee?''

''I explained why.''

''But surely you have trusted friends who are more qualified than I am.''

''It has to be family.''

''But... I'm not... I can't....''

''Matt, Brynn!'' Ruth rushed up to them, her face both anxious and relieved. ''I'm so glad I found you.'' She leaned against her son for support. ''Your father wants to see you. The doctor says it's a good sign.'' Then she reached out to clasp Brynn's hand. ''And you. He wants to see you. He misses Gregory, but by seeing you, Frank knows he's all right. We all do.''

Guilt and pain battled for prominence.

Ruth studied Brynn's anxious face. "I hope it won't bother you to see him this way."

"Of course not. I'm...I'm pleased he asked to see me."

Together the three of them headed toward the intensive-care unit. And Brynn tried not to bow under the pressure. How had it gone this far? And how in the world was she going to fix it?

BRYNN IGNORED THE QUIET, along with the concerned faces of her animals as she continued to pack. The three pets were unusually subdued as they watched their mistress. It was a cowardly time to flee, with the family camped out most of the time at the hospital, but Brynn knew she had to seize her moment. It wasn't as though leaving with three animals could be done with stealth. She had to choose a time when the family was away. A time like now.

Pleading a headache, she'd escaped the hospital before signing the trust papers. That she simply couldn't do. Her conscience rang for relief. While she couldn't rid herself of the remorse for having ever started the charade, she couldn't take this final step.

Brynn folded the oversize broomstick skirt she hadn't worn in weeks. Matt would find someone else to be trustee—someone more appropriate, someone they wouldn't despise once they learned of her deception.

She reached for a scarf, and a piece of construction paper floated to the floor. Picking it up, she stared at the drawing. It was a rendering of Lancelot, drawn by Andy, entitled *My New Friend*. She smoothed the paper, placing it carefully in a folder with her important work files. It was a treasure she wanted to keep.

As she reached for a blouse to fold and pack, she heard a knock at the door. Knowing the family was at the hospital she assumed it was one of the employees. "Come in."

Miranda entered, a tired smile spreading across her face until she spotted the open, half-filled suitcase. "What's going on?"

Brynn wished Miranda hadn't been the one to discover her. "I'm packing."

"Why?"

As she reached for another blouse, Brynn's hand faltered. "I have my reasons."

"Which are?"

Brynn considered the truth, then chickened out. "It's almost Thanksgiving and I'm going home to spend the holiday with my mother."

Miranda reached over to pet Snookems. "I know that your mother plans to spend Thanksgiving with her young boyfriend." She met Brynn's shocked gaze. "Don't think we've been spying. Ruth accidentally overheard and she's been worried about you ever since. She thinks of you like one of her own. But then Ruth's always been ready to mother the world."

Brynn cringed, hating to think they knew about her pitiful relationship with her mother. "You've found me out. I'm not going to spend Thanksgiving with my mother. But I still have to go home. I have all kinds of work to do."

"Haven't you been getting it done here? I thought that's why you've been holed up so much lately."

"Well, I have. But the truth is, I've got a yen to get home."

"Not to pick at a scab, but isn't this the time of year to be with family? And that's how all of us regard you. You're one of our own."

Brynn's lips trembled. She had no defense against kindness. "I'm...not who you think I am." Her eyelids flickered shut briefly. "I've deceived you all and once you learn the truth...you'll all despise me."

"You mean because you're not Gregory's wife?"

Brynn's eyes flew open in shock. "You know?"

"I guessed. I wasn't positive until you confirmed it."

"How long have you known?" Brynn turned, pushing her hand through unruly curls. "How did you—"

"Guess?" Miranda tilted her head. "It wasn't anything, and it was everything. I know the love of a good woman can change a man, but from what you told us, Gregory's transformation made Jekyll and Hyde sound dull. And much as I love my nephew, he couldn't be as sensitive and bighearted as you made him out to be if he'd had a personal visitation from a saint. It's just not in him. Of course, his mother believed it because she's his mother. And she's always seen him through a filtered lens, but then I guess it's a good thing somebody does."

Brynn bent her head. "I want to say that I can explain, but I don't think I can."

"Why don't you try?"

The story spilled from Brynn's lips. At times she stumbled through the words, at others she nearly cried. When she finished, she was exhausted but oddly relieved. It had been a terrible strain, keeping the story to herself.

Still her eyes filled with sadness as she looked at Miranda. "So I'm leaving, before I have to tell Matt the truth. I certainly can't sign as a trustee for Frank's medical trust."

"Why not?"

Brynn stared at her, wondering if stress had caused Miranda to lose her hearing or her sense. "You've got to be joking."

"Like I said, you're part of the family now."

"After what I just told you?"

"You're in love with a MacKenzie—you just picked the wrong brother to begin with."

This was unsteady ground. "What do you mean?"

"Don't kid a kidder. I know how you feel about Matt."

"But..."

"Just like you knew how I felt about Edward."

The stinging reminder echoed between them.

"Even if that were true—" Brynn battled to steady her voice

"—Matt would never be able to forgive me. I've deceived him…all of you. How could he live with that?"

"Maybe you're underestimating him."

"I won't be around to find out. I've already made too big a mess of things."

Miranda's lips firmed. "You'd be a fool to throw away his love. I know. I'm an expert."

Brynn worked nervous fingers, finally shoving them into her pockets. "I said too much about Edward—built up your hopes—interfered in something I didn't know about—"

"That's neither here nor there. The point is I fled from love once and I've been paying for it ever since. Don't walk away thinking you won't spend your entire life looking back. Because you will."

"I just don't know, Miranda."

"Even though things haven't worked out as I might have liked with Edward, this time it was real. Before, I dreamed about Neil's love—built it into something impossible to match. And now I know that the real thing's better than a dream."

"I do, too," Brynn admitted. "I look at the pictures in the wedding album and I see strangers." She lifted troubled eyes. "But that doesn't excuse what I've done."

"I know we've been playing on your guilt, telling you how much the family needs you. The truth is—Matt needs you. He's facing the biggest crisis of his life. I don't think he can handle having you leave in the middle of it."

"But ultimately I'll just hurt everyone that much more."

"We can't think about 'ultimately'—it's all we can do to live through today. Can you give them that much more?"

Brynn bent her head. "I don't know why you're doing this. You should be angry."

Miranda clasped Brynn's shoulder. "Sometimes families aren't born—they're made. From love and hope and caring. You've shown all that for us—however things started. So, you see, you are one of our own."

"Oh, Miranda!"

"Then you'll stay?"

Brynn swiped at her moist eyes. "You're hard to refuse."

Miranda cleared her suspiciously gruff voice, then patted her hair—set in a softer style since she'd met Edward. Chasing away their tears, she grinned. "That's what all the fellas say."

Chapter Eighteen

Frank MacKenzie looked exhausted but pleased as he settled into his own room at Eagle Point. The long journey from the critical-care unit to regular patient care, and finally home, had been an arduous one; yet he had never complained. Although a donor had not yet been found, he'd had surgery—a balloon procedure that had bought him time.

And he was responding better to this surgery than his previous one, surprising everyone by returning home in less than two weeks.

Everyone had hovered at first, but Frank had put a quick end to that. *"I'm not at my best, but I'm also not at death's door. You can quit fussing over me because it makes me think you're all waiting in line to be the doorman. Now, can we act normal?"*

His irreverent words had startled them out of their oversolicitous behavior. And, things had returned to normal—or as close to it as possible, with the worry never far from their minds.

Brynn almost confessed a dozen times, but Frank's weakened condition, coupled with the hope on everyone's faces, stopped her. She'd come too far to literally pull the plug on Frank.

Restless, on the edge, she'd thrown herself into the preparations for opening day of the season, volunteering for every

job, large or small. She supposed it was some sort of penance—
or escape. But she couldn't remain in her room, surrounded by
her guilt.

Although she gave her comic strip ample attention, each time
she thought about her self-imposed hibernation, she cringed,
then found another job to volunteer for. And as she worked
she hoped she could forget the ever-growing tangle of lies.

MIRANDA WAS BUSY MAKING last-minute changes, then ap-
proving the final Thanksgiving menu. Tomorrow was the biggest day of the year for Eagle Point. Ruth had turned the responsibility for the day's celebrations over to Miranda, her own
concern over Frank's precarious condition paramount.

Guests had been arriving all week, many of them the previous day. The lodge and all the cottages were packed. As were
all the ski runs. Even though the season officially opened the
following day, lifts were operational.

The day had dawned beautifully. Clear, sunny, with an abun-
dance of the greatest snow on earth. Powder fanatics had hit
the slopes, their enthusiasm spilling over to the employees. Traditionally, it had been a day charged with hope and enthusiasm.
Today was no different—except that Miranda's hope centered
around her brother.

Since their father's death he had been the constant in her
life, the only man she'd been able to count on. She wasn't sure
what she'd do if she lost him. And despite his stopgap surgery,
she was terrified that he'd lose this battle.

Brynn knocked, then poked her head inside the office doorway. "Am I interrupting?"

"Of course not." Miranda studied Brynn's pale face, the
shadows that ringed her eyes, the worry that never left her
expression. "I thought you were resting."

Brynn slipped into the chair facing Miranda's desk. "I can't
sleep."

None of them slept well these days. "You won't help Frank

by falling apart. Ruth is counting on us to keep things running smoothly." Purposely Miranda gentled her voice, knowing the guilt that ate at Brynn. "Matt has everything under control, but she and Frank were always the glue that held everything together. I'm afraid you've been drafted without hope of leave."

"I like helping out. I guess I'm just overwhelmed by how fast everything is happening." How quickly Matt had insisted on her signature. Papers she'd shakily signed, certain she was dooming herself with each stroke of the pen.

"This isn't the kind of family that sits on the sidelines. Once you're a MacKenzie so to speak, you're sucked in. After a while you forget the time when you weren't a part of the family."

That was painfully true. "Have you heard any news about a donor?"

"Not yet, but I know we'll hear soon. Frank wasn't meant to leave us this soon." Her lips trembled before she firmed them. "He can't abandon an old spinster like me."

Brynn's heart went out to the woman who now ached from two fresh hurts; a woman who'd stood by Brynn even though she didn't deserve it. "He won't."

A sudden knock on the door startled them.

"Come in," Miranda called out.

Edward West filled the doorway, shocking both women.

Brynn recovered first, quickly rising from her chair. As Edward approached Miranda, Brynn darted toward the door. Glancing between them quickly, she disappeared.

"Edward?" Miranda's voice was shaky and she firmed it. "You should have told me you were coming for Thanksgiving. Reservations have been flying in. We're all booked up."

"I found that out last week when I called. But I'm not here for Thanksgiving."

"You're not?"

"I would have been, but I couldn't get a room. I'm here because of Frank."

Miranda's voice quivered. "You are?"

"I know how close you two are. I didn't want you to be alone."

Hope trembled. "You didn't?"

"If you'll come out from behind that desk I'll show you."

In a moment she was in his arms, her head buried against his shoulder. "I wasn't sure you'd be back."

"Neither was I."

She lifted her head cautiously, studying his face.

He took her hand, absently encircling each finger. "I wasn't sure I was ready to let go of Sylvia's memory. We were married for thirty-two years. It's not easy to shut the door on such an important part of your life. Then I told myself I could just come out for Thanksgiving—that it didn't have to mean anything—and I found that I was too late to get a reservation. I called yesterday and heard about Frank. I didn't want to be too late again. And I don't mean for a room."

Miranda wanted to simply accept his words. But she couldn't. "I can't keep having…interludes. I care about you, more than I thought I ever could. But I can't bear to keep watching you walk away, taking little pieces of me with you until there's nothing left."

Edward planted his hands on her shoulders. "I don't want to walk away. That's why I'm here, to ask if you'll consider having me…for the rest of our lives."

Miranda could hardly hear over the thundering in her heart and the joy singing in her consciousness. "Are you saying what I think you are?"

"I'm asking you to be my wife. I love you, Miranda."

Their kiss was a seal of commitment, and the fluttering promise of tomorrow.

Watching through the glass door of Miranda's office, Brynn found a tear trembling in her eyes. A hopeless romantic, she rejoiced in the happiness she saw shining in their faces, grateful her interference hadn't cost Miranda this well-deserved joy.

Each MacKenzie had found a special niche in her affections. Aching with the knowledge of how empty she would be without those connections, Brynn turned away, hoping this holiday would truly bring a Thanksgiving for the family. Knowing that what she wished for would mean Gregory's return and her subsequent unveiling, she looked for the courage to face both.

BRYNN STARED IN fascination as the trail groomers defied the darkness to smooth the trails, tilling and moving snow, leveling the bumps, and covering the bare spots. The operation would go on all night as they groomed each trail before morning so that the skiers would wake to picture-perfect runs.

But now the grooming machine was completing the steep grade that Brynn was observing—the one that would be used for night skiing.

Surface hoar crystals glimmered in the oblique light. As Brynn watched, euphoric skiers lined up at the top of the run. With headlamps beaming they began their descent, chasing one another through the sparse pines, around the curves and over the creek crossings.

The moon rose over the resort, the all-encompassing soft white light adding its extraordinary glow. Torchlights crystallized in the air, outlining the winding trail.

Moonlight powder-skiing.

It was enchanting, it was awesome. It was romantic.

Brynn shivered in the evening air, wishing for a strong, warm body to be seated next to hers. And it wasn't just anybody's body she wanted. She wanted one particular man to share this aura of romance.

As though in response to her silent bidding, a shadow darkened the bench she sat on. An accelerated heartbeat told her it was Matt. Lifting her eyes, she beckoned him to join her.

As he did, her loneliness vanished.

Matt was quiet, watching the gentle dance of the skiers, their sure waltz as they descended the slope. "I never get tired of watching this," he finally said. "In some ways it's better than being part of it."

"What's night skiing like?" she asked, wanting to hear his voice, to hold it close.

"When the moon's full, the light refracts on the cratered beacon and it drifts over the mountainside, making it seem brighter than a summer day."

Her eyes smiled for her. "That sounds wonderful...very poetic."

Matt held her gaze. "If the moon sinks above the cliff, we ski blind. Not so wonderful. And sometimes we seem like the shadows of ghosts." His teeth flashed white in the darkness. "But mostly it's like flying in your sleep."

"That sounds nearly as difficult as catching stars."

His tawny eyes roved over her face, resting on the bow of her mouth, then searching for the telltale pulse at her throat. "And as invigorating."

"Do many things invigorate you?" she asked, urged on by the full moon to be daring.

His gaze zeroed in on hers. "More things than you could know."

She took her heart and placed it in his hands. "You might be surprised at what I know...and what I want."

Pain obviously battled with desire. "We can't always have what we want."

"Even if we want it badly enough?" she whispered, only a breath away from him.

"Sometimes that makes it more impossible."

The hard line of his body pressed into hers, his muscular thighs comforting and tantalizing her at the same time. She wanted to shout the truth, flail at the unfairness of their situation. Instead she tilted her head, allowing herself the pleasure of resting it on his shoulder, drawing comfort from his presence.

Unable to stop himself, Matt stroked the sweep of her long,

dark hair. In his mind he saw her silhouetted in the moonlight, her naked alabaster body belonging to him. Bending to breathe in the scent of her hair, he knew those dreams would remain in his thoughts—just as she would remain forever out of reach.

Snow fell gently from the sky, giant flakes that brushed their skin, collected on the slope, dusting the skiers as they wove down the course.

Matt watched for the opening-night fireworks he knew would start momentarily. A burst of color suddenly flared, followed immediately by others, splashing across all the quadrants of the sky. The falling stars and ribbons were brilliantly defined at first. Then they blurred with the falling snow, creating slanted rainbows, fractured blooms.

Watching pyrotechnics while it snowed was a rare event—one Matt had hoped he would share with Brynn. He could see the beauty through her eyes...and in her eyes.

The fireworks continued to light up the sky, sounding off the silent cliffsides, echoing their unspoken thoughts—and illuminating their need.

Chapter Nineteen

The morning of Thanksgiving Day at Eagle Point lived up to all its promise. Excited skiers clattered down the stairs, filled the dining room for an early breakfast, then attacked the freshly dusted slopes. While no one was glued to a television set watching the Macy's Day parade, there was no mistaking it was "turkey day."

The tang of ginger, cloves and cinnamon from baking pumpkin pies floated out to tantalize the appetite. The chef and his staff had been baking all night. Rows of turkeys were lined up on the counters like plucked soldiers waiting their turn. Onions and celery sautéing in butter promised dishes of well-seasoned dressing. Several pounds of cranberries came to a boil, ready to be added to a rum-raisin concoction. Flaky croissants, dinner rolls and loaves of bread lent their yeasty aroma to the ambience.

Accustomed to a pared-down version of the holiday, Brynn was charmed by all the preparations and bustle. While she doubted the Pilgrims boasted skis, state-of-the-art boots, and designer ski wear, there was a true Thanksgiving spirit.

The family gathered in midafternoon for their celebration, allowing enough time for the lunch crowd to disperse and plenty of time before exhausted skiers gave in to the encroaching darkness and their appetites. Many of the hearty revived on dinner and then returned for night skiing. And the Mac-Kenzies wanted time for the family in between.

A golden-brown bird decorated the center of the table and all of the accompaniments crowded every other available inch. No employees assisted in serving the meal since it was also an Eagle Point tradition for the employees and their families to congregate in the large banquet room for an identical dinner. A skeleton staff kept the main dining room operational, but even they took turns dropping in at the employee celebration.

So the MacKenzie table was intimate, with everything served family style in bowls and serving dishes Brynn was told had come west in covered wagons. All the tradition both overwhelmed and warmed her. Although she had a few precious mementos from her grandmother, there was little she could claim as family heritage. Brynn pictured her mother, no doubt outfitted in the latest ski wear, swooshing down the slopes with her latest young lover. Hardly a Norman Rockwell image.

A knot formed in her throat as Brynn thought of giving up warm moments like this; of not sharing more days with Matt; of walking out of his life forever.

As if in unspoken agreement, her eyes met his.

Although they were all grateful for Frank's shaky presence at the table, Brynn noticed that Matt, too, was quiet. Feeling their time ticking away as though a pendulum marked each second, she sensed a desperation hovering darkly over the gay voices and happy chatter that ringed the table.

The wide double doors leading into the dining room were closed in order to keep the public out. Only the serving door to the kitchen was ajar. So when the double doors were suddenly flung open, everyone at the table reacted in startled confusion.

"Surprise!"

Silence filled the room before a babble of excitement and cries of joy erupted as nearly everyone jumped from their chairs.

Gregory stood at the entrance, as big as life. His mother, aunt, sister, and youngest brother hung all over him like birds on a scarecrow. Frank rose painfully to his feet, not bothering to check the tears that silently ran down his cheeks as he embraced his oldest son.

Brynn met Matt's eyes, saw the indecision there before he, too, rose to hug his brother, then pound his arm in an age-old gesture of affection. Only Brynn remained rooted to her chair.

Well, the jig is up, she told herself. *And the reckoning is now.* She tried to summon up some of the feelings she'd had for Gregory—the hopeless infatuation that had fueled so many fantasies. But nothing stirred.

The MacKenzies took turns hugging Gregory, then hugging him again, before examining him, commenting on his thinness, then hugging him again. Brynn knew she should be happy for them. And in a strange, detached corner of her emotions, she was. But her joy for them was overwhelmed by her own despair.

Wishing she could escape, disappear into a quiet puff of invisible smoke, Brynn had to sit quietly since both entrances were blocked. The main door was filled with the family, the kitchen door blocked by beaming staff dying to share the special moment.

As the babble lowered to a mild roar, Gregory glanced around the room. When his puzzled gaze landed on her, Brynn straightened her spine, calling on her courage, wondering where the bottom of her stomach had disappeared to.

"Who—" Gregory began.

But Miranda clasped his arm, enfolding him in another hug. "You rotten boy. You've worried me sick."

"Aunt Mir, you're just put out because I didn't send you chocolates from Paris like I promised." Gregory's smile flashed, lighting his handsome face, and gave her a tight hug.

"Why didn't you tell us you were coming home?" Ruth demanded, sniffling away happy tears.

"I swore the State Department and my firm to secrecy. Thought it would be a nice holiday surprise." As he spoke, Gregory glanced meaningfully at his father.

Frank returned his gaze with a steady look of his own. "Now we truly have something to be thankful for."

Gregory clasped his father's shoulder. "We all do." From the telling gesture, it was clear that Gregory had learned about Frank's close call and his still-precarious situation.

Turning back to the table, Gregory's gaze landed again on Brynn. "You'll have to intro—"

"Gregory!" Miranda practically shrieked. "I know you barely got here, but I need to drag you away for a minute." Not allowing him to answer, she literally tugged him through the doorway.

A chorus of voices protested.

"Miranda! But Brynn hasn't even—"

"Won't be a minute," Miranda called out cheerily, slamming the dining-room doors.

Gregory walked along with her, a look of concern on his face. "Auntie Mir, are you okay?"

"That stands to be seen," she replied, guiding him across the lobby to the library, leading him inside and then locking the door.

"Another kidnapping?" he joked.

But she took his hands, ignoring his light tone. "You know I love you dearly, Gregory. You've always been very special to me—my favorite nephew, in fact."

He nodded.

"Even though you're one of the most selfish people on earth."

Gregory pursed his lips. "This isn't *exactly* the homecoming I'd envisioned."

"I'd break this to you gently, but there's a roomful of people in there—not to mention a turkey waiting to be carved—that demand immediate attention. So here's the scoop."

Quickly she outlined Brynn's appearance in their lives, the reason, and her subsequent attachment to all of them and their attachment to her. "So you see," Miranda concluded. "You can't go in there and just blow everything."

"I don't want to sound selfish, but it sounds like she set herself up for this fall," Gregory replied.

Miranda shook her head as she stared at him. "The fact that this all began because Brynn thought she was in love with you didn't even make a dent, did it?"

Without waiting for his answer, she continued: "But then, you've led your life with thoughts of only yourself—not that I'm suggesting you're the bad seed—but being self-centered makes it hard to see something through another person's eyes."

The expression on Miranda's face firmed as she went on. "You left Eagle Point without a care, dumping the entire load on Matt. Without asking you for help, he shouldered all the responsibilities, while watching firsthand as your father deteriorated day by day."

Gregory hung his head for a moment. "I knew he was sick— I just didn't know how seriously until the State Department briefed me."

"You'd have known if you'd been in touch more. But Matt knew. And he still didn't ask for your help—even though by tradition the responsibility belongs to the oldest son. Matt knew your dream wasn't tied into Eagle Point so he didn't burden you—because he loves you."

Gregory had the grace to look embarrassed. "Aunt Mir, you talk like I don't care about him."

"I know you do. But you've got to know something else. Matt's in love. With Brynn."

Gregory's mouth opened, then echoed with hollow laughter. "You're kidding."

"No. And she loves him."

"Sounds cozy."

"That's exactly what it isn't." Miranda leveled him with a

look he recognized from childhood. "And even though Matt fell in love with her, he did everything in his power to facilitate your release. He called out every favor, every card in his deck."

"His friend in the State Department," Gregory murmured. "I heard his name, knew my case had been given priority status, but I didn't think..."

"Matt." Miranda filled in the blank. "Despite how he feels about Brynn, he never stopping working to get you home. And he never let himself step over the line with the woman he thought was your wife."

Gregory shrugged. "Well, now that I'm home and everybody knows we're not married, they've got free rein."

"Hardly."

Gregory stared at his aunt. "Why not?"

"Because Matt and the rest of the family will think Brynn deceived them."

"Well, she did."

"How can you be so smart in business and so dense in life?"

"I hope there's a good part coming, because frankly I can't take much more of your enthusiastic welcome."

She swatted his arm. "You know damn well how glad I am you're safe. Now shut up."

Gregory rolled his eyes.

"It's up to you to get Matt and Brynn out of this impossible situation."

He lifted his brows. "You got any ideas about how to do that?"

"Well, of course. I can't leave all the planning up to you."

"I'm guessing you've given this some thought. Which means you figured out the truth. Why didn't you nail Brynn?"

"Because she's a love. She's sensitive, sweet, charming and genuine. And she needs us as much as we needed her. She kept your father going and because of it, we all blackmailed her into staying, playing on her soft nature. She doesn't deserve to lose everything. And Matt doesn't deserve to lose her.''

Gregory sighed. "Okay. So what's the plan?"

By THE TIME THE DOUBLE doors opened again, Brynn was ready to bolt from the table as though jet-propelled. Feeling like a prisoner being led to the gallows, she watched as Gregory approached. She swallowed, waiting for the noose to tighten.

Instead, Gregory picked up her hand and kissed it lightly. "Brynn, I don't know how to thank you."

"I'm not sure—"

"It couldn't have been easy, pretending to be my wife."

Brynn froze, afraid to look at the others.

"But you knew how important it was and the plan worked. You convinced everyone you really were my wife."

Darting a glance around the table, Brynn saw the stunned amazement on everyone's faces, the betrayal etched on Matt's. She tried to speak.

But Gregory wasn't through. "By convincing everyone you were my wife, you kept my real fiancée safe. Despite the State Department's precautions, she wouldn't have been completely protected from the kidnappers if they'd believed she was still my fiancée." He smiled easily, enjoying his role. "Of course, that's why we had to go through with the wedding photos, having some of them published in the paper. South American connections in this country are strong. She could have been snatched at any moment. I owe you a debt of gratitude for saving her life."

The MacKenzies continued to stare, unable to take in the information, unable to process what it meant. From the corner of the room, Miranda sent Brynn a discreet thumbs-up. Of course, her ally.

It was an easy way out. A graceful escape that could allow her to salvage her relationship with the family and perhaps begin one with Matt. But it was a lie. And if living with Charlene Magee had taught Brynn anything, it was that a life based on a lie was worth nothing. Less than nothing if you spent the rest of that life chasing happiness that would always remain elusive.

Slowly Brynn withdrew her hands, then met Gregory's eyes. "Thank you. I'm not sure why you did this, but I have a pretty good idea." Briefly she looked at Miranda. "And I appreciate your trying to save me from my own deception, but your family deserves the truth."

Slowly she lifted her head, her gaze gliding around the room, touching on the faces that had become so familiar, so dear. When she reached Matt's, she faltered for a moment. Then she began, knowing she had to before her courage deserted.

"Part of what Gregory told you is true. I'm not his wife. But he wrapped the reasons for my tricking you into a pretty package. It's not pretty, though. I didn't pretend to be his wife to save his fiancée. I'm not even sure he has a fiancée. You see, I fell in love with an illusion—Gregory's illusion. It certainly wasn't his fault." Her saddened voice faltered. "I doubt he ever knew I existed. But I built this fantasy world around him, believing one day he would know me. That's why I had the wedding album made. It was just supposed to be my silly little secret. I never dreamed the photographer would send you a copy."

Brynn lifted her hands plaintively, then lowered them to her sides as a helpless note crept into her voice. "And then when you all came and took me into your family, I knew it was wrong to keep on deceiving you. But by then I cared so much about all of you. I wanted to give you hope about Gregory. I wanted to be part of your family. I didn't count on caring so much about you...or falling in love with your other son." A hitch crept into her voice, breaking up her words. "I'm just so sorry." Her gaze met Matt's. "So very sorry."

Biting down a sob, she ran from the room, not aware of the

silence she left in her wake, the sense of disbelief. Or the babble that broke out a few minutes later.

Upstairs in her room, Brynn threw her things into a suitcase, not bothering with clothes, gathering only her work papers, not wanting to be loaded down with more than she could manage. Tears ran unchecked down her face as she snapped leashes on Lancelot and Snookems, then secured Bossy in his cage.

Using the back stairs, she crept down to the employee entrance. Spotting Dustin, one of the employees she knew fairly well, she approached him. "I know it's Thanksgiving and I know how busy you are, but can you drive me to town, please? Just to Logan. I can get to Salt Lake from there. I wouldn't ask if it wasn't an emergency." A hiccup punctuated her words and tears continued to stream down her face.

In typical male fashion, Dustin looked helpless in the face of female tears. "Sure. I'll just tell Matt where I'm going—"

"No! I mean, is that necessary?"

"I'm on this shift," he replied, obviously ill-equipped to handle a near hysterical woman. "I can't just leave."

Brynn felt her tears increase, barely able to focus as she tried to wipe them away. A cool hand clasped her arm.

"I'll drive her."

Dimly Brynn recognized Tracy, the girl who'd been so kind since her arrival. "I'd—" Brynn's voice hitched uncontrollably "—really appreciate it."

"I just finished my shift," Tracy told her. "And I'm going to Salt Lake to see my grandmother. She wasn't well enough to come here for Thanksgiving—she had a hip replacement not long ago. My uncle and his family went to see her, but I'm staying with her tonight and coming back tomorrow afternoon. So, I can take you all the way into Salt Lake."

Tears swam in Brynn's eyes as she tried to express her appreciation. Tracy competently picked up Bossy's cage along with Brynn's suitcase, leaving her to handle the leashed animals. Within a few minutes, they'd left the resort behind.

Brynn craned her head backward once, looking longingly at the place that had become her home. Finally she stared forward, unable to believe how much it hurt, knowing that Matt would never be hers; and remembering the look on his face when he'd learned the truth—a look she'd never forget.

Tracy glanced over at her, her young face wreathed in concern. "Sometimes things seem worse than they are."

Brynn continued to stare unseeingly into the road, silent tears still creasing her cheeks. "And sometimes, things are worse than they seem."

Chapter Twenty

Brynn erased the last frame of the comic strip, stared at the paper, then sighed as her gaze drifted again to the window. She missed having a mountain right outside. The Wasatch Range had seemed so close before. Now they were unbearably distant. A few birds braved the cold, flitting to the bare branches of the trees. They, too, looked lonely, out of place.

She'd replaced her drafting table, reconstructed her working files and turned blindly to her work. Gradually, Stephanie had reclaimed herself. Only now, she'd gained a slightly bitter edge—one Brynn disguised with biting humor. Her agent and editor were thrilled. The strip had been picked up by another syndicate and a huge marketing deal for everything from Stephanie pencils to nightshirts was in the works. It simply made Brynn sadder.

There was no thrill in her success; no satisfaction, since she had no one to share it with. Before living with the MacKenzies, she'd escaped to her fantasies, shared her hopes and dreams with imaginary heroes. Now there was no escape. And there were certainly no heroes.

To add to her melancholy, the city rang with Christmas preparations. The streets were hung with lighted garlands, and her neighbors' homes overflowed with holiday cheer and decorations. Their gaiety was a constant reminder that this would be her loneliest Christmas yet. She knew there was no point in contacting her mother. Charlene Magee had made it clear that she had no interest in a family celebration. The best Brynn could hope for was a postcard from Hawaii or whatever island destination her mother had chosen.

Brynn had hung the stockings she'd collected in previous years for her pets, but she couldn't bring herself to buy a tree. While she detested self-pity, she also knew there was nothing more depressing than a tree without a single present beneath it. And though a fire now burned steadily in the fireplace, the stockings seemed like a neglected reminder of what she was missing.

Spending most of her time wondering what the MacKenzies thought of her—if any of them had forgiven her yet—Brynn could only hope they had salvaged Gregory's homecoming. A picture of each shocked face was seared into her memory, but it was the hurt on Matt's face that haunted nearly every moment.

What had she been thinking, keeping the truth from him? In her mind, she'd played out a thousand alternatives to her behavior, but her daydreams couldn't change what had happened. Nothing could.

Her doorbell rang suddenly, startling her and sending Lancelot into a frenzy of barking. As the dog dashed to the window to look outside, she opened the door.

Matt filled the doorway, every familiar line of him.

Brynn couldn't speak. All the words she'd ached to say suddenly locked in her throat.

But Matt spoke. "May I come in?"

Dumbly she stared at him, nearly tripping in her haste to move backward. "Of...of course."

He stepped inside, this time seeming to fill the room. Although the old apartment was roomy—certainly adequate for her—now it seemed close. Faintly she wondered how one person could make such a difference.

When he looked around as though taking inventory, it struck

her that he'd never seen her apartment before. She grasped at the ordinary. "Would you like something to drink? Hot tea or—"

"I'm not thirsty."

Brynn couldn't read anything in his words or voice. Like someone parched in a desert, she drank in the sight of him. Impossibly, he looked even better than she'd remembered.

She licked her lips, then struggled for words—words that could somehow set things right. But Lancelot was running across the room, flinging himself at Matt.

At first Brynn feared the dog was attacking him, but then she saw that the only danger Matt faced was being licked to death. Relief made her laugh shakily, easing a fraction of her tension. "I guess he missed you."

As soon as the words were out, her tension shot back up to the breaking point. As she met Matt's gaze, she willed him to know how much she, too, had missed him.

Matt patted the dog, his countenance somber. "I have some papers for you to sign."

Brynn's heart fractured, along with her hope. The trustee papers. Naturally he wanted her name removed. Erasing her last link with the MacKenzies.

She tried to be brave, ignoring tears that prickled behind her eyelids as she forced her voice to remain steady. "Of course."

He pulled out a folder she recognized. How could everything be so familiar, yet at the same time so strange? she wondered. Blindly she accepted the pen he offered, then the paper he held out.

"It's the last line," he told her.

Barely able to see, she turned to the drafting table, scrawling her name across the bottom of the page. "I guess that's it."

Matt's voice changed slightly. "I guess so." He patted Lancelot again. "Except for one question. Why didn't you tell me?"

No glib excuses came to mind. Instead, the truth lodged in

her conscience and found its way into her words. "I was chasing a fantasy. I didn't expect to find reality. When I knew…" She clutched at control. "When I knew I'd fallen in love with you, I was convinced I couldn't tell you the truth. I couldn't face seeing the recrimination in your eyes—the expression I saw that last night at Eagle Point. So I kept putting it off, logically knowing that would only make it worse. But I didn't want it to end. And the night it did, I nearly died."

"Didn't it occur to you to give me a choice?"

She stared at him. "What kind of choice would that be? To accept me as Gregory's wife or as an impostor?"

"But it would have been a choice. Instead you shut me out."

Brynn's voice rang with regret. "My relationships have all been in my daydreams. And daydreams aren't very good at teaching you how real people tick."

"I tick whenever I'm around you," Matt informed her, moving a step closer.

"You do?" she managed to croak.

"Sometimes you tick me off."

"Oh?"

"And other times you have my heart ticking like it's going to bust out of my chest."

Hope raised a wary head. "Oh?"

"And sometimes I'm so ticked I could just shake you."

"Oh?" she repeated yet again, unable to utter more than the one-syllable word.

"And sometimes I'm so ticked I could kiss you until I forget why."

Hope was gaining ground. *"Oh?"*

"Can't you say anything else?"

Numbly she shook her head.

He closed the last remaining space between them, his arms snaking around her, pulling her close. As their lips met, it was hard to tell who drank from the other with more desperation.

When they finally broke apart, Brynn's words were little more than a sob. "I thought I'd never see you again."

"When you walked away from Eagle Point you took the best part of me with you."

She sagged against him again. "Can you ever forgive me?"

"On one condition."

She braced herself. "Which is?"

"That you come home with me."

Relief nearly made her crumple. "But your family... What must they think of me?"

"Who do you think sent me here? Remember, they were the ones who had your address, not me. If I come back without you, they'll have my hide."

"I can't believe they'd still want me."

"You're one of their own. That didn't change when you ran away."

Gratitude battled with disbelief.

Matt tipped up her chin. "But you're not a very astute businesswoman, Brynn."

Distracted she gazed at him. "I'm not?"

"Do you sign everything anyone puts in front of you?"

"I don't understand."

Matt withdrew the paper she'd signed. Her eyes followed his as he held up the document. "This, for example."

"Release of trustee—I understand why you'd want that signed."

"Are you sure that's what it is?"

Confusion clouded her eyes. "Of course. What else would it be?"

He brought the paper closer. "Maybe you should read it."

She was too happy not to humor him. "It says right there: 'Release...'" Her eyes focused on the words, but her brain refused to accept them. "This is a marriage license!"

"So it is."

She continued to stare at the suddenly all-important paper. "And it has your name and mine on it."

"I think that's the way it works."

Brynn was beginning to feel like a salt-water factory as more tears threatened. "Is this what I think it is?"

"If you think it means I'm asking you to marry me, then it is."

She threw her arms around him, crushing the paper as their bodies met. Then she drew back, smoothing the paper with something close to reverence.

A thought sprouted and she met his gaze. "What if I'd said no?"

He pushed one hand through his hair as his expression fell just short of abashed. "Then I'd have been pretty embarrassed." He rocked back slightly on his heels. "The family has a full-tilt ceremony planned for next week at the lodge. They're just waiting for you to come home."

Overcome with emotion, she buried her head against his shoulder. "I don't deserve you... Or them."

Pulling her face back, he lifted up her chin. "You deserve the world. It's time someone gave it to you. I hope a wedding at Eagle Point is all right. I thought about Ireland, but Dad couldn't make the trip and I guessed you'd want to share the day with the whole family."

"Eagle Point is where I want to start our life together," she replied. "It's where it began, and where we belong. Where our family is."

The promise shining in her eyes made him want to toss aside the niceties, to savor the intimacy they'd both craved for too long, but he had one more surprise for her. "And Edward's joining that family."

Brynn's face lit with delight. "He is?"

Matt smiled at her excitement. "They're getting married soon. And Eagle Point inherits one of the premier PR men in the country. Edward's dying to come out of retirement and he wants the resort to be his new project and investment.''

"I'm happy for them. And you.'' Her eyes shone. "This means you're going for it! You're taking Eagle Point into the next century.''

Matt brought her a bit closer. "And you'll be along for the ride.''

"To fulfill the promise of the next generation,'' she murmured.

"Something that we'd better start on now.''

His meaning hit her, along with a wave of anticipation.

Matt pulled the drape—enough to give them privacy, but not far enough to shut out the few remaining rays of sun that clung to the short winter day.

Moving away from the window, they clung together, sharing their first urgent kisses. Then they slowed the fevered pitch, savoring each touch, each new discovery.

Matt had waited for so long…he knew he could take his time. His hands molded around her shoulders, pushing aside the portrait collar blouse she wore. As he'd imagined, her skin was like alabaster, the stuff of fantasies he could now play out. His fingers lingered over her fragile collarbones, able now to study her beating pulse at will. As it had before, it spoke of her excitement, as did the flush that glowed from her ivory skin.

Matt met her gaze, murmuring endearments as he kissed her eyelids, then caressed the long column of her neck. Her wild curls danced between them, scattering silk over his hands, spreading the scent of captured flowers.

Brynn accepted each touch, strained toward every caress. No daydream had prepared her for the reality, for the waves of sensation his slightest touch ignited. How could there be such sheer joy between two people? How could she have been so blind to this wonder?

Matt gently unfastened the row of tiny buttons that held her cotton shirt together. The flush beneath her skin grew, seeming to glow in the deepening shadows of dusk.

Breasts, covered in satin and lace, rose with the rapid breaths she took. Although no false sense of propriety stood between them, he knew she was unschooled in the ways of love. He wanted this experience to be one of joy—the first of many they would share.

Hesitantly her hands ventured toward him, her fingers reaching for the buttons of his shirt. Each sweet, untrained movement was torture. When all of his buttons were freed, the tails of his shirt loosened, his breathing had deepened along with his need.

Her fingers curled over the muscles of his chest, the silkiness of his skin. Reminded of buttered steel, she continued her exploration, curiosity and desire propelling her motions.

Unable to repress a groan, Matt bent toward her breast, cupping the still-covered mound in his hand. When she responded with a shudder, he gently kissed the breast, letting the smooth fabric abrade her skin as it dampened and moved over her nipple.

"Matt," she pleaded, not knowing what she asked for, yet knowing he could somehow guess; and certain he could satisfy.

He opened the clasp on her bra, allowing her breasts to slip free. Exposed to the air, her already swollen nipples hardened further and he bent to taste them.

Brynn arched toward him in delight. As his mouth worked its magic, she felt an unfamiliar dampness at her core.

Then his hands roamed over her torso, tantalizing her as they danced over her ribs, to her waist, past her hips, continuing downward. His clever fingers skimmed over her skin until she wondered that she didn't explode from his touch.

Matt filled his eyes with the sight of her, his fingers with the satin of her skin. As she moaned in pleasure, he slipped her blouse off, tossed away her bra, then shrugged away his own shirt before reaching for the fastening of her jeans. Something deep inside stirred as he realized she still adopted the clothes he'd asked her to wear.

Closing his mouth over hers, he brought their bare chests together, luxuriating in the feel of her breasts, acquainting her with the feel of his naked skin. When her body moved of its own accord, sensuously weaving against his, his control slipped. Sinking his teeth into her shoulder, he nipped gently, eliciting another low sound of satisfaction.

He reached again for the snap on her jeans, then slid her zipper free. She didn't protest as he quickly removed the jeans. Picking Brynn up, he carried her to the bed and together they slid against the mattress. For a moment he let himself savor her long legs, as shapely as he remembered. Then his hands traveled over them, cupping the firm flesh of her calves, his mouth reaching to tease the tender skin behind her knees.

Her cries of pleasure punctuated each movement, each new discovery. As he felt her hands fumble at the fastening of his jeans, he sensed both her hesitancy and desire.

He held her mouth in a deepening kiss, scraping his tongue over hers, tracing each curve, each undiscovered recess. While he kept her lips captive, distracting her, he unfastened his jeans, breaking away from her only long enough to dispatch them.

Great expanses of naked skin now yearned to touch, to feel, to meld.

Brynn's eyes roved over his beautiful body, wanting to caress, wishing to pleasure. When her unskilled touch made him shudder, a shaft of pure feminine power shot through her, at once amazing and satisfying her. So she, too, could make him feel this intense pleasure. Pleasure so acute she thought she'd die from the wanting of it.

Then his hands began a new journey, teasing the sensitive flesh of her inner thighs, cradling the curve of her hips. The possibilities in her mind expanded, then leaped out of control.

Matt teased the last wisp of silk she wore. His fingers danced over the curved valley of her waist, then slipped beneath the fragile silk barrier. Despite his growing hunger, he kept his moves gentle, not wanting to frighten her. But when he cupped her heat, she arched against his hand, welcoming his touch.

Then her lips were near his ear, her breath a whispered caress, her murmurs an invitation—one he accepted, his fingers encountering her engorged flesh, the moist welcome that signaled her readiness. Almost immediately her body collapsed in shudders, her fingers digging into his shoulders, her words a wonder of trembling.

"I didn't know," she breathed.

His eyes met hers, demanded that she focus on his. "You still don't."

Stripping away the scrap of lacy panties, Matt pulled her close, letting her fully feel his arousal. He heard her expected gasp, but her low moan of desire surprised him. Tracing the contours of her face, he felt her hands return the caress, then bracket his jaw.

She had waited for this moment, dreamed of it. She wasn't going to let her shyness stand in the way. "I want you, Matt. All of you."

The last of his control was hanging by a quickly dissolving thread. He wanted this to be special, memorable, enjoyable. Yet the demons of his own desire drove him and his patience was slipping away.

Gently he parted her thighs, feeling her brief initial resistance fade away as he cradled her between his legs. Poised to enter her, he reclaimed her mouth, then her gaze. "I love you, Brynn Magee."

Pure pleasure split her face as he deepened gentle strokes, claiming her in a ritual as ancient as life itself. Instinctively, her long legs curled over his back, their strong muscles holding him close.

Brynn wondered that she didn't die of the exquisite joy. The brief pain was already forgotten as she felt the building pressure, the bursts of incomparable wonder, the race toward an edge she didn't yet recognize.

Then her body bowed, surprising her as a whipcord of ecstasy struck...stunning her as it was followed by a flood of shuddering and inexplicable satisfaction.

Matt reached for the pleasure and found it. Her body quivered helplessly beneath him, snapping his control, thrusting him over the edge, carrying her with him.

Moonbeams pushed past the parted drapes, casting a silver glow that battled with the golden embers of the fire. Gentle fingers of woodsmoke drifted over them, along with the light from the evening stars, bathing them in shared wonder.

The magic of the early moonrising combined with their joy, caging their wild hearts, capturing them for all time.

Epilogue

Brynn stared out at the wild cliffs of Moher, glints of blue fire radiating from the diamond on her left hand. The previous day she and Matt had exchanged wedding vows—their marriage beginning appropriately on New Year's Day. A day of new starts, new resolutions and new promise.

A day that had convinced her for all time that the MacKenzie family completely welcomed her. A healthier-looking Frank and a happily teary-eyed Ruth had called her "daughter." Miranda, with Edward by her side, had simply said: "Welcome home."

Then, with overwhelming generosity, they'd presented her with the Irish lace wedding dress once worn by Gallagher MacKenzie's young bride. A dress that fit Brynn as though it had been sewn just for her. A dress she could use to initiate her own family traditions. It was something old.

Heather, the one so very close to Gregory, had given her a beautiful golden heart locket engraved simply with the word Sister. The gift signaled her acceptance. And provided something new.

Ruth, apparently overcome by an imp of her own, had lent Brynn the garter she'd worn on her own wedding day. As Ruth grinned and then winked, Brynn saw a glimpse of her own future—with its promise of the unexpected. And she'd happily accepted something borrowed.

And dear Miranda had made a gift of her grandmother's diamond earrings—the ones that sparkled with blue flame. Ones that would forever be tied to the Harvest Ball so meaningful to them both. A very special something blue.

Matt, who'd stunned her with the beautiful solitaire, managed to reduce her to tears with his simple contribution to the ceremony. He'd chosen a local guitarist to strum the notes of "Dream Weaver"—a song that suited Brynn to perfection. A magical day from beginning to end, she wondered if it had been spun of those dreams.

While Matt had explained his choice of Eagle Point for the ceremony, he'd saved their honeymoon as a surprise, giving her a piece of the legacy she had so craved. Now they traveled down the west coast of Ireland, her heart swelling as she imagined her grandmother smiling down from heaven, pleased that her "lass" had made this pilgrimage.

Pinching herself until she was nearly black-and-blue, Brynn could still scarcely believe Matt was hers. Remembering how the family had welcomed her back like a prodigal daughter, complete with their version of the fatted calf, she had to blink back a tear. Brynn didn't know what she'd done to deserve such happiness, but she knew she would never take it for granted. She planned to embrace each day and hold on to her happiness with a firm grasp, never allowing it to become an elusive quest.

Matt slipped an arm around her waist. "Happy?"

"Almost unbearably so."

He pointed ahead to the rugged sweep of raw rock that soared toward the sky, the spray of the ocean challenging each elements-battered cliff. "We could have our picture taken there—it'd make quite a backdrop."

Her eyes danced as they met his. "The first picture in our own wedding album?"

He turned her toward him, his fingers lacing through her wildly blowing hair. "You're way behind, love."

"I am?"

"I started taking pictures of you the day we met."

Surprised, she reached out to touch the familiar planes of his handsome face, the intriguing dent in his chin. "You did?"

With his other hand, he picked up hers, placing it over his heart. "They're imprinted here."

Brynn battled the catch in her throat, swamped by the love that filled her. "You're an answer to all my daydreams, all my fantasies."

"That was Gregory," he reminded her.

"No. He was never the culmination of everything I've wanted and needed my entire life." She traced the contours of his firm, strong lips. "But you are. I didn't know it until it was nearly too late—"

His fingers touched her mouth, stopping the flow of words, the regret she still lived with. Then his thumb eased gently over her lips. "I don't need a camera to know this is a picture I plan to keep. I don't mind if you get lost in your daydreams...as long as you find your way home...to me."

Brynn reached up, her arms winding around Matt's neck, her lips meeting his. The wild Irish wind whipped about them as they sealed the promise. And began a living dream. One that no fantasy could touch.